Gabriel Hawke Novels

Murder of Ravens

Mouse Trail Ends

Rattlesnake Brother

Chattering Blue Jay

Fox Goes Hunting

Turkey's Fiery Demise

A Gabriel Hawke Novel

Book 6

Paty Jager

Windtree Press
Hillsboro, OR

TURKEY'S FIERY DEMISE

Contact Information: info@windtreepress.com

Windtree Press
Hillsboro, Oregon
http://windtreepress.com

Cover Art by Christina Keerins
CoveredbyCLKeerins

PUBLISHING HISTORY
Published in the United States of America

ISBN 978-1-952447-48-8

Special Acknowledgements

Special thanks go to Judy Melinek, M.D. CEO, Pathology Expert, Inc. for answering my questions about a body left in a car for a week and Tara Johannsen Assistant Fire Marshal for answering my questions about the burning vehicle and what a Fire Marshal would look for and find while investigating. Also thank you to my brother and sister-in-law who know the Troy area well, for their insights into the best place to "lose" a vehicle.

Author Comments

This book was inspired by the ride-along I did with a Wallowa County State Trooper with the Fish and Wildlife department. He showed me the spot at the same campground where a vehicle had burned with a body in it. He told me how it ended up being classified as an accident but he and other law enforcement members had felt it wasn't. The D.A. at the time hadn't felt there was enough evidence to classify it as a homicide. This book is my way for righting a wrong, even if it isn't for the real person.

Chapter One

"Hawke. County Dispatch. There's a vehicle on fire at Grizz Flat."

"Copy."

Gabriel Hawke, Oregon State Trooper with the Fish and Wildlife division, put down his infra-red binoculars and started up his vehicle. He'd been watching for poachers. Dale Ussery, a rancher in the Flora area, had asked the Fish and Wildlife to keep an eye on his property. He'd found the guts, heads, and legs of two does at the edge of one of his grain fields inside the tree line the last two weekends. It was April. This wasn't hunting season for deer. The does had been pregnant when they were killed, leaving behind two fetuses.

Nothing irked Hawke as much as wasted life. His Nez Perce and Cayuse ancestors, and many of his people today, made sure every bit of an animal was used or given back to the earth to replenish. You never killed a pregnant animal. That would be taking food away from your family another year.

He headed to the gravel road that zig-zagged down the canyon to the Grand Ronde River and the small town of Troy, Oregon. A car on fire could start a forest fire even though there were still a few shaded areas with snow this early in spring.

This weekend was the Muzzleloader Rendezvous at Grizz Flat. There shouldn't be any vehicles at the camping area. They camped and held all the events as if it were the 1800s.

The tires on his truck slid around a corner on the gravel. He slowed his pace slightly. The road from Flora to Troy was steep, switch-backed, and narrow. He kept a close watch for headlights coming up out of the canyon.

Twenty minutes later, a black plume of smoke hanging over the trees was revealed in his headlights as he turned to drive through the short street that made up Troy's main street. He crossed the bridge over the Wenaha River. The road to the camping area was a 180 degree turn back the way he'd come. He followed the dirt road, his headlights illuminated people waving their arms.

"Down there!" A man in buckskins said as Hawke lowered his window.

He followed the road down to the flat and took the first left driving toward the dull glow, smoke, and crowd of people.

He stopped with his lights on the flames and steam shrouding a vehicle sitting over a campfire ring. The grill and back end, that weren't engulfed in the flames, resembled a Jeep Wrangler. A line of people passed buckets of water to the man standing closest to the raging flames. He threw the water and more steam mixed with the black smoke.

"Stop throwing water on the vehicle!" Hawke called out. From experience he knew water did little to put out a vehicle fire. With the flames, smoke, and steam, he couldn't see if the vehicle was occupied. It was too late to save anyone who was inside and unless a fire truck arrived with fire retardant, all they could do was wait for the fire to stop. The small fire extinguisher he carried wouldn't even put a dent in the flames.

He walked over to the man tossing the water. "Try to put the flames out in the pit and wet down all around the pit. Let's keep this from spreading."

The man nodded and began dousing the campfire and the area around it.

The man at the end of the water brigade line was in his late thirties, clean shaven, wearing a soot smudged white shirt and buckskin pants.

Hawke asked him, "How did this happen?"

The man shook his head and walked to the side to toss water on the ground on the other side of the fire. "I don't know. Never heard the Jeep start up. It must have rolled over the fire. I was in my tent over there." He pointed to a white canvas tent thirty yards from the smoking vehicle. "I heard a funny 'poof' and the side of the tent lit up. Stepped out and saw the Jeep on fire."

A scream pierced the air.

Hawke spun back to the vehicle. Smoke curled toward the sky, but the flames had begun to die. The inside of the Jeep was revealed.

The charred remains of a body leaned on the steering wheel.

"Oh no!" A woman in a flannel nightgown ran toward the Jeep. Hawke caught her before she disrupted any evidence.

"Ma'am, who do you think that is?" Hawke asked, holding the shaking woman in his arms.

A younger man walked toward the Jeep.

"Don't anyone go near this!" Hawke called out. "Is there someone here who can make sure no one goes near the vehicle?" He glanced around at the men and women in buckskins and flannel.

"I'll keep an eye on things." A large man dressed in a night shirt over what looked like knee-high moccasins.

"Your name?" Hawke asked.

"Grizzly."

Hawke studied him, trying to determine if the man was being secretive. "That's your name?"

"Here, at the Rendezvous, I'm Grizzly. Real name's Adam Jolly." He stood with his arms crossed, reminding Hawke of a big grizzly bear studying the lay of the land.

He focused on the woman sobbing in his arms. "Who are you?"

"School Marm up here. Kristen Pruss in Alder. That's my husband, Sure Shot, James." She glanced toward the vehicle and shuddered.

"How do you know it's your husband?" Hawke set her away from him. He scanned her face. There were traces of makeup around her eyes. As far as he knew women didn't wear makeup in the early 1800s, especially one calling herself School Marm.

"That's his Jeep. He'd been acting funny today. We had an argument. He stormed off to drink with his buddies."

"What time was that?" Hawke knew he needed to call in the Fire Marshal, the Medical Examiner, a deputy, and another State Trooper to get all the statements and gather all the evidence. This was a crime that needed to have all law enforcement entities involved.

"I don't know. Seven?" She sniffed. "I got ready for bed and read for a little while. I was asleep when all the commotion started."

He got a feeling she wasn't telling the truth. In his peripheral vision he caught a man hovering along the edge of the onlookers. His best guess was the man wanted to comfort the woman.

"Grizzly, don't let anyone near this. I have to call it in. I'll be right back." Hawke scanned the people standing around. "Go back to your camps. When I get reinforcements, someone will be around to take your statement."

They mumbled and didn't seem to want to return to their tents. Even though it would be warmer than standing around here.

"Everyone, go back to your camps, except the first people to hurry to the fire." He left the crowd discussing who were the first to the scene and walked to his truck.

He picked up his mic from the holder on the dash. "This is Hawke."

"Dispatch. Copy."

"I need the Fire Marshal, the Medical Examiner, a deputy, and another State Trooper to Grizz Flat. There's a body in the burned vehicle."

"Copy. Will instruct and let you know their ETA."

"Copy." He attached the radio to his belt, the microphone to his shirt, and grabbed his evidence kit before exiting his vehicle. It was a good thing he hadn't come on duty until 6 PM. It was going to be a long night.

He returned to the group of half a dozen people standing a short distance from the charred vehicle.

Grizzly had the group gathered around him. The victim's wife stood next to him. Hawke doubted anyone would tamper with the still smoldering car and body. He walked over to the group to get their statements while the evening was still fresh in their minds. He'd gather evidence later when the remains had cooled down.

"I'd like to speak with each one of you separately." He motioned to the youngest member of the group. The man was in his twenties and stood at the edge of the group wearing more modern clothes. "You, come with me." Hawke pointed to the young man and walked in the direction of the metal storage container. From previous visits to the flat when the muzzleloader group was practicing, he knew it was where they kept all the targets and tents used for this event.

He stopped when they were far enough from the group to not be heard. Hawke opened his logbook, holding it and his flashlight in the same hand, giving enough glow from his light to see to write and keeping the beam to the side of the young man's face, to be able to see his expressions.

"Name?"

"Hardtack."

Hawke studied the young man. "The name on your I.D."

Hardtack crossed his arms and pressed his lips tight.

"I care more about what you saw than who you are." He'd let the kid think that and find out from someone else his real name. "Where were you when the fire started?"

"Biscuit and I were up the hill a little ways." He pointed to the hill to the east of the camping area.

"Did you have a clear view of the fire?" He circled Biscuit as a person to talk to.

"Not really. It was the fireball that caught our attention. Then the smoke. I ran down toward it and saw Grizzly, Buckskin Bob, and Sourdough shouting orders about getting a bucket brigade going." He shrugged. "Other people came running up, and I stepped into line."

Hawke glanced over at the group waiting to be interviewed. "Are Buckskin Bob and Sourdough over there waiting to talk to me?"

The young man nodded. "Don't tell Sourdough I was with Biscuit. He's been shooing me away when I try to talk to her."

"I take it he's Biscuit's father?"

"Yeah."

"You may go, but tell someone else to come over here." Hawke watched the young man walk up to the oldest looking man who wore all buckskins and had a raccoon fur cap.

That person wandered over to Hawke.

"Not sure I can be much help," the man said.

"Name?"

"Buckskin Bob."

Hawke sighed. "Does it say that on your I.D.?"

The man grinned. "Yes sir, it does. Had my name legally changed to that twenty years ago."

"Bob, what were you doing when you noticed the fire?" Hawke studied the man. He appeared to be an open book. His eyes held interest, no wariness. His features were lax.

"I was cleaning my gun. The big shoot off is tomorrow. I wanted my rifle to be ready to go."

"What alerted you to the fire?"

"There was a bright flash of light. I looked out my tent flap and saw the flames around the Jeep sittin' on the campfire. My first thought was 'Why in Sam Hill didn't Sure Shot leave his vehicle parked across the river like the rest of us. We all drive in and unload then drive over and leave our vehicles at the parking area across the river. You know, so it feels like the 1800s."

"How do you think the vehicle ended up over the fire?"

"I guess he got something out of it, bumped the gear shift, and it rolled." Buckskin Bob glanced back at the vehicle. "But why would he be in it? Unless he got drunk and School Marm kicked him out of the tent." He chuckled. "That's happened before."

"He got drunk often?" Hawke asked, making a note in his book to check on this.

"Sure Shot liked alcohol and women." The man glanced toward the group. "The fight he and School Marm got into wasn't because he was drunk. He's been 'rendezvousing' with some married women at this event every year."

"Names."

The man roughed up his beard and studied the ground. "You didn't hear this from me or I won't tell you."

"I'm pretty sure if you know so do several other people. Possibly their spouses." Hawke waited for the man to spill, what he could tell Buckskin Bob was dying to tell, even though he stalled.

"Seamstress Sue. That's Sourdough's wife."

Hawke circled the name he'd already written down as the father of Biscuit.

"The other is Chessie, short for Winchester. She comes by herself, but she's married. I happened to see her with her husband at another event."

"Are all of the people here locals?" Hawke asked.

"No. They come from all over the Pacific Northwest to this Rendezvous. Sourdough and Seamstress Sue are from Eagle. Chessie is from somewhere in Washington. Sure Shot is… was the president of the Wallupa Muzzleloaders. Shit! That means Smokepole is going to be the president. We only made him V.P. to keep him from being a pain in the ass." The man kicked at the dirt and started to walk away.

"Send someone else over," Hawke said loud enough for the man to hear him.

Buckskin Bob threw a hand in the air to signal he'd heard.

Chapter Two

The next person to walk up to Hawke was a young woman, that he guessed from the beam of the flashlight to be in her early thirties. She had long blonde hair, loose around her shoulders and reaching her waist. She wore a buckskin dress without any adornment.

"Name?" Hawke asked.

"Swift Arrow." She crossed her arms and stared at him.

"I understand that is your name for your time at the Rendezvous. What is your name on your identification?" He studied her cool demeanor. She definitely wasn't the woman who'd screamed when the steam evaporated and the body was revealed.

"Swift Arrow is the name given me at my naming ceremony fifteen years ago."

"Who are your people?" Hawke asked.

Her eyebrows rose. "Only another Indian would ask me that."

"I'm from the Confederated Tribes of the Umatilla. Nez Perce and Cayuse ancestors." Hawke was proud of his heritage even though many times during his life, he'd had to fight for respect due to others preconceived beliefs he was either dumb or out to kill them.

"Warm Springs."

"Do you travel to many of these Rendezvous?" Hawke was curious about the woman coming to such an event.

"And Powwows. I make and sell long bows. At Rendezvous, I shoot my bows in the competitions." She smiled. Confidence in her workmanship made him wonder how well she shot.

"How did you do today?" he asked, seeing she had lost her unwillingness to talk to him.

Another smug smile tipped her lips. "I won the long bow round today. Came in first in the woman's knife throwing."

"I'd say you are an accomplished woman." He smiled. "And what is the name on your birth certificate?"

She frowned. "Cherrie Pearson. But you won't tell anyone will you?"

He studied her. "Why?"

"Cherrie doesn't sound like a woman who can shoot an arrow or throw a knife well." She shrugged.

He would have laughed if he hadn't been interviewing her about a dead body. "How did you come to be one of the first people to the fire?"

She pointed to a teepee he'd missed while driving toward the fire. It was about fifty feet from the charred remains. "I saw the flash of light. Brighter than a flashlight, which we all have but try not to use."

"When you saw the flash, what did you do?"

"I threw open the flap on the teepee and stepped out. That's when I saw Grizzly and Sourdough running toward the fire. Grizzly shouted 'Get your buckets' and I grabbed mine and joined the line to the river."

"You saw Grizzly and Sourdough. Anyone else?" He watched her. Her teepee was in a direct line across from the victim's tent.

"I thought I saw someone in the shadow of Sure Shot's tent."

"Man or woman?"

"I couldn't tell. It was just a movement."

"Thank you. Send someone else over." Hawke watched her walk back to the group and talk to a short round man while pointing back at him.

The man waddled over, held out his hand, and said, "Gravedigger."

Hawke studied him. "And your real name?"

The man sighed. "I prefer using my Rendezvous name while I'm at these events."

"A man has died. I need full cooperation from everyone," Hawke said, wondering if the little guy had any run-ins with the victim.

"Harold Gavin."

"Thank you. I understand you were one of the first people to see the fire. What can you tell me?" He didn't want to bring up the shadow Swift Arrow saw. If the man saw it, Hawke wanted him to mention it himself.

"The front of my tent lit up, and I opened the flap to see what it was. That's when I saw the tall flames and realized there was a vehicle in the fire. I was worried about School Marm's tent being so close. When Grizzly yelled for us to grab buckets, I picked up my bucket and headed for the line that was forming toward the river."

"Is that the usual protocol for putting out a fire?" Hawke asked. It seemed they all did what was asked as if it were second nature.

"We, the Wallupa Muzzleloaders, have practiced at our monthly meetings in case a tent catches on fire from an overturned lantern." Pride filled his voice.

"I see. Have you had a tent catch on fire at one of these rendezvous?"

"Not at a Rendezvous but one of the monthly campouts. Sourdough's boys got to wrestling in the tent and knocked over a lantern. We got the fire out right away with the bucket relay."

"Did you see anything that seemed odd when you first walked out of your tent or while standing in line handing the buckets along?" Hawke wasn't getting much to go on with his questions. He glanced at his watch. The M.E. and deputy should be showing up soon.

"A vehicle on fire. In the line everyone just kept their eyes on the buckets going back and forth."

"Thank you. Would you send the next person over?" Hawke shook out his hand that had been holding the logbook and flashlight.

Gravedigger walked back toward the smaller group waiting to be interviewed. He talked to the one person Hawke had yet to meet from the group. It must be Sourdough.

A man in his early fifties strode over to Hawke. He was fit, wore a military haircut, and had a pissed off expression.

"Gravedigger said I needed to come talk to you?"

The man had a belligerent attitude to start the conversation.

"Your name?" Hawked asked, again, knowing what he'd get.

"Sourdough." The man stared at him in the peripheral beam of Hawke's flashlight.

"The one on your I.D., please."

"Jake Levens."

"Where do you live, Mr. Levens?" Hawke asked.

"Eagle. Why does that matter?"

"I'm just gathering information. What alerted you to the fire?"

"I saw the bright light." He wasn't offering more.

"Where were you when you saw the light?" Hawke wondered why this man was being so evasive when the others had been forthcoming.

"I was looking for my daughter." The tone indicated that was the real reason he was pissed. He had a teenage daughter that had been out in the woods with someone.

"Where were you looking?" Hawke didn't plan to let the man know where his daughter had been.

"I had gone around to the families of the kids she talks to. None of them had seen her. I was headed to Swift Arrow's teepee when I saw the bright light and looked over."

"Why Swift Arrow?"

"Biscuit had been hanging around her the last couple of days. Trying out some bows and acting as if she was finally interested in one of the activities. Thought she might have gone to talk some more." The man lost some of his anger as he talked about his daughter embracing what it was evident the man enjoyed.

"What exactly did you see when you noticed the fire?"

"I noticed the Jeep on fire and laughed. Served Sure Shot right having his Jeep burned up. We all told him he was ruining the 1800s feel of the event by stashing his Jeep behind the storage shed. It was bad enough to see that metal box when we were trying to replicate 1840." The man showed he took the whole rendezvous seriously.

"Why did he insist on having his vehicle here and not parked with the others?" Hawke had wondered that from the moment he'd seen the burned vehicle.

"Something about he was the president and if he wanted to keep his vehicle close by it was his prerogative." The man snorted. "Prerogative. Hell, I didn't think he even knew such a word. Mind you, I don't usually talk bad about a person after they die, but he kind of got what was coming to him."

Hawke studied the man. Sourdough didn't show any malice. His eyes were thoughtful and his stern facial features had softened a bit. "How so?"

"Take insisting on keeping his Jeep here just because he was the president. Flaunting his affair with Chessie in School Marm's face, and then crowing like a rooster this afternoon when he out shot Red Beard. You don't do that. You shoot your best, if you do well you encourage the other contestants. You don't talk down to them and act as if you were so skilled no one would ever beat you."

"The deceased sounds like he was boastful about his shooting and his affairs." He watched the man. His wife had been linked to the deceased. Did he know?

There was a twitch at the right side of his mouth. He knew. Another reason for him to wish the man dead.

"Back to the fire. Did you see anything out of the ordinary, other than the Jeep on fire?"

The man started to shake his head then his eyes widened. "I caught the backside of Smithy going behind the tent next to Sure Shot's."

"Is he a friend of the deceased?"

Sourdough laughed. "No. He's not even a member of the Wallupa Muzzleloaders. He shouldn't have been over here. He's camped there." He pointed to the area near the beginning of the flat. "He comes to the rendezvous, but he does more nighttime games than the daytime ones, if you know what I mean." He winked.

"He comes here to fool around?" Hawke thought it was kind of an odd way to meet up with a lover.

"He only fools around with one person. School Marm."

Hawke glanced over at Grizzly and the deceased's wife standing side by side, staring his direction.

"Mrs. Pruss said she and her husband had an argument around seven. Did you happen to hear what it was about?" Hawke wondered if the argument had been meant to send the man to his Jeep.

"No. At seven I was helping my wife clean up from dinner and getting the boys to settle down."

"Thank you, would you send Grizzly over and tell Mrs. Pruss she can go to her tent and wait for me to come see her." Hawke could see the woman was shivering. The temperature had dropped to freezing due to the clear night sky.

The man strode back to the other two. The woman headed to her tent, Sourdough walked down the road, and Grizzly walked toward him.

"You want to grab a coat before we start?" Hawke asked the man.

"I'm good." He stood with his arms crossed, waiting.

"How did you come to see the fire?" Hawke asked.

"I had just turned off my lantern and crawled into my sleeping bag when there was a flash of light. I thought some of the kids might have been messing around, so I got up and looked out the tent flap. That's when I saw the Jeep in flames. I knew it was Sure Shot's. I hollered for people to get buckets, and we started relaying buckets of water to throw on the fire."

"How did you know the deceased?"

The man swallowed and his eyes glistened. "He's been my best friend since high school."

"Where do you live?"

"Promise. I have three-hundred-and-sixty acres I farm." Grizzly's arms dropped to his sides. "Sure Shot sold me all of my pickups since I got my driver's license. His father owned the car dealership in Alder before Sure Shot and his mom took over a few years ago."

The deceased's best friend. Time to see if he knew all of his friend's flaws.

Vehicle lights entered the campground.

"Which is your tent?" Hawke asked.

"That one." Grizzly pointed to the tent next to the teepee.

"I'll come find you after I catch the new arrivals up to speed." Hawke closed his logbook and turned off his flashlight as he walked out to meet the convoy of law enforcement vehicles arriving.

Chapter Three

"You haven't taken any photos yet?" State Trooper Shoberg kidded Hawke.

"I've been interviewing the first people on the scene," he said, trying not to show he was unhappy with himself for not getting photos before everyone showed up. It meant they had to all stand back until the initial photos were taken.

"I'll take them if you want to keep interviewing people," Shoberg offered.

Hawke nodded and captured Deputy Novak's attention. "I've talked to most of the people in the tents right around the crime scene, you can start from the tent three over from the teepee and ask what they know from seven o'clock this evening until they learned about the fire."

Novak started to walk away.

"And let me know where Chessie, Smithy, and Hardtack's tents are located."

"Those are names?" Novak asked with skepticism.

"You'll find they take staying in character at this thing important. You'll have to ask them all for their real names." Hawke grinned and faced Dr. Vance and the Fire Marshal. "Everyone says it was a bright light that caught their attention to the fire." He motioned toward the burnt Jeep and fire ring. "Any idea what would cause that?"

"Most likely it was the fumes in the gas tank catching fire. There would have been a poof and a fireball. No explosion, unlike how the movies and T.V. shows always portray vehicle fires," Fire Marshal Wes Florry said, his gaze remaining on the charred remains. "Do you know how the vehicle ended up over the campfire yet?"

"No. That's what I need to figure out." Hawke glanced at his watch. One. He'd let Grizzly and the victim's wife know he'd talk to them in the morning and get busy looking at the vehicle tracks to see how the Jeep had ended up where it did.

He scanned the area for Shoberg and walked over to the other trooper. "I'll go tell my last two witnesses that I'll talk to them in the morning, then I'll come check out the tire tracks and take photos of those."

"Copy." Shoberg snapped another picture.

Hawke walked over to the victim's tent first. He knocked on the canvas. "Mrs. Pruss, it's Trooper Hawke."

The woman stuck her head out the flap. Her makeup was smeared even more and her eyes were red.

"Ma'am, I'll be by in the morning to take more of your statement. I need to go after the evidence right now. Try and get some sleep."

She nodded and her head disappeared.

He wondered if the man called Smithy was in his tent or in this one. Walking over to Grizzly's tent, he spotted a light on in Swift Arrow's teepee. What was she doing in there? He wondered if the competitions would continue tomorrow with the investigation going on.

The tent flap flopped open when he was two steps from the canvas structure.

"Trooper, I've been waiting for you." Grizzly was dressed in full buckskin.

"I came to tell you to go ahead and try to sleep. I'll come by in the morning and continue the interview. I need to gather evidence while it's still fresh."

"I understand. I hope you find out what happened. I really don't think Sure Shot would do something as stupid as run his Jeep over a campfire and sit there while he burned up. He wasn't a quitter."

"Thanks, I'll keep that in mind." Hawke walked away from the tent, wondering how a man who seemed so smug and boastful would allow someone to incapacitate him long enough he would burn up in a fire.

Behind the vehicle and fire, Hawke swept the beam of his flashlight back and forth across the ground, looking for tire tracks. It would have been easier in daylight, but he wanted to see if there had been someone pushing the vehicle. He wondered if the shadow Swift Arrow saw was that person or the man presumedly leaving the Pruss tent after the fire started.

He found the tire tracks. The tread on the tires was what some called angry. It was made to dig into the ground and pull the vehicle through all types of terrain. With his flashlight trained on the tracks, he took a photo.

"You didn't happen to bring any floodlights with you?" he asked Shoberg.

"In the back of my vehicle," the trooper replied, not looking up.

By now Dr. Vance and the Fire Marshal were allowed to examine the body and the fire.

As Hawke walked by, the Medical Examiner waved him over.

"He didn't get into this Jeep on his own," she said.

"How do you know?" Hawke had worked enough cases with the woman that he would side with her findings any day.

"His hair and skin are burnt, but see this?" She pointed to a crack in the skull that could be seen where the broken skin had shrunk from the heat and flames. "Looks like blunt force trauma incapacitated him enough to then finish him off in the fire. I've no doubt I'll find he was still breathing when he was consumed by the flames."

Hawke shuddered. Burning to death wasn't something he'd care to have happen to him. "Thanks for the information. I'll keep it in mind to look for blood. That kind of a gash in the scalp would have bled a lot."

At Shoberg's vehicle, he opened the back and found two battery-powered floodlights on expanding stands. He hauled them both behind the burnt Jeep and set them up, lighting the area behind the vehicle.

He could see the tire tracks in the dirt easily with the lights. Taking several photographs from different angles, Hawke also took in all the area between the tracks. That would be where someone would have walked if the vehicle was pushed over the fire. What he didn't understand was why the man was left to burn? Was it because the blow hadn't finished him off? But couldn't there have been another blow struck if whoever did it had planned to kill the victim?

He didn't see any definite footprints, but there were indentions from someone digging the toe of their moccasin-clad foot into the dirt to get more traction. The vehicle had been placed over the campfire. This was proof. He took photos of the indentions and moved the floodlights closer to the steel container.

The tire tracks stopped where the Jeep had been parked. The passenger side appeared to have been only the length of the side mirror from the container. With the vehicle tucked so tight to the container, only the driver side would have been accessible to put the body in.

He aimed one of the lights at the area where the driver's side would have been. The dirt, grass, and small plants were trampled and dug up as if a struggle had dislodged the plants. *A struggle*. From the gash on the head, he should have been unconscious. Had the person putting him in the vehicle struggled because they weren't strong?

That opened several possibilities. The women in the victim's life.

But where had the head wound occurred?

Hawke turned on his flashlight and ran the beam along the ground, starting at the point of the struggle to put the victim in the Jeep. A few dark spots in the dirt proved to be blood.

Running the beam of his light over the container box, there was a dark spot on the far back corner.

He took photos of the foreign substance, then removed his pack and pulled out a swab kit and a small paper envelope to scrape the residue into. This appeared to be the point where the victim was incapacitated. From the scene, Hawke could imagine an argument, the victim was shoved, hit his head, and maybe slumped to the ground.

But if it had been an accident, why had the person who shoved him then put the body in the Jeep and shoved the vehicle over the fire? Had they planned to kill him or just scare him?

The beam of the flashlight surveyed the area as Hawke flashed the thoughts through his mind. The ground was trampled, no tread marks from any type of shoe. Since most of the participants had been wearing moccasins, there would be little chance of matching anything more than foot size if he found a sharp impression.

"Dr. Vance is taking off. The wagon showed up to collect the body," Shoberg said, walking toward Hawke.

"Has the site cooled down enough for the fire marshal to sift through it?" He wanted to do some looking himself.

"Yeah, he's already checking for an accelerant." Shoberg waved a hand. "Did you find something."

Hawke pointed to the corner of the container. "That's where the victim hit his head. Not sure why he was put in the Jeep and shoved over the fire."

The state trooper made a low guttural sound. "You rarely know what triggers a person to kill another."

"Yeah." He popped out the SD card from his camera and handed it to Shoberg. "Take this and these samples I collected to forensics. I'm going to hang around here to check out the fire and talk to more people." The sun cast a yellow glow on the horizon. "They should be rising soon."

"Will do. I'll fill in the lieutenant and the D.A." Shoberg took the items Hawke held out to him and headed back toward the crime scene.

Hawke took one more look around and walked back to the charred vehicle. He found Florry sifting through the ashes, a camera dangled from around his neck.

"How's it going?" Hawke asked, watching the man do his job.

"Gasoline was used to make this fire take off. It wasn't a leaking gas line. I can smell the gasoline still in the seats. Gas fumes are what burn, not the gas. This vehicle was doused with gasoline and the heat from the fire under the vehicle lit the fumes."

"The witnesses all saw a ball of fire that caught their attention." He'd witnessed vehicle fires. When the fire got to the gas tanks it would 'whoosh' and make a ball of fire.

"The thing is, did they see one or two? The gas tank would have done that when it caught fire. But there should have been a surge of fire when the fumes in the vehicle ignited."

"There was only mention of one flash. Could the tank have exploded at the same time as the vehicle?" Hawke shuddered. "From what you've said, this was intentional and pre-meditated if the perpetrator rigged the vehicle to make sure the victim died."

Florry dropped items into evidence bags. "This was well thought out."

Chapter Four

Rather than disturb the victim's wife, Hawke walked over to Grizzly's tent. He knocked on the canvas. "Trooper Hawke."

The tent wiggled and the flap opened. As the man stepped out of the tent a waft of warm air came with him.

Hawke had a suspicion the man wasn't "roughing it" as much as portraying a mountain man from the 1800s.

"Mr. Jolly, I have some questions for you," Hawke motioned to his truck. He'd left the tailgate down on his way over to the man's tent. They could sit on the tailgate, since there were only upturned logs to sit on.

The man followed him to the truck and sat on one side of the tailgate.

Hawke sat on the other end, glad he didn't have to use his flashlight to write in his logbook. The sun bathed the meadow, trees, and river in a yellow glow as it slowly rose behind the hill.

"Did you figure out why Sure Shot parked over the firepit?" Grizzly asked.

Looking up from his logbook, Hawke studied the man. He seemed confused. "Did he usually park in the Rendezvous encampment?"

"The last couple of meetings, when we were preparing for this event, he'd kept his Jeep by the container, but we all had vehicles in here. We were hauling tools and targets back and forth as we fixed them or made new ones."

"Why did he have his Jeep here, in the camping area, for the Rendezvous?"

Grizzly scrubbed his bearded face with his palms. "He said the last time he'd left his vehicle in the parking area across the river, things had been stolen. I told him to put the top on." The man shook his head. "He said that wouldn't stop anyone. Sure Shot wasn't one to let anyone get the best of him twice."

Hawke glanced toward the widow's tent. "Did he know his wife was having an affair?"

Grizzly stared at him, anger igniting in his eyes. "Who told you that?"

"Is it true?"

"If it is, that's Kristen's business and not ours." Grizzly's face, that could be seen, had turned nearly as red as the wool belt around his waist.

It seemed this man had feelings for his friend's wife. Hawke had witnessed the two standing together as they'd waited, but Grizzly hadn't put an arm around the woman and she hadn't huddled close to him.

"What about your friend? I also heard he spent more time with other women than his wife."

The color heightened on the man's cheeks, neck, and ears. "He was my friend. Had been since high school, but I didn't condone his sleeping around. We've been in several heated discussions about that."

"Did you have one last night?"

He scrubbed his palms over his face, again. Settling his large hands on his knees, he stared at his feet nearly touching the ground. "Yeah. Sure Shot came to me complaining about Kristen throwing him out of the tent because she caught him flirting with Swift Arrow." He shook his head. "I asked him why he had to chase every female that came to these things." His gaze latched onto Hawke. "He said, 'Because I can.'"

"What you're telling me is every man here, who has a wife, girlfriend, maybe even a daughter, could be a suspect for the death of James Pruss?" Hawke didn't like the idea of having so many suspects and a short amount of time to find the killer. It could be someone from anywhere in the Pacific Northwest or farther.

"And then there's the shooters who he's put down every chance he could." Grizzly peered at him with sadness in his large brown eyes. "He was my friend, but he could be an asshole."

"You're not making this any easier for me." Hawke saw the flap at the victim's tent flutter. "I'll be catching up to you later. Thank you for your time." He hopped off the tailgate and strode over to the tent as School Marm stepped out.

"Good Morning, Mrs. Pruss. I'd like to ask you a few questions."

She pointed to the outhouse. "When I get back from there."

Hawke nodded and sniffed. Someone had coffee

brewing. Scanning the ten or so closest tents, he spotted Swift Arrow crouching in front of a small campfire. He sauntered over to her campfire.

"Is that coffee I smell?" He sat on an upturned log by the fire.

"It's just about ready." Her gaze moved from the fire to him. "If you have a cup, I can fill it for you."

"I happen to have a cup. Be right back." Hawke strode over to his vehicle and grabbed the travel mug he'd filled last night before starting his surveillance for the poacher.

Back at Swift Arrow's camp, he noticed the victim's wife exit the outhouse, but she headed north, toward the other camping areas. Was she avoiding him on purpose?

Swift Arrow crouched before the fire, she took his cup and filled it. "Do you have more questions for me?"

"I know you aren't part of the Wallupa group." He glanced around the group of tents making up their own village of sorts. "Why are you camping with them?"

She shrugged. "While these are family-oriented events, there is some drinking that goes on and I feel safer if I'm near Grizzly."

"The drinking gets out of hand at these events?" The only mention he'd encountered was the victim drinking too much.

"Usually the last night, after all the competitions. The men and some women party. But there are a few who drink every night." She scrunched up her nose. "Mostly the ones who come alone. Leave their spouses behind."

"Do you happen to know how things were between Sure Shot and his wife? You mentioned Grizzly made you feel safe, I got the feeling he has more than friendly feelings for Mrs. Pruss."

"Mrs. Pruss?" Her brow wrinkled as she studied him.

"School Marm."

"Oh! The wife of the dead man." She nodded. "It was no secret he spent more time in other people's tents than his own." Her gaze became dark and angry. "The first year I came to this event, he tried to get in my teepee. If Grizzly hadn't been with him, I'm pretty sure Sure Shot would have gone to jail on charges of rape. I didn't want his attention, but he seemed to take me saying 'no' as a spear jabbed in the ground."

"He took your resistance as a challenge." Hawke was getting the picture of a man who liked a challenge and didn't give up on getting what he wanted.

"I guess you could say that. I would say, he was a bad loser."

This intrigued him. "Are you talking about women or shooting?"

"Both." She nodded toward the other tents. "Red Beard threatened him yesterday after the adult round of muzzleloaders. He accused Sure Shot of cheating."

Hawke sipped the coffee and studied the woman. "Cheating? How does one cheat with a muzzleloader?"

"That's what I was wondering. But I never had a chance to see if Grizzly had any ideas." Swift Arrow nodded toward the large man's tent. "He and Sure Shot wandered off after dinner. I didn't see either of them again until the fire. Then it was chaotic." She nodded toward the other tents. "School Marm is coming back."

Hawke twisted to look over his left shoulder. The woman was hurrying back. Her gaze landed on him, and she veered his direction.

"I'm sorry I took so long." She stood back, not looking at either of them.

"Thank you for the coffee," he said to Swift Arrow.

"You're welcome."

He stood and motioned toward Mrs. Pruss's tent. "We can talk over at your lodgings."

She glanced at him before walking slowly toward her tent. About ten feet from the charred vehicle, she hastened her pace, hurrying by the area wrapped in crime scene tape.

Stopping in front of her tent, Mrs. Pruss held up a hand. "I'll grab two chairs. I don't want to hide in my tent."

He wondered where the woman came up with the idea others would think she was hiding in her tent.

She stepped out carrying two wooden folding chairs. Handing one to him, she deftly opened the second and sat.

Hawke studied the workmanship of the chair. There wasn't a nail or staple in it. Everything was put together with wood dowels. "Nice chair."

She smiled. "My brother made them. He likes to do woodworking in the winter when he isn't farming."

"You're lucky to receive such gifts from him." Hawke sat and pulled out his logbook. "Can you tell me all you know about your husband's actions yesterday and last night up until the fire?"

She nodded, thought a moment, and said, "We were up early. James wanted to make sure all the targets were ready and the scorekeepers had what they needed." She studied her hands. "He returned about nine, I guess, to get his gun, powder, and balls. He was whistling and he kissed me on the cheek asking me to wish him luck." A tear trickled down her cheek. "I told him 'Good luck' and then gathered my money box and headed to my vendor tent."

"You don't shoot?"

"No. I don't like competing. I like constructing period adornments from photos I see. I sell them at the Rendezvous." She smiled. "I even sell them online. They've become so popular, I'm having a tough time keeping up with orders."

"When was the next time you saw your husband?" Hawke asked.

"Not until after all the shooting had finished. Red Beard arrived at the tent first, looking for James. I told him I didn't know where he was. He stormed off. About twenty minutes later, James showed up drunk, boasting how he'd bested Red Beard." She shook her head. "I could tell he'd had too much to drink. When I mentioned it, he became defensive and told me to mind my own business. Adam must have heard him yelling. He arrived and they walked off together. That's the last time I saw him before…" She put a hand to her mouth.

"Did your husband get drunk often?" Hawke wondered if the man's alcohol loosened lips got him in trouble. He wouldn't be the first, nor the last, man to say something that got him beat up, or in this case, barbecued.

"He didn't often, but when he did, it was like he couldn't stop. And he did things that I think he regretted afterward." She wrung her hands in her lap.

"What kind of things?" Hawke studied her.

The woman kept her face downcast. He couldn't read her eyes.

"He would boast, antagonize, say hurtful things."

"To you as well?"

She raised her face and peered into his eyes. "Yes. The last time, I told him I was leaving him. He told me to go ahead and leave. I had my clothes and some of the items I wanted to take with me all packed when he returned from work the next day. He begged me not to leave and promised he'd never drink again." She swiped at a tear and shook her head. "I gave in and told him just the one chance. He'd been doing better, then this weekend." Standing quickly, she said, "I hate this club."

"Why the club?" Hawke had a feeling he already knew considering so many people mentioned how the deceased had been sleeping with other women at these events.

"Ever since James became president, he's been lording it over everyone and using his 'status' to force people into doing things they normally wouldn't."

Hawke grasped onto her words. "What do you mean by that?"

Her pale complexion flushed. "I shouldn't have said that. I'm probably just thinking that because James complained so much about some people."

"Which ones?" He wasn't going to let that go. This was another motive.

"Smokepole, Sourdough, and Dead-eye Duke. They are the ones in charge of each event. Smokepole the archery, Sourdough the roundball, and Dead-eye the knife throwing. James wanted to have a trophy for the highest score in each of the events. We've always just brought items everyone purchased throughout the year and tossed them on a blanket, like the original

Rendezvous. The highest score picked off the blanket first then on down. James wanted the highest scorers to get something more than a pick off the blanket. Some of the old-timers were against changing the pattern of the rendezvous. He was in arguments with them all the time."

"I don't think someone would kill him over changing the way things are done, do you?" Hawke studied her.

"Some of the people here take staying true to the original Rendezvous seriously." She walked into her tent.

Chapter Five

"Smithy is in the third tent on the left after the Y in the road. Chessie is clear on the far side. You can't miss the wind chimes made out of shell casings. Hardtack is the small non-canvas tent at the very end of the last group of tents." Deputy Novak reported to Hawke.

"Thanks. Anyone have anything interesting to say?" Hawke asked, hoping someone might have noticed something out of the ordinary.

Novak tapped his logbook. "The victim wasn't very well liked by some and too well liked by others, if you get my drift."

Hawke nodded. "Sounds like what I've been hearing. The victim was last seen walking through the campsites with his best friend. Anyone say they saw the two after dinner?"

"No. It is as if no one saw him last night until…" he flipped open his logbook, "the flames vanished and a burnt-up person sat in the Jeep."

Hawke nodded. Flipping thought his notes, he asked. "Did you talk to a family going by Sourdough, Biscuit, and Seamstress Sue?" The names sounded like characters in a children's book.

"I talked to the two women. They were both upset but didn't comfort one another. They avoided eye contact with me or each other. I got the feeling they both had more to say but not with the other one present." Novak closed his logbook.

"Could be because I know where the girl was when the fire was discovered. And the woman's name has been linked with the victim." Hawke added Novak's comments to his logbook. "Hear anything about the event continuing or if people were pulling up stakes?"

"It sounded like most were pulling out after giving their statements." Novak scanned the area. "Do you need to keep any?"

"As long as we have addresses and phone numbers, no. I have a feeling this has to do with the local club and not the people who traveled here." Hawke watched as a family of four, the boys appeared about ten and twelve, and the parents, hauled items out of their tent.

"I'll go talk to Smithy and Chessie. You might as well go file your report and clock out."

"Copy." Novak strode toward his vehicle.

Hawke turned and followed the Y to the left, counting three tents. A man stepped out of the tent carrying a duffel bag. "Are you leaving?" Hawke asked, making the man jump.

The man, Smithy, regained his composure and held out a hand. "Smithy, err, Blake Roberts."

"Mr. Roberts, where are you from?" Hawke felt a slight tremor in the man's hand as he shook.

"I told the deputy, Anatone. Just up the highway."

Only an hour's drive from here. Close enough for an affair with the victim's wife. "How did you know Mr. Pruss?"

"I told your deputy. From Rendezvous. I'm a gunsmith by trade. My hobby is rebuilding original muzzleloaders. I come to these events to promote my business."

"How long have you known him?" Hawke jotted down the information.

"Five, six years."

"And his wife?"

The man's cheeks and ears flushed. "The same length of time. She attends the events with him."

"And I heard that you and she have been meeting up at these events." Hawke didn't give the man time to think. "Did you get along with Sure Shot?"

Roberts gave his head a shake as if to clear his thoughts. "As well as anyone else who came across him."

Hawke studied the man. "Then you didn't like him. Was it because of how he acted or because he was married to the woman you are having an affair with?"

The man's eyes narrowed. "You're tossing out a lot of accusations?"

"Not accusations. I'm trying to get to the truth. Enough people have told me about you sneaking into the Pruss tent that I am certain it is a fact." Hawke flipped the pages of his logbook as if counting the different statements.

Roberts shrugged. "They all know that her husband slept with more than one woman. At least Kristen is faithful to me."

Hawke quirked an eyebrow. "How do you know she is faithful to you? I had a witness say they saw a man slip out of her tent when the fire was noticed."

The gunsmith grinned. "Because that man was me. As soon as her drunk husband left, Kristen called and asked me to keep her company."

"I see. What did you and Kristen do while her husband was away?"

"You're kidding me, right?" The man's jaw dropped as he stared at Hawke like he was a fool.

"No. Did you talk? Maybe plan how to get rid of her husband?"

"Hey! We did no such thing! We drank wine and made love. The bright light, that we later learned was her husband's Jeep, stopped all the love making. She slipped into a nightgown, and I went out the backside of the tent, went around behind a couple of tents, and joined the bucket brigade."

"I saw you hovering at the edge of the crowd wanting to protect Mrs. Pruss." Hawke allowed a bit of sentiment to inch into his words. This man was easy to read. The more he could get out of him the better. Right how he'd given the wife an alibi, but the spouse is always the first suspect in a murder.

"It's hard to keep my distance at these things," Roberts added.

"Do you see her other than at Rendezvous?" Hawke wondered if the victim had figured out his wife was serious about someone, and not liking to be bested, had made an ultimatum.

"We'd meet in Lewiston once a month. She'd tell her old man she was going shopping." The man smiled.

"She didn't think he'd caught on to that?" Hawke

would wonder why his friend Dani was going to a town two hours away to shop once a month. Was he more skeptical than most men?

"She's a teacher. There are more places in Lewiston than in Alder for her to purchase supplies and craft projects for her class. She would go to a couple of places for those items first, then meet me for dinner, a movie, and spend the night."

Hawke shook his head. "You're sure he didn't know about you two? Everyone else here does."

Roberts glared. "I doubt any of them would have told. No one likes him and everyone knows how he treated her."

This piqued Hawke's attention. "How did he treat her?"

"Like a possession. He told her what she could and couldn't do, except when she met me in Lewiston. She flat out told him, she had to go there for supplies." He smiled. "She stood up to him for me."

Hawke made a note to talk to Mrs. Pruss about those trips and if she had any inkling her husband knew about them. He was too controlling to not have found out about her affair. "Thank you for your answers. What's your number in case I have any other questions?"

Roberts rattled off his phone number and his face slackened with relief.

Hawke wandered along the road until he found the tent with empty rifle cartridge wind chimes. Wooden boxes, and what looked like bedding, were stacked in front of the tent.

He knocked on the side of the canvas. "State Trooper Hawke."

No one answered. He called out again and pulled the flap back. The inside was empty. He spun around slowly taking in the camps around this one. They were all in the same state of being taken down.

A plume of dust appeared above the tree tops along the road into the flat. It appeared many had gone to get their vehicles. He remained where he was as a pickup rolled on by and parked three camps down. Then a small SUV appeared and stopped at another camp. After six vehicles arrived in the area, an older model SUV pulled to a stop in front of him.

A woman with copper curls and the clothing he'd seen in photos of Annie Oakley, stepped out of the pickup and walked up to him with her hand held out. "Chessie," she said.

"Trooper Hawke," he responded, returning her firm handshake.

"Horrible what happened here last night." She released his hand and headed to the boxes, picking one up.

As she headed back to the truck, Hawke said, "You aren't too shook up about the death of a man I heard you were having an affair with."

She placed the box in the back of the SUV and slowly spun toward him, a smile on her face. "Affair. That means, I didn't give him my heart. I used him when he was available."

"I see. Did he know you were using him? From all the people I've spoken with he was the user." Hawke determined this was a straight forward woman and he'd get further with her by being straight forward back.

She laughed. "That's what he liked about it. I didn't get weepy if he decided to conquer someone new. I didn't need him to prop up my ego."

"So, you held no grudges against him?" Hawke had a feeling this was the first honest person he'd questioned so far.

"Not a one. We've known each other a long time. He never wanted the car dealership, and he never wanted to stay in Wallowa County. But his dad died suddenly and his mom needed help with the business. When he married Kristen, I thought he'd finally learn to be happy. Then we met up at these things and I learned he wasn't happy. That's why he slept around, bossed people around, and basically acted like an ass. It was his way of making life more interesting."

Hawke jotted all she said down. "Did he know about his wife and Roberts?"

Her face scrunched into a puzzled expression. "Roberts?"

"Smithy."

She grinned. "Yeah, he thought it was great once that happened. That way Sure Shot could fool around and Kristen didn't care."

"Are you sure she didn't care about his fooling around?" Hawke had yet to see a woman who didn't mind their man -married or not- fooling around. Dani had made comments since they'd been sleeping together that she'd prefer it if she were the only one. Which she was. He had never been a bed hopper.

"How much does a wife care about what the husband is doing as long as he's leaving her alone?" Chessie gave him a wry smile.

There was something more she wasn't telling him. "What is the story behind that remark?"

"Sure Shot could get physical. Lots of pent up

aggression."

"He hit his wife?"

"I can't say one way or the other. I can only say how he acted when we were together, and I'm pretty sure he would be rougher with his wife, who couldn't walk away as easily."

Chapter Six

Hawke knew he needed to clock out and go home to sleep, but he wanted to talk to two more people before he slept on what he knew so far.

He walked back to the area where the local muzzleloaders were camped. Many of them were also pulling up camp. It appeared this year's event had been cancelled.

Sourdough, Mr. Levens, was shoving items into the back of a box trailer hitched to an older suburban. "Mr. Levens, where could I find your wife and daughter?"

The man stared at him. "What do you need to talk to them for?"

"I'm talking to everyone who is a part of the Wallupa Muzzleloaders to learn all I can about the deceased."

"They don't know anything about Sure Shot." Levens moved between Hawke and the tent.

"I'm sure the women get together and visit during

the weekends here." Hawke peered into the man's eyes. "I'd like to see if Mrs. Pruss ever confided in your wife or if your daughter ever overheard anything."

"Oh, like woman to woman stuff?" Levens seemed uncomfortable talking about that topic.

"Yeah."

Levens moved out of the way. "I think School Marm did visit with Wendy a time or two." He walked to the tent. "Wendy, Biscuit, come on out here," he said, sticking his head into the tent.

The man walked back over to the stack of camping gear by the trailer.

Two boys around eight and ten ran out of the tent.

"Sorry, mister," the first one said, when he bounced off Hawke.

"He's not a mister, he's a cop," the second one said, standing back, staring.

"What did you want, Jake?" Mrs. Levens stepped out and stopped when her gaze landed on Hawke. The daughter stepped out behind her mother.

"Mrs. Levens, Biscuit, I'd like to have a few words with you over by my vehicle." He knew they'd never speak up with the husband and father standing within earshot.

"I'm not…" The woman started.

"It's okay, he wants to know about School Marm," Levens said.

The daughter linked her arm with her mother's. "Come on, Mom." The two women walked ahead of Hawke to his pickup.

At the vehicle, he motioned for the two to sit on the tailgate. They did. The woman stared at her booted, swinging feet. The young woman studied him.

"I'd like to know what you saw or heard last night from about seven pm on," Hawke thought starting with the easy question might get more out of them than confronting them with what he knew.

Mrs. Levens muttered something.

"What was that?" Hawke asked, his pen poised on his logbook.

"Jake and I finished cleaning up from the meal and put the boys down. He went out looking for Sara. She'd disappeared right after we ate." The woman glanced at her daughter. "I worked on a vest for a client and waited for them to come back."

Hawke settled his gaze on Sara. "And you? Where did you go when you left?"

She glared at him and crossed her arms. "That's no one's business but mine."

"A man was killed here last night. If you can't account for your whereabouts, I'll have to assume you had something to do with it."

The mother and daughter inhaled at the same time. And they exhaled both talking at once.

Raising a hand, he stopped the two. "I need to know where you were, and if you were with anyone who can vouch for you."

Sara huffed out a chest-full of aggrieved air. "I was with Hardtack."

"You know your father forbid you to see that boy," Mrs. Levens said, studying her daughter.

The daughter glared at her mother. "He forbid you to see Sure Shot and you still did."

"How?" Horror sculpted the woman's face and rounded her eyes.

"I'm not stupid. When he came to see you about a

new pair of buckskins." The young woman made a face. "You never took your other clients in the bedroom to measure them. And when he picked them up? I wasn't at Megan's. I saw him arrive and not leave for over an hour."

The woman's shoulders slumped. "It's not something I'm proud of. He had a way of making me feel…" Her gaze darted to her husband. "Desired."

Hawke wondered how some marriages survived when one or both parties were so unhappy or unfulfilled. "We'll get into that after I talk to Sara." He shifted his position to look the young woman straight in the eyes. "Where were you and Hardtack when you realized there was a fire?" He wanted to see if her answer was the same as the young man's.

She pointed to the hill the sun had peeked over as he drank coffee with Swift Arrow.

"What did you do when you realized something was wrong?"

"At first, we just saw brightness, then we hurried down the hill and saw the fire. Hardtack told me to go back to camp, and he ran down to help."

"Did you see or hear anything before the flash of light?" Hawke needed to figure out how soon before the fire the man had been shoved into the corner of the container.

The young woman closed her eyes, then opened them and shook her head. "No. We walked up the hill. I heard something rustling and worried it was Dad, but then a turkey gobbled and Hardtack laughed at me for being scared of a turkey. We were looking for a downed log to sit on to talk, when the light flashed."

"Thank you. You can go help your dad pack up. I

have a couple more questions for your mom." He waited until the young woman threw a glare at her mom before slipping off the tailgate and walking toward her father.

"Mrs. Levens, were you still having an affair with the victim?"

The woman's face crumpled, and she raised her hands to cover her falling apart. "Yes. Sure Shot said if I didn't continue to sleep with him, he'd make sure Sourdough was run out of the club. This club, this re-enactment, is what Jake lives for. He loves the shooting, the dressing up, and camping with minimal equipment."

Hawke studied the woman. Had she done it for her husband or for herself? "I didn't get the opportunity to see what the victim looked like, but from all I've learned, I believe he was a good-looking, fit man, who knew how to make a woman feel desired. Could it be you let him think you were trying to save your husband's first love so you could see him more?"

She didn't answer, just sat there with her face buried in her hands.

"You were no different than most women, wanting a little excitement. Sure Shot was the bad boy who didn't miss an opportunity to bed a woman. Especially one where he could rub the affair in the face of the husband."

Her hands dropped and her eyes glared at him. "What do you mean? Jake didn't know anything about our affair."

Hawke tapped his logbook. "Your daughter stated your husband forbid you to see Sure Shot."

The woman stared at him, her eyeballs quivering as she tried to find a way around the facts.

"Even if your daughter hadn't said anything, I've heard from enough people camped in this area about your affair with the deceased that there is no way your husband didn't know." Hawke's first impression of this woman being fragile had changed. It changed when her daughter walked away, and he felt, rather than saw a transformation in the woman.

"It doesn't matter what others said. I had stopped seeing Sure Shot. He told me now that everyone and my husband knew about the affair, it wasn't as fun to sneak around." Her gaze bore into him.

Was she mad the man had only used her when it was an illicit affair or had she wanted him to think that? He held the stare, trying to figure out which.

She finally dropped her gaze. "I need to help my family pack."

"Where do you and your family live?" he asked.

"Eagle." She slid off the tailgate of the vehicle and walked back to her husband, placing a hand on the man's back and saying something to him.

Hawke walked over to where Grizzly was taking down his tent. "Can you tell me where I can find Red Beard, Dead-eye Duke, and Smokepole?"

The man faced him and pointed. "That's Dead-eye's place. Two over is Smokepole, and Red Beard is with the group over there." He swung his arm toward the group of tents where the road first entered the flat.

"Thanks." Hawke nodded toward the Pruss tent still standing twenty feet from the charred vehicle. "Anyone going to help Mrs. Pruss pack up?"

"I will when I finish here. She's not in any shape to do it," Grizzly said, staring at the tent.

"That's kind of you." Hawke was trying to see just

what kind of feelings the man had for his best friend's wife.

"It's what any brother would do."

"Mrs. Pruss is your sister?" Now it clicked. The closeness but not that of lovers. And she'd said her brother had made the chairs when he wasn't farming.

"Yeah. I'm the one who introduced her to James. There have been several times I'd wished I hadn't. Like now. He's dead and she's going to have to deal with her mother-in-law alone." Grizzly didn't look as large and intimidating as he talked about his sister.

"Why? Do you think the mother-in-law will accuse your sister of her son's death?" Hawke hadn't thought about the deceased's family. But they would need to be included in his investigation.

"I'm sure of it. Mrs. Pruss has never liked Kristen." Grizzly scrubbed a hand over his face. "You'll find out when you question her." He returned to taking down his tent.

Chapter Seven

At the camp Grizzly pointed out as being Dead-eye Duke's, Hawke introduced himself to a man in his sixties, with a long gray beard and shaggy gray hair. The man wore buckskins that looked as if they'd been dug up during the raid of a mountaineer's grave.

"Dead-eye Duke," the man said, shaking hands. "Bet you're here about the commotion last night."

Hawke studied the man. "I am. What can you tell me about James Pruss and the last time you saw him?"

The man shook his head. "Seen him about seven last night when he and Grizzly walked by. I was cleaning out my rifle. They were having what looked like a deep conversation."

"When did you see the fire?" Hawke asked.

The man's cheeks, that could be seen above the beard line, reddened. "I didn't see the fire. I had a couple swallows of Jim Beam and passed out. Didn't know anything until this morning when I seen the Jeep burnt up and asked someone what had happened."

Hawke raised an eyebrow. "Kind of hard to throw a knife with a hangover, isn't it?"

Dead-eye bristled. "I've been tossing knives since I was big enough to lift one. There's more to it than strength and a steady hand."

"Really?" Hawke knew an alcoholic when he saw one. His stepfather had hit the bottle as soon as he'd rose out of bed in the morning. It was amazing some of the things they could do while hungover. It was as if their body did it without them having to use their minds.

"I'm packing. Anything else you want to know?" Dead-eye turned his back to Hawke.

"How did you and Sure Shot get along?"

The man swung back around. "We got on just fine when he wasn't tryin' to change everything."

"What was he trying to change?" Hawke flipped open his book and wrote what he'd already learned while waiting for the man to continue.

"What you writing down?" The man tried to look at the book.

"Your answers. I am investigating a murder." Hawke stopped writing and glanced up.

Dead-eye's bushy gray eyebrows rose and his mouth made an o shape surrounded by the long wiry gray hairs of his beard. "I just thought the Jeep burned up. Thought that was funny. You mean Sure Shot was in it?"

There was no denying the surprise on the man's face. "Yes. I thought someone told you what happened?"

"Smokepole only said the Jeep caught on fire."

Hawke closed his book. "Where can I find

Smokepole?"

Dead-eye pointed to the man who had been at the head of the line throwing water on the fire the night before.

"Thanks. For the record. Did another police officer talk to you?"

The man shook his head. "You're the first I seen."

"What's your real name?"

"Floyd Covey."

Hawke wrote that in his logbook and headed over to talk to Smokepole. He'd expected another older member of the group, not one close to the age of the deceased.

"Trooper, how can I help you?" Smokepole asked, stepping forward and extending a hand when Hawke walked into his campsite.

"You were at the front of the bucket brigade last night. Didn't you see there was a body in the vehicle before you started tossing water on it?"

"No. All I saw were four wheels and flames filling the vehicle. Then the steam after I tossed the water on." The man motioned to two up-turned logs.

Hawke said, pulling out his logbook to write. "What's your real name?"

"Todd Hudson. Like I told the other officer, I live in Winslow and I work part-time at my family's farm and the rest of the time I make art out of scrap metal."

"I understand you and the deceased didn't get along." He waited for the man to tick through who had said that.

Sighing, Hudson said, "It's common knowledge Sure Shot wanted to make big changes to the club and this rendezvous. I didn't mind some of the changes, but giving out fancy trophies isn't how it was done in the 1800s. Neither was using fancy targets. He wanted to get electronic targets that kept score rather than the way we do it now."

"Why was he pushing for things to be modernized?" Hawke asked.

"Hell, if I know. He joined the club saying he loved history. Then when he was voted in as president, he started trying to change us into a regular gun club rather than a muzzleloader club."

"And that's the only beef you had with him?" Switching up the conversation did what Hawke wanted, caught the man off guard.

"What do you mean?" He was stalling.

"Pruss didn't hit on your wife or girlfriend? Or maybe you saw him being mean to that pretty wife of his?"

The man scowled. "If you're trying to say I didn't care for the man, I didn't. He was a worthless piece of shit who treated everyone like they were his servants, and that included his wife. But I didn't kill him. He wasn't worth wasting my life over."

The man said all of this peering straight into Hawke's eyes. He was speaking the truth.

"Thank you for your time." Hawke stood, closed his logbook, and walked over to his truck. He needed to get out of here, go home, and grab some sleep if he was going to be back in Flora tonight to watch for the poacher.

At his vehicle, he took off his hat, and slid in behind the steering wheel. He'd catch Red Beard on his way out.

Before he closed the door, he felt a presence beside

him. He turned his head and found Swift Arrow standing between his door and him.

"Did you have more to tell me?" he asked, grabbing for his logbook.

"I think I know who the person was I saw by Sure Shot's tent." She nodded her head.

"Who?" Hawke already knew the answer but he wasn't going to say so.

"I think it was Smithy. The more I think about it, I'm sure it was him."

"Do you think he would kill Sure Shot?" He studied the woman to see if she was trying to manipulate his way of thinking or she really wanted to help.

"He and School Marm have been messing around a long time. He might have wanted to make room to become School Marm's husband. Then they wouldn't have to sneak around. And everyone knows Sure Shot wasn't nice to her." Swift Arrow backed up.

"What about her? School Marm. Do you think she'd torch her husband?" He was seeing a grudge against the dead person from Swift Arrow. But he wasn't sure it was enough to make her kill. But you never knew when someone would snap. He planned to have her checked out as thoroughly as all the others that made him suspicious.

"A woman can only put up with so much and they snap." With that the woman strode back to her loaded vehicle.

Hawke wrote down the conversation in his logbook and headed out of the camping area, following other vehicles. When he reached the spot where Grizzly had pointed to where Red Beard was camped, the space was empty. He'd have to get the man's real name from the report and contact him later.

"What's this I heard about you catching a homicide when you were supposed to be catching a poacher?" Sergeant Spruel asked when he walked into the State Police side of the Fish and Wildlife building in Winslow.

"I was watching for the poacher and a call of a vehicle on fire at Grizz Flat came in. There was a body in the vehicle." Hawke walked to the breakroom to grab a cup of coffee.

Spruel followed him into the room. "Get the report written up and get some sleep. I'm tired of Dale calling in here every morning wanting to know what we're going to do about the poacher."

"Did he call in this morning?" Hawke would have rather sat in his vehicle watching for the poacher than deal with the homicide. His thoughts did an abrupt halt. Who was he kidding? He'd become addicted to following the leads in a homicide and finding the killer. It was a lot like following tracks in the wilderness.

"No. I think all the commotion at Grizz Flat may have kept the poacher away." Spruel poured himself a cup of coffee. "Get the report finished and go home and get some sleep." The sergeant strode out of the room and down the hall.

Hawke walked out to his desk, one of four along the same wall, and flicked on the computer monitor. He pulled the drawer out with the keyboard and logged in. Sipping coffee, clicking into the homicide investigation document Shoberg must have already started, he began to type in his findings. His stomach grumbled. He picked up his cell phone and scrolled through the numbers, looking for the Rusty Nail Café, his favorite spot to grab a quick bite in Winslow.

"What'cha want?" answered the seventy-something owner in her usual non-hospitable way.

"It's Hawke. I'd like a cheeseburger, fries, and piece of pie to go in an hour."

"What kind of pie? We got cherry, apple and banana cream."

"Apple, please."

The phone on the other end clunked down. And that was the charming Merrilee, who made up for her poor people skills with good food.

He returned to typing in the information. After inputting what he'd learned, he wrote a list of names down. Ones that he wanted to know more about. He'd typed the first one into the database when the phone on his desk buzzed.

"Hawke," he answered.

"Hawke, there's a woman out front who said she's delivering your order," Marsha O'Dell, the receptionist for the Fish and Wildlife, said.

"I'll be right out." He hung up the phone and glanced at his watch. It was forty minutes past when he'd said he'd pick up his meal. He walked into the Fish and Wildlife side of the building.

His friend, Justine, stood on the other side of the counter. When she spotted him, she held up a brown paper bag.

"I lost track of time," he said, by way of greeting.

"You know Merrilee, it was blocking the shelf between the kitchen and dining room," Justine replied.

Hawke laughed. "I bet she called me a few choice

names."

"None I'll repeat." Justine laughed.

"How much do I owe for this?"

"Twenty would cover a tip." She raised her eyebrows.

He laughed some more. "Here's twenty-five. Did you just get off work or actually come here just to deliver the food?"

They exchanged the money for the bag.

"I'm on my way home."

"How did you know I was here?" Hawke opened the bag and started munching on the fries. That's when he realized Marsha was listening into the conversation.

"I figured if you had called in for an order to go, you were working at the office. It's the only time you know when you will be by exactly. Only this time…"

"Yeah, well, thanks." Hawke cut the conversation short. He and Justine were just friends. Had been for several years, but it seemed as if every time they talked in public his name became linked with hers. He was in a relationship with Dani and didn't want the fiery ex-pilot to think he was two-timing her. Even though she and Justine called themselves the Hawke Fan Club. He liked living and all of his body parts.

"Okay, see you around." Justine frowned, but headed to the door.

Before Hawke cleared the reception area, Marsha said, "Is she your girlfriend?"

He spun around. "No. She's a friend."

"A pretty good one to bring you food." Marsha slid her chair forward and started typing on the keyboard.

Hawke sighed and walked back over to the State Police side of the building.

Chapter Eight

The unnerving buzz of the alarm clock pulled Hawke from a deep sleep. As he grew older, his body and mind required more than a few hours of sleep each night, or in this case, day. His mind was muddled. Why was he sleeping in the afternoon? And why did his clock wake him up?

Dog, his wire-haired mixed mutt, whined and poked his nose in Hawke's face.

"Yeah. Yeah. Any idea why I'm getting up?" As he slid his hand back and forth across Dog's head, his mind began to focus. He needed to watch for a poacher at Dale Ussery's and while he waited, he'd check out the information that had come in so far on the homicide last night.

He scrubbed his hands over his face and sat up. Putting on his uniform, his stomach grumbled. A grilled cheese and milk shake from the Shake Shack would be good. He'd pick that up on his way through Alder headed to Flora.

First, he needed to feed his horses and mule.

"Come on, Dog." He headed to the door. When it opened, Dog shot by him and down the steps to the barn floor below. Hawke rented the small apartment, paddock, and run from Herb and Darlene Trembley. He wasn't home much and his animals needed care when he was working the Snake River in a boat, went on a vacation, or worked long hours away from home. Otherwise, the animals went with him when he worked the wilderness areas.

"Hey, boys. Looks like Darlene has been taking good care of you." He scratched Jack, an appaloosa, on the forehead, Horse, the mule, around his long ears, and his newest, younger appaloosa gelding that he'd traded his skittish gelding, Boy, to Darlene for, on the neck. The newest horse was more personable than the one he'd traded out. Hawke had a good feeling about, Polka Dot. He cringed whenever he thought or said the name, but his little friend, Kitree, named the gelding when she saw him. She had given Hawke fits about the names he'd given his pets from the first time they'd met, when he was tracking her and saving her life.

"Are you headed out again tonight?" Herb asked from behind him.

"Yeah, didn't get a chance to catch the poacher last night before all hell broke loose at Grizz Flat."

"So we heard. I can't say I didn't see it coming." Herb walked up and patted Jack on the forehead.

"See what coming?" Hawke not only had the best landlords in terms of them helping care for his animals, they also knew just about everyone in the county and heard all the gossip. This knowledge had helped him a time or two when it came to finding suspects and killers.

"James Pruss being murdered. That boy, and now man, has always rubbed people the wrong way. If his mother didn't keep a close eye on the dealership, I would bet you my land he would have been bringing in stolen vehicles and selling them." Herb gave one curt nod. "Yep. His untimely death doesn't surprise me in the least."

Hawke shifted to lean against the gate and study his landlord. "Did you hear anything about how he treated his wife?"

"You don't think Kristen had anything to do with his death, do you?" Herb spun to face him.

"I'm just in the asking questions stage. I haven't made any decisions one way or the other." Hawke wandered to the hay he purchased from his landlords to feed his horses. After filling a wheelbarrow, he headed to the outside run.

Herb followed along behind him, while Dog ran after a barn cat that had the misfortune of jumping off a baler as the dog approached.

"Kristen comes from a good family. I can't see her harming her husband. If so, she would have done it years ago, not now."

"Do they have children?" Hawke always worried about murder victims who leave behind children. Something sordid always popped up when he investigated a homicide. He tossed the hay over the fence to the horses.

"No. That's why I say she could have done away with him or left him at any time. Don't see her murdering him to get out of the marriage. All she'd have to do is wave the tablet full of women's names he'd slept with."

Hawke had wondered if that was as common knowledge in the county as it had been with the muzzleloader group. "What about her brother? Adam Jolly?"

"Big guy, but his heart is just as big. Good farmer and even better wood craftsman." Herb followed Hawke back to the barn.

Hawke placed the empty wheelbarrow back in the barn. "I need to get going. I want to be in place before dark."

"Sure thing. I'll see if Darlene's heard anything that might help you." Herb strode out of the barn, like he was on a mission, Dog trotting at his heels.

The animal had smelled the cooking roast Hawke had caught a whiff of while walking back to the barn. His stomach grumbled. No home-cooked food for him tonight.

With his truck hidden in a grove of trees at the edge of the field Dale Ussery had found the dead does, Hawke sat in the driver's seat reading the reports that had come in on the burned body found in the Jeep.

As he'd noted, the head had hit a pointed object and the medical examiner agreed it could have been the corner of the storage container as there were flakes of paint in the victim's hair. They had been sent off to the state forensic lab along with the evidence gathered by the fire marshal and a DNA sample.

Hawke's list of suspects was long. The victim had few friends and many enemies. He did have Red Beard's real name, Wylie Lambert. He lived in La

Grande and was part of one of the rival muzzleloader clubs.

Glancing at the time on his laptop, Hawke decided it would be best to wait until morning to call the man.

A light flashed to his left. Hawke closed the laptop and slipped out of the vehicle. He waited. There it was, another flash of light. It appeared the poacher had come back tonight.

Staying in the trees, Hawke made his way toward the light.

He was close enough to see the beam land on a doe feeding in the field.

The "crack and thump" of a high-powered rifle fractured the silence.

The doe dropped.

Hawke remained hidden until two men walked to the animal, studied it, and then placed their rifles on the ground and began dressing out the animal.

Walking slow and quiet, Hawke stood within twenty feet of the men with his Glock pointed at them.

"State Police, hands in the air!" he called out.

One man started to reach for his rifle.

"If you want to get shot, grab the rifle. Right now, you just have a poaching violation. You shoot at me and it's going to be a lot worse."

The man jerked his hand back.

"Kneel with your backs to me." As the two turned around, Hawke strode forward, grabbing the wrists of the smaller man, who had made a grab for his gun, and cuffing him.

As soon as he finished that, he cuffed the larger man.

"Stand up," Hawke ordered. He walked them ahead

of him back to his vehicle. There was evidence to pick up, and he didn't want the two sitting in his vehicle the whole time. He grabbed a rope out of the back of his truck and walked them over to a tree.

"Stand with your back to the tree," He motioned to the two.

They backed up to the tree. Hawke moved them so they were directly across from one another and couldn't see or touch the other around the large pine. He slipped the rope around the chain between the handcuffs and tied it tight to the tree trunk.

"I'll be back." He drove the truck as close to the doe as he could get without ruining the crop in the field. Taking photos, he felt for the animal. Not only was it killed just because the fool thought he could, the body wouldn't even have been revered for the bellies it filled, the warmth the skin would have provided as clothing, and the beauty of a teeth necklace. Hawke picked up the carcass and placed it in the back of his vehicle. After taking photos of the rifles, he stored them in the toolbox behind the cab.

Using his flashlight, he followed their tracks and found their vehicle. He checked the registration. It said the vehicle belonged to a man he'd caught before for poaching. But neither of the men he'd cuffed tonight were that man.

He didn't see any keys in the ignition. Locking the doors, he hoped one of the two had the keys.

Driving back to where he'd left the men, a call came over the radio.

"Reckless driver called in on the North Highway," dispatch said.

"Copy. This is Hawke. I'm bringing in two

poachers. Can someone else grab that?"

"Copy," Ward Dillion, another Game Warden replied.

Hawke stopped with his headlights on the two. Neither one looked familiar. Perhaps one was a relative of the person who owned the pickup.

"You can't tie us to a tree and leave us," the smaller one complained.

"You got a dog?" Hawke asked.

"Yeah."

"You tie him to a tree or post?"

"Yeah?" The man smiled as if it were something to be proud of.

"This is how he feels when you tie him up." Hawke pulled a knife out of his boot sheath and sliced the rope to let the two loose. "I should leave you here for Mr. Ussery to find. He isn't very happy you've been poaching on his land."

"We weren't poaching. We have a right to hunt wherever we want," the larger man said.

"How do you figure that?" Hawke asked, staring at the man while he held them both by an arm.

"I found out I'm Indian - Native American. We can hunt when and wherever we want." The man planted his feet.

Hawke stopped and shoved the man next to the hood of his vehicle. "Stay put. I want to talk to you." He turned to the smaller man. "Are you also Native American?"

"No. I came along to help."

"With a gun? One you were going to point at a law enforcement officer?" Hawke let the words settle in as he opened the door and helped the man into the vehicle.

He latched the handcuffs to a chain he had bolted in the floor.

He returned to the other man. "I'm going to reach in your back pocket for your wallet to see your I.D."

"Go ahead. I've never been arrested before." The big man stuck his left hip towards Hawke.

Plucking the wallet from the pocket, Hawke flipped it open in front of the man. "It says here you are Ronald Waite, age thirty-five, and you live in Tollgate. What are you doing over here, Ronald?"

"These are my ancestral lands. I can hunt and fish here anytime I want."

Hawke studied the man. "What tribe?"

"Warm Springs."

"That's not a tribe, that is a confederation of tribes." Hawke studied the man in the beam of his headlights.

"I was told my Paiute side of the family is Warm Springs," the man said stubbornly.

"Then you are Paiute. They did not hunt in this area. They were in Southern Oregon, Idaho, Northern California and Nevada." Hawke led the man to the back door of his vehicle on the passenger side. "Besides, no Indian would leave the waste when killing an animal like you did."

He closed the door and walked around to the driver's side and slid behind the wheel. "Even Natives have to hunt the same time during the year as everyone else. But they are allowed to hunt on public land. You were hunting on private land."

The larger man groaned and the smaller man started in bashing his friend for getting him into trouble.

Hawke tuned the two out, thinking about his friend

Dani who grew up off the reservation and was starting to become interested in her heritage. They'd talked about attending the Tamkaliks Powwow this summer.

"Hey, this isn't the way back to Alder," a loud voice said.

Hawke focused on the road and realized he was headed downhill to Troy, not back to the North Highway.

Something about last night's death was bothering him. But what? Something that had him taking two suspects in custody toward a crime scene.

"The nights you came out to Flora to poach, did you see anyone else?" Hawke studied the two in the rearview mirror.

"We wouldn't tell you. That's more against us," said the smaller man. The more Hawke studied him, the resemblance to the poacher who owned the truck they were using appeared. When he put this man's name in the system, there was a good chance he'd come up with priors.

"There was one of those compact SUVs, dark blue, came down this road the last two times we came out here," Waite said.

"When was that?" Hawke didn't want them to know the days were important. He crossed the bridge and turned left toward Troy.

"I saw the SUV on Monday and again Tuesday," Waite said.

He heard a scuffle in the back and glanced in the mirror. It appeared the smaller man didn't want Waite telling how many times they'd been out here poaching.

"Did you see who was in the vehicle?" He turned, driving the short street of Troy and turning left into the parking lot that had been full of vehicles the night before.

"A woman was driving. There was a passenger, but I only glanced at it. Figured it was someone who lived here." Waite glared at the other man as he talked.

"It probably was just a local." Hawke turned the vehicle and headed back to Flora. He'd drop these two off at the county jail and write up his report.

Chapter Nine

Hawke spent Sunday morning sleeping before heading to the office in Winslow. He'd arrested the poachers and needed to finish writing up the report and wanted to read anything that came in on the Grizz Flat homicide.

Since it was Sunday, he had the office to himself. The other two officers on duty were on patrol. Sergeant Spruel had the weekends off. That's what being higher on the payroll got him. Not that he had any less stress with his job. Hawke preferred being out of the office. Especially patrolling the wilderness. This time of year, it was mostly checking that the turkey and bear hunters had proper tags and were hunting in the specified areas.

He pulled up the report he'd started last night at the county jail to get the two poachers locked up. He finished the report and noticed they would be arraigned in the morning. He wrote Ronald Waite's information in his logbook with the other people to contact about the fire victim. If he found the vehicle that had traveled to Troy two nights in a row, he could see if Waite recognized it. The prospect was a long shot, but he suspected there was a reason the man brought it up. More than that car had to have driven that road, why had Waite mentioned it?

With that report out of the way, Hawke opened up the Grizz Flat homicide and read his input, Deputy Novak's, and Trooper Shoberg's. Then he pulled up the M.E.'s initial findings. Blunt force trauma to the head before suffocating from smoke. Body charred beyond recognition. Dental records requested. Some missing teeth. Appeared to have been knocked out perimortem.

Hawke leaned back in his chair. If the victim was shoved and hit the back of his head on the container, how had he lost his teeth? Which teeth were they? He found Dr. Vance's phone number on his cell and called.

"You've reached Dr. Gwendolyn Vance's voicemail. Please leave a name and number and I'll call you back as soon as possible. Thank you."

After the beep, Hawke left his name and number then continued reading the reports. Fire Marshal Florry's report stated what he'd told Hawke that night. The fire had been escalated by dousing the inside of the Jeep with gasoline.

Had the gasoline come from a can on the back of the Jeep? Or had someone stashed it somewhere with the plan of using it? If it had been a spur of the moment decision to finish off the already unconscious man, then the gas had to have come from some place handy. Would the murderer have syphoned it out of the vehicle? Why was the victim so insistent his Jeep had to remain at the camping area?

So many questions. The best way to get answers to them was to visit Mrs. Pruss.

Hawke logged out of the computer and headed to the door. His phone buzzed. A quick glance at the name and he smiled.

Dani.

"Hawke," he answered, as he always did.

"Hey, I'm flying back into the lodge tomorrow, do you have time for dinner tonight?" Dani asked, getting right to the matter of her phone call.

That was what he liked about the woman. She only talked when she had something worthwhile to say. And she didn't expect a commitment out of him. They were two independent people, who found they melded well together.

"If you make it a late dinner. I'm working until eight."

"I don't want to clean up a cooking mess that late. Want to meet somewhere?"

"The only place open late on a Sunday would be High Mountain Brew in Alder." Hawke tried not to frequent places where people knew him when he dated Dani, but he wanted to see her and that was the best place on a Sunday night to get something to eat that late. If he was lucky Desiree Halver, a young woman he knew at the establishment, wouldn't be working tonight. She wasn't a gossipy woman, but she'd have many questions, and he preferred not to answer any.

"That sounds perfect. Want me to pick you up at your place at eight-thirty?" Dani's tone didn't sound like a question, it was more an order. You could tell she'd been an officer in the military. Air Force pilot, to be precise.

"I'll be ready. See you then." He ended the call and continued out to his work vehicle. On his way to the Pruss residence, he did a drive by of the Wallowa Valley Car Sales owned by the Pruss family.

It was as he remembered. Lots of flags and signs talking about good deals and newest features. Because the county had a small population, the one dealership had several different automobile company franchises. What would happen to the business with James gone? He'd check it out tomorrow.

The Pruss residence was on the hill overlooking the town of Alder. He parked his vehicle in the driveway and wondered if the victim and his wife had taken separate vehicles to the event.

Walking up the sidewalk to the house, he heard raised voices.

Hawke stopped on the porch and listened. The voices were too muffled to make out words, but one was definitely angry. He knocked before noticing the obscured doorbell.

The stomp of feet could be heard on the other side of the door before it swung open.

Mrs. Pruss stood with one hand on the door and the other on the door jamb, staring at him with relief. "Trooper Hawke. I'm glad you came around."

He not only saw the woman's relief but felt it immediately. Whoever she'd been quarreling with, she didn't trust.

"Mrs. Pruss, I have some more questions I'd like to ask." Hawke stepped into the house as soon as the woman backed up.

A tall thin woman with silver hair and an outfit, he knew hadn't come from any store in the county, walked out of a room Hawke presumed was the living room. "What are you doing about my son's murder? Are you here to arrest this woman?" A long bony finger pointed at the victim's wife.

The younger Mrs. Pruss slid a little behind him. She was scared of her mother-in-law.

Hawke made introductions with the matron of the family. "State Trooper Hawke, I'd like to ask you some questions Mrs. Pruss." He waved for her to return to the room and shifted to face the younger woman. "Mrs. Pruss—"

"Kristen, please, I don't want to be associated with that woman," hissed the victim's wife.

"Kristen, would you get me a cup of coffee, please." Hawke wanted a few minutes with the older woman. It was evident she didn't like her daughter-in-law. He'd seen more hostility in her in the last three minutes than he'd witnessed in the younger woman over hours.

Kristen spun on her heels and headed down the hall.

Hawke entered the living room, which was like looking at a magazine ad for furniture or flooring. Everything was in its place except for a small ball of yarn and knitting needles.

Mrs. Pruss paced.

"Ma'am, take a seat please. I have some questions for you." Hawke sat on a chair and motioned for the woman to sit on the fancy couch.

She reluctantly sat, her butt perched on the edge of the cushions and her back straight as a board fence.

"Before your son went to the Rendezvous, did he say or do anything that had you concerned?" Hawke asked.

The woman hesitated for only the blink of an eye. "No. He was excited as always to get away for a week and shoot his great granddad's old gun. I never saw the charm of a gun that took so much work to load."

"The week? I thought the Rendezvous was only over the weekend?" Hawke pulled out his logbook.

"He was the president of the club and had to make sure everyone did their job," Mrs. Pruss replied.

Kristen entered the room carrying a tray with three cups of steaming coffee.

Hawke could tell by the smell it would taste better than anything he made or the Rusty Nail served.

While the older woman watched with pursed lips, Kristen handed a cup to Hawke, then placed a cup, sugar bowl, and creamer in front of her mother-in-law.

"What day did your husband go to Grizz Flat?" Hawke asked the woman who'd just joined them.

She sipped her coffee as if she needed the caffeine and said, "Wednesday. We both went up to help set up the targets and our camp. We had to be ready to sign people in on Thursday morning and start the competitions."

"Then he was at home on Monday and Tuesday getting things ready?" Hawke asked.

She studied him. "No. He went to work Monday and Tuesday." She faced her mother-in-law. "He worked late. Said you had him finding items the CPA had asked for."

"My son wasn't at work. He asked for the whole week off." Mrs. Pruss stared down her nose at Kristen.

"It seems he lied to both of you. Do you have any ideas why?" Hawke watched the two. Knowing a man they both had loved had duped them, he would have thought it would bring them together. However, the older woman glared at the younger woman, who seemed to shrink.

"If he wasn't at the car dealership and he wasn't here, where do you think he was?" Hawke glanced back and forth between the two women.

Kristen spoke first. "He could have been out at Adam's, but he would have told me when I mentioned James had worked Monday and Tuesday."

"It's obvious to me, he wanted time with someone before spending so many days with you," Mrs. Pruss snapped at the younger woman.

"It's been perfectly clear from the day James introduced me to you that you felt anyone was better suited to your son than me. Well, you won't have to put up with me anymore. I'll sell the house and move far from here. There are nothing but bad memories here anyway." Kristen popped to her feet and ran out of the room.

Mrs. Pruss's smug expression brought out the anger in Hawke.

"It's evident she is grieving more than the victim's mother."

"How dare you say I'm not grieving for my only child!" Mrs. Pruss tipped the cup of coffee as if she planned to throw it on Hawke.

"You're treating the woman your son loved and married as if she were some vagrant." Hawke stared, daring her to toss the coffee on him.

She tipped the cup back toward herself. "He never loved her. She was a conquest. Once he won a woman's affections, he moved on. How she conned him into marrying her, I'll never know. But she was the only one he stayed with long enough to put a ring on her finger. His father was delighted James had married into an old county family. He said we'd be sure to get more sales from the locals with so many being related to us." She laughed. "He was wrong. It took shrewd dealing to get low end vehicles to keep the locals buying here and not out of the county."

"Are you the shrewd dealer?" Hawke asked.

"Yes." She said the word proudly. "James became a salesman in high school. He could sell anything to anyone. He knew what made people tick and how to play their weaknesses and their strengths to seal a deal."

"I see. And was he still happy with being a salesman or had he taken over the business?" Hawke had Jolly's version of this which would have come from the victim.

"I still had my hands on the reins. James didn't like it, but I wanted the family reputation to remain intact." She sniffed and sipped the coffee.

"You mean James was tarnishing the family's reputation? Was it because he slept around?"

The woman flipped her hand as if that accusation was nothing. "He liked to work with shady people."

"Do you think his shady dealings got him killed?" This thought had been in the back of Hawke's mind since it had been mentioned two nights ago.

He'd caught the woman's attention for the first time.

"You think whatever he was doing outside of selling cars might have caused his death?" She finally appeared to be shook up over her son's murder.

"That's a possibility I plan to look into. Can you

give me any names of the shady people he's been dealing with?"

"No names. But I know he met with someone every Monday night and parts would arrive on Wednesday that cost us less than through the manufacturers." She frowned. "I didn't care for doing business that way, but the parts haven't been inferior, so I didn't say anything."

"Who did he meet?" Hawke was getting a lot of suspects. Too many.

"I don't know the person's name, but they met at the Blue Elk in Winslow." She narrowed her eyes. "If that is who killed him, I'll gladly add any charges his merchandise can provide."

Hawke wondered at the woman's ability to not see she was also an accomplice in purchasing and using what was most likely stolen automobile parts. "Are there any other unscrupulous things you should tell me about your son?"

She glared at him, but hesitated before saying, "Nothing." She rose. "I need to get home and make arrangements for his body and the funeral."

"Shouldn't Kristen be in on that? He was her husband."

The woman scoffed. "He was my son. The woman he married has never behaved like the wife of a pillar of the community. She would hardly give him the funeral he deserves." The woman strode out of the room. The door opened and closed.

Kristen walked into the living room and heaved a sigh. "I couldn't get her to leave before you arrived. She kept asking me why I killed him." The woman stared straight into Hawke's eyes. "I didn't kill him and

I don't know who did." She plopped down on the couch. "I listened in on what James' mother said. He always told me he was playing cards with the boys on Monday night."

"Did that include your brother?" Hawke asked.

She stared at him. "I don't know. I never asked. I just assumed it did. James and Adam have always been close. So close it took me a while to convince Adam, James wasn't treating me right."

"Physical abuse?" Hawke asked. His stepfather had been a physically abusive alcoholic. He often wondered if his biological father had known how his son and wife would end up in a bad relationship if he would have changed his ways to keep his wife with him?

"No, he never laid a hand on me, but his words. He could be charming one minute and making me feel less than human the next." She once again stared him square in the eyes. "I can't say I'm sorry he's dead, but I wouldn't wish burning like that on anyone."

"Why didn't you leave him if you were so unhappy?" His mother had left his biological father when she'd learned he had a gambling and womanizing problem. The womanizing was why Hawke didn't like his name connected with any woman, especially ones he only called friends.

"James liked being married. It kept his 'conquests' from getting serious. He would tell me I couldn't leave because he would spread rumors about me that would get me booted out of my teaching and I'd never get a job again." She stared at her hands. "The Prusses have contacts all over the state and with people in prominent places. I couldn't chance not being able to teach. I love kids. When I discovered I couldn't have children, knowing I could still spend every day surrounded by them with teaching, I could endure being sterile."

"Did James want kids?" Hawke was having a hard time figuring their murder victim out.

Kristen laughed. When she got under control, she said, "No. He thought kids were an anchor. I think it's because his mother was more interested in the car business than her son. He went to work there to spend more time with his parents. Once he was pulled in, he couldn't get loose. He wanted to start his own dealership in La Grande, but his mother stopped him. She wanted him here, where she could keep an eye on him."

"From what she said about him purchasing stolen parts, it might be a good idea she kept him under control."

The woman laughed again. "Please, she didn't care that he was purchasing stolen parts. It made her money. She just didn't want him doing something stupid to tarnish the family name."

Hawke wondered if the mother had withheld more information about her son. He'd go by Wallowa Valley Car Sales tomorrow and see what he could find out from the other employees.

Chapter Ten

Sitting in his vehicle in front of the Pruss residence, Hawke looked up Adam Jolly's phone number and called.

Voicemail picked up.

"Mr. Jolly, this is Trooper Hawke. I would like to talk to you about the Monday night poker game James Pruss attended every week. Give me a call."

He hung up and his phone buzzed. Not Jolly. It was the county M.E., Dr. Vance.

"Dr. Vance, thank you for returning my call," Hawke answered.

"I believe it must have something to do with the fire victim from Friday night?" she replied.

"It does. Reading your report, I saw that several teeth were missing. And I believe the wording meant they were missing before he was in the fire."

"Correct. The trauma to the jawbone makes me suspect they were either knocked out, like in a fight, or taken out on purpose, and not by a dentist."

Hawke soaked this information in. "Have you received the victim's dental records?"

"I'll get them tomorrow. And those will be the first teeth I check records on."

He smiled. The woman was thinking the same as him. "Thank you. And let me know what you find out."

"I will. Enjoy the rest of your Sunday, I plan to."

The call ended. He sat in his vehicle wondering who the victim had conned into driving him to Grizz Flat Monday and Tuesday and why they made the two trips. A glance at his watch said he wasn't going to have time to run out there and look around and get back in time to meet Dani for dinner. Unless…

He pulled out his phone and dialed his dinner date.

"Hello?" Dani answered. "Are you cancelling on me?"

"No. That is if you are up for a picnic at Grizz Flat."

He went on to explain how she could get there from her place outside of Eagle and that he'd bring the picnic. After ending the call, he headed to the Firelight and waited for two rib dinners to be cooked and packaged to go.

"Who you feeding tonight?" the new owner of the Firelight asked.

"Myself." Hawke paid for the meals and left.

On the drive to Troy and Grizz Flat his stomach grumbled, smelling the ribs and all the fixings that went with it.

He spotted Dani's car sitting in front of the Troy store. She wasn't in it. He didn't want to go inside and have people speculating about the two meeting clear out here.

Pulling his vehicle in behind hers, he waited.

Ten minutes later, she came out of the store carrying a brown paper bag. She nodded to him and he pulled out, passing her vehicle and crossing the bridge.

She pulled out and followed.

Taking the hairpin turn onto the road to the flat, he grinned, thinking it had been a long time since he'd invited a woman out to the woods. In fact, the last time he'd invited a female, they were both in high school. That had been a fun afternoon and evening.

Until Dani, he'd still visited Linda from time to time to get his itch scratched. She'd turned out to be a good friend, but also a woman who sold her body. He didn't judge her. She'd needed to make ends meet when her husband left her with two small children. Now the kids were grown and gone, and she didn't feel inclined to worry about what others thought.

Hawke stopped his vehicle near a picnic table and stepped out.

Dani parked her car behind his and walked over to the table, carrying the bag from the store.

"What do you have in there?" he asked, nodding toward the bag.

"Drinks. Did you think of that when you bought dinner?" Her gaze landed on the large brown bag he'd placed on the table.

"No. Good thing you did." He glanced in the direction of the metal container.

"You need to look around before it gets dark," Dani said, picking up both bags. "I'll put these in the car while you look around. You need my help?"

"Possibly. Sit here until I decide."

She nodded, walking toward her car.

Hawke set out toward the container. The contents were checked and documented by Shoberg, but he hadn't been looking for traces of gasoline at the time.

A cheap padlock hung from the handle. Hawke pulled out a set of lock picks and had the door open in minutes. The inside was like a dark cavern with darker shadows of the objects inside. The smell of gun powder, animal hides, and wood filled his nose when he inhaled. He turned on his flashlight, surveying the contents. The targets, wood structures, and miscellaneous boxes were all shoved into the container haphazardly. He wondered that the local group had even taken the time to put the items back in the container as fast as everyone left on Saturday.

He closed the doors and replaced the lock.

Biscuit, Sara Leven, had said she heard something when she and Hardtack were up on the hill. He glanced up. The area the two had been was almost directly above the container.

"Want to go for a hike?" he called to Dani.

She stood from where she'd been sitting at the picnic table watching him, and strode over.

"I suppose you expect me to go up hill?"

He grinned. "We're looking for a gas can. Most likely hidden in a bush."

"You mean the person was burned?" She pointed to the Jeep still standing over the campfire.

"Intentionally."

She shuddered. "How do you deal with all the things you see?"

Hawke started up the hill. "By knowing I'll put the person who causes others harm in jail."

She grunted and moved to the right of him. They went no more than thirty feet up the hill and Dani called out. "Here."

Hawke maneuvered around the bushes and rocks to get to her. The woman had keen eyes. Barely three inches of red could be seen where a metal gas can had been shoved under a bush next to a boulder.

"Good eyes." He pulled out his phone and took photos before pulling on a latex glove and lifting the can out of the bush. "Let's go."

He carried the can back to his vehicle where he placed it in the tool box in the bed of his truck. "Time to eat."

Dani walked over to her car and brought back the two brown bags, placing them on the picnic table. "I hope whatever you bought tastes good cold."

"Me too," he said, wiping his hands with a sheet from a container of disposable wipes. He kept the wipes in his vehicle for when he dealt with dead animals and wanted to get the blood and stench off his hands.

Dani took one of the wipes, cleaned her hands, and then opened the bags. "Smells like barbecue ribs."

"I hope you like the ones from the Firelight." They'd had several meals at the restaurant, but he didn't remember her ever ordering ribs.

"That's why you brought the wipes out. Not because we needed to clean our hands but because we'll need to clean them when we finish." She set one of the food containers in front of him and the other in front of herself. "I like ribs, but it's not a food you eat on a date."

He laughed. "You really think I'd never ask you out again if you ate ribs in front of me? I enjoy watching you enjoy food."

She stared into his eyes for several minutes before they both opened their containers and dug in.

As they ate, he asked how preparations were going for the opening of the lodge for late spring and summer guests. The sun set behind the ridge to the west. Cold air blew up the river.

"We better get going," Hawke said, compiling all the trash into the big brown bag.

"Yeah. I think I'll follow you out to the highway. I don't know if I could find my way over all the dirt roads in the dark." Dani rubbed her hands up and down her arms.

Hawke wrapped an arm around her shoulders. "Ok. I'll be stopping to talk to the farmer who called in the poachers I caught last night. You just keep on going when I turn on my blinker."

"I can do that. When do you have days off?"

"Tomorrow and Tuesday."

"I could stick around until Tuesday if you want to do something tomorrow?"

The wistfulness in her tone almost had him saying yes. But he wasn't sure if he'd be totally free. If Dr. Vance called with something about the teeth, and he'd need to drop the gas can off for it to go to forensics…

"I'd like that, but I have a lot to get done tomorrow. I need to ride Polka Dot."

Dani laughed. "I bet your teeth grind every time you say that."

"It's getting easier the more I say it, but yeah. Never thought I'd have a horse named Polka Dot. I'm thinking of just calling him Dot. Easier and faster to say."

"I'm sure Kitree would understand if you do."

They stopped at the driver door of her vehicle.

"Thanks for agreeing to the change of plans." He leaned against her car, one arm still around her shoulders, the bag of trash in his other hand.

"I could tell you had something you would ditch me to go check if I didn't agree." She slipped out of his arm. "I understand being married to your job. I had that for twenty-five years. I loved what I did. But now I enjoy enjoying life." She stared up at him. "You're ten years older than me. You might want to think about retiring, you have enough years, you'd have a good pension."

Hawke scowled. She was beginning to sound like his mother. "I will, when I quit liking my job." He opened her car door, and she dropped down onto the seat with a huff.

"See you the next time you come to town," he said and closed the door.

Damn! The evening had been enjoyable until Dani's last comment. He stomped over to his vehicle and slid in, tossing the trash in the back seat.

Good thing he had to stop and give Dale Ussery an update on the poaching. It had given him an excuse to not follow her home. As much as he liked Dani's company, he liked his freedom more.

Hawke parked in front of the Ussery home. Two border collies charged around from the side of the house barking.

He stepped out of his vehicle and greeted the two dogs. "Hey boys, anyone else around?" Talking to the animals calmed them down. One ran back to the house and up to the screen door. He pounced twice on the door and a minute later, Dale stepped out onto the porch.

"Trooper, I heard from your boss you caught the poacher." The man motioned to one of the wooden chairs on the porch.

Hawke took a seat. "I did. The one supposedly doing the shooting wasn't from around here. The other one is working his way toward many more poaching violations, I figure."

The farmer shook his head. "I don't begrudge a man the need to feed his family, but they should have been shooting bucks this time of year, not does, and not leaving behind so much good meat."

"It wasn't anyone who needed the meat. Just someone who thought he had the right." Hawke would have been more lenient on the poacher if he had been an Indian who had been living the truth of his ancestors and needed to feed his family. The man he'd caught had used his just learned heritage to try and get away with something.

Hawke shifted the conversation to what he really wanted to ask. "Dale, you've been around here a long time."

"My whole life, except when I was away fighting in 'nam."

"I bet you know the vehicles the locals drive."

The man grinned. "That I do. You can hear old Horace Beckman's rattle can of a pickup from a mile away."

"You know anyone in the area who drives a dark blue compact SUV?" Hawke pulled his ball cap off his head and ran a hand over his brow before replacing the cap.

"No, but I saw it driving fast the night you were called to the fire at Grizz Flat."

Chapter Eleven

"Did you see what make it was? Possibly the license plate?" Hawke knew it was a long shot the man would have noticed any of that. It was after dark when he'd headed to Grizz Flat. And he didn't remember passing anyone coming up the hill.

"It was a Ford, not sure the exact model. No license plate." Dale nodded his head.

"What time did you see it?"

"Close to ten. I'd driven out to see if you'd caught anyone and saw you were gone. I was getting ready to turn around when I saw the lights coming. I had my lights off and watched as the vehicle went by. I thought it might have been the poachers. That's why I remember the make and no license. I was going to give you a description."

"Thanks. You shouldn't have any more poachers." Hawke stood, shook hands, and walked back to his vehicle.

He had another reason to go to Wallowa Valley Car Sales tomorrow. Not only to see what the other employees thought of the victim, but to see if there was a dark blue Ford compact SUV missing from the dealership.

Hawke rose late Monday morning. It was his day off, even though he had a lot he wanted to accomplish and most of it was related to work.

After feeding the horses, he transferred the gas can to his personal pickup.

Herb wandered out of the tool shed, holding a wrench in a rag. “If you got a minute, Darlene has hot apple coffee cake and some information.”

It was hard to pass up anything Darlene baked. She had won best baker at the county fair off and on her whole adulthood.

“I can always spare some time to eat something your wife has made.” Hawke whistled to Dog, who sat by the driver’s side door, waiting to go for a ride. The animal loped toward him. “We’ll go pretty soon,” Hawke told the dog and fell in step beside his landlord.

“Good, Herb told you about the coffee cake,” Darlene said when the two men entered the kitchen through the back door.

“You knew that would get me over here just as easy as you having information.” Hawke placed his Stetson on the chair beside him. Dog lay down at his feet.

The woman smiled. “Gossip, coffee cake, and coffee. That’s the best way to start a day.”

Hawke grinned and shook his head. This couple

had kept him in the loop of more things than he could remember. They both grew up in the area, knew everyone, and while they gossiped to him and their closest friends, they were respected. Which led them to learn more than the average citizen.

With a large piece of coffee cake on a plate in front of him, a steaming cup of coffee above that, and a fork in his hand, he waited.

Darlene placed a plate with cake in her spot and sat down with her cup of coffee. "Herb told me you were interested in the Pruss family. I can tell you that Mrs. Pruss has always been the brains behind the business. Both her husband and her son were the charmers. The ones who could get people to sign papers for vehicles they couldn't afford."

"I met Mrs. Pruss yesterday. She isn't a people person." He studied both his landlords.

They burst out laughing.

"No, she isn't," Darlene said when she stopped laughing. "She thinks she's better than anyone else and is proud to tell them so. She's not from around here. I'm not sure where Jim met her. I don't think he went to college?" Darlene peered at her husband.

"No. Jim never went to college. I think they met at a car convention or something like that." He shoved a large bite of coffee cake in his mouth.

"Is that why she hates her daughter-in-law? Because she is from around here and respected?" Hawke had known there was more underlying hatred in the older woman for the woman her son married.

"Yes. Mrs. Pruss wanted James to marry someone with money and status. She even sent him to college hoping he'd find someone. But he came back here and pursued his best friend's sister." Darlene raised an eyebrow. "I can't believe Adam let Kristen marry James. He knew what his friend was like."

Hawke shrugged. "Maybe he thought James would treat her better because they were friends?"

Herb shook his head. "He knew better. James used Adam all the time in school. He knew his friend liked to be the victor at everything."

"I find it interesting no one has had anything nice to say about the victim." Hawke glanced between his two landlords. "Did you find out anything that I don't already know?"

"Selma's granddaughter takes care of the paperwork at the dealership. She said there was a huge fight on Friday between James and his mother. She threw something at him, and he took off out of there saying he wasn't coming back." Darlene picked up her coffee cup. "Is that something you didn't know?"

Hawke grinned. "Yes, and what I'd hoped to hear from a visit to the dealership today. What is Selma's granddaughter's name?"

"Stay," Hawke told Dog as he opened his vehicle door and stepped out. After talking to Herb and Darlene, he'd dropped the gas can off at the state police office in Winslow to be taken to state forensics to be dusted for prints and any other evidence. Now he planned to act like he was looking for a new vehicle and talk to the employees about their deceased salesman.

An older man wearing a windbreaker with the Wallowa Valley Car Sales logo, slacks, and cowboy boots strode toward him, his hand extended.

"Burke Harris, at your service," he said, shaking Hawke's hand. "You looking for a new vehicle? Or perhaps a used, but new to you, vehicle?"

"Mr. Harris—"

"Burke. We're all friends here at Wallowa Valley Car Sales." Harris smiled even bigger.

Hawke saw the mercenary gleam in the man's eyes.

"I was dealing with James, could you tell him I'm here?" Hawke said, watching the man.

"I'm sorry, he is no longer with us. I'd be happy to help you with your car needs." The man didn't stop selling.

Hawke pulled his badge on a chain out from under his shirt. "Then maybe you can tell me why a dark blue Ford SUV wasn't reported stolen from here?"

The man's eyelids flickered open and closed as if he were a computer that had just malfunctioned. "I-I don't know what you're talking about." He gathered himself together. "Did James steal the Escape that was missing?"

"Someone here did know it was missing."

"Mrs. Pruss was yelling and accusing everyone on Friday of taking off with one of the vehicles. It wasn't until I'd walked the lot, I figured out which one." He glanced toward the building. "I'd noticed a discrepancy in the miles on it when someone test drove it on Thursday. But I didn't want to say anything to the witch and get boiled in oil."

"Did you mention it to anyone else?" Hawke wished he'd brought his logbook with him. He'd have to remember all of this to put in his report.

"I was about to tell the state trooper who was here

yesterday, but Mrs. Pruss came out of the building and pulled him into her lair."

"You don't talk well of your boss," Hawke said.

The man had the decency to blush. "If you ask her about me, she won't have anything good to say either. I started this business with her husband. Jim and I were doing just fine. Then he married her. Next thing I know I'm demoted to salesman and before Jim's grave is covered in grass, she's grooming that delinquent son for what should have been my position all along."

"I heard James liked to purchase stolen parts. How many people here knew that?" Hawke studied the man. It appeared to be news to him.

"Really? That doesn't surprise me one bit. For all his charm, he always got the best for himself and not the customer."

"Do the other employees feel the same about James and his mother?" Hawke caught a glimpse of Mrs. Pruss staring out the window at them.

"There are two other salesmen. James and I were the only two who worked forty hours. The other two work weekends. Cindy takes care of the contracts and books. It didn't take Cindy long to see through James' charm. I think that's why Mrs. Pruss keeps her. She's good at what she does and her head wasn't turned by James."

"I'd like to speak to Cindy. Where do I find her?" Hawke walked towards the building.

Burke fell into step beside him. "I'll introduce you."

Mrs. Pruss met them at the door. "Trooper, I thought that was you. Are you looking for a car or trying to wiggle answers out of my employees by pretending to be a car buyer?"

"It's my day off, but I wanted to come by and see the dealership. Speak to a few people." Hawke stared the woman straight in the eye. "I like to stay on the trail of the evidence even if it's on my own time. I think as a business woman, you'd understand."

Her eyes narrowed, but she gave a slight nod.

"I'll take you to Cindy," Harris said, moving around his boss.

The woman whipped around. "Why are you talking to Cindy?"

"I'm talking to all of the employees. Are there others here?"

"Juan and Charlie in the service department," she said, quickly.

"Good. I'll visit with them after I talk to Cindy." Hawke had the impression Mrs. Pruss would send Cindy on some errand to keep the bookkeeper from talking to him.

Burke strode across the floor and knocked on a door marked contracts.

"Come in," called a female voice.

The salesman opened the door and motioned for Hawke to enter. It appeared the salesman was going to go about his business.

Hawke glanced at the name plate: Cindy Albee, and the woman in her thirties sitting in the chair behind the desk.

"I'm State Trooper Hawke. I'd like to ask you some questions about James Pruss."

She nodded and drew her hands away from the keyboard. "What do you want to know?"

"Did James and his mother get along?" Hawke

decided to start with what Darlene had given him.

She glanced at the door. This room didn't have any windows, so it was hard to believe she might have seen anything.

"They have never seen eye to eye about anything in this business. Mrs. Pruss wants to get as much out of every customer as she can get. James just wants, wanted to make enough to have some fun." She shook her head. "Not that I wanted to have any fun with him. He hit on every woman who walked through the doors. And from what I overheard during some of his follow-up phone calls, I think they got more than a car out of the deals they made with him."

"Is that the fun you were talking about?" Hawke cursed in his head that he hadn't brought his logbook. He glanced at the printer beside her desk. "Could I borrow a piece of paper?"

"Sure." She reached over, grabbed a piece and handed it to him.

He folded it in thirds and drew out his pen. "The fun he wanted?" Hawke wrote what Burke had said and caught up to where he was with Cindy when she started speaking.

"He wanted out of here. He talked of traveling. Seeing the world. Lots of us who grew up here have that dream. For some it comes true, for others they go and come back. And a few never leave."

"Which are you?" Hawke had a feeling he knew the answer.

"I left, but had to come back to help out when my parents died." She stared at something behind him.

Hawke craned his neck and stared at a large poster of a tropical island.

"Someday, I'm going there and never coming back." She sighed. "But for now, I'm helping with the medical bills from their accident and my husband is keeping the farm going."

Hawke waved a hand. "This is a pretty isolated room. How did you see the argument between James and his mom a week ago Friday?"

She stared at him. "Who told you?"

"I have my sources. What happened?"

"I had just told Mrs. Pruss there was a discrepancy in the books. As I left her office, James came down the hall. Mrs. Pruss called his name. He turned in the office. I hadn't told her I believed James had skimmed money. But she must have figured it out." Cindy folded her hands together. "There was shouting from both of them. I heard something hit the wall, later I cleaned up a vase that had been sitting on Mrs. Pruss's desk with some cut flowers. James stormed out of the office, shouting she'd not see him again." She leaned back in her chair. "It was as if he knew what was going to happen to him."

Hawke had a different idea. "Do you have any way to trace the money that you said was missing?"

She stared at him. "No. Why?"

"Just a hunch. Can you give me the bank account number for the business?"

She shook her head. "You'll have to ask Mrs. Pruss for that. Or bring a warrant."

"Can you call her in here?" He tapped the phone on the desk.

"I can, but you'll have to do the asking."

He nodded.

Chapter Twelve

"I'll not hand over the dealerships bank account numbers," Mrs. Pruss said, before Hawke finished asking the question.

"Then I'll get a warrant for all of your records." Hawke stood. "It was nice meeting you Mrs. Albee. Mrs. Pruss." He walked out of the office and stopped over by the service department. He pulled out his phone and dialed Shoberg.

"Hawke, why are you calling me on your day off?" Shoberg asked.

"I'm down at Wallowa Valley Car Sales, the dealership the victim's family owns. There is money missing and the vic had planned to leave. It would be a good idea to get a warrant for all their records. And the vic was dealing in stolen auto parts."

Shoberg whistled. "You've been busy for not working."

"It's easier to stay on one thing when you don't

have to answer the radio calls." Hawke had learned that over the years. Leg work was easier to do when you weren't being called from one end of the county to the other for traffic wrecks, domestic disputes, trespassing, and all the other things they dealt with as troopers when they were still trying to do their game warden job as well.

"I'll get the D.A. to issue the warrant. Take the rest of the day off."

"I have two more people to talk to, and then I will." He ended the call and stepped into the service department.

Burke stood in the service area talking to a man in his fifties sporting the gray overalls of a mechanic.

"Here's the state trooper," Burke said, motioning to Hawke.

Pulling the folded paper out of his pocket, Hawke asked, "What's your name?"

"Charlie Porter. I've worked here for nearly as long as Burke. I started out of high school."

"Then you've seen all the changes through the years?" Hawke watched as the two men glanced at one another.

"You could say that. I seen Burke get kicked out of the partnership when Mrs. Pruss arrived. Then shoved even further down the ladder when her boy was old enough to sell cars."

"Why do you work here if you don't like your bosses?" Hawke had wondered that from the beginning. So far the employees he'd talked to have had their jobs here long enough to have seen a lot of change. Why stick around?

"There's not a lot of jobs in the county. I tried to

get on with the county crew, but they hired in house. All I know is the inside of a vehicle." Charlie pulled a wrench out of his back pocket and polished it.

"Where's the other mechanic, Juan?" Hawke asked. He wanted both men together when he asked about the stolen parts. Though Burke could have mentioned it to Charlie already.

"He's in the can. He'll be out shortly." Charlie grinned at Burke like it was a joke.

"Go knock on it and tell him to come out now." Hawke pointed to Burke.

The man shrugged and walked to a door at the back of the service area. He knocked. "Juan, there's a state trooper out here who wants to talk to you."

"Okay." Came an accented voice.

Burke walked back to where they were standing.

"Have you ever seen anyone get angry with James Pruss?" Hawke asked Charlie.

"Yeah. Anyone who ever dealt with him was angry." Charlie twirled the wrench like it was a baton.

"I heard he was a charmer?"

"At first. Then the customers would see through that whole thing and realize he'd conned them."

Hawke studied Charlie. "What do you mean by conned?"

A short, thin Hispanic man walked across the concrete floor toward them. He had on the same gray mechanic jumpsuit, but the closer he walked, the acrid scent of cigarette smoke grew. The man had been in the bathroom smoking.

"Juan, this is State Trooper Hawke." Burke made the introduction.

"Sir." Juan held out his hand to shake.

Hawke obliged. The man had a firm shake and his gaze held Hawke's. He had nothing to hide other than his smoking habit it appeared.

"I was wondering if either of you knew that James had been purchasing stolen auto parts?"

Juan glanced at Charlie. They knew.

"Why didn't you tell the authorities?" Hawke asked.

"He was the boss. I didn't want to lose my job," Juan said.

"Ditto," Charlie shoved the wrench in his back pocket. "I told you there isn't a lot of jobs for a mechanic in the county. You have to keep what job you have."

"Do you know where he got the parts from?" Hawke studied them. Juan's gaze looked over Hawke's shoulder. "You know. Where was he getting them?"

Juan glanced at Charlie and Burke. They both nodded.

"I came back one night after I'd realized I'd left something. James and another man were arguing beside a white van back here by the bay doors. I realized this must be where he had been getting the parts. I wrote down the license plate. I don't want to be sent back to Mexico for something I didn't do." He shoved his hand through the slit in the overalls, and felt around for his back pocket before producing his wallet. Juan opened the wallet and pulled out a worn piece of paper and handed it to Hawke. "This was the number on that van. I don't know if they used the same one every time or not."

"Thanks. Did any of you see any change in James the last week?" Hawke leveled his gaze on each one.

"He was talking up the Rendezvous he was in charge of. You'd have thought it was the damned Olympics the way he talked about it. How he was coming back with trophies and putting the Wallupa Muzzleloaders on the map," Burke scoffed.

"I take it no one else here was into muzzleloaders?" Hawke asked.

They all shook their heads.

"But you two would know how to make a car catch on fire." He waved his finger from one to the other of the mechanics.

"Hey! I didn't like him, but I didn't hate him enough to burn him," said Charlie.

Juan made the sign of the cross and said, "I would never take a life."

Hawke spun to Burke. "What about you? It appears he took your half of this business."

Burke raised his hands. "I like my freedom too much to kill that dumb ass. You should be looking into the women he's charmed and their husbands."

The mechanics nodded.

Hawke folded the paper and put it in his pocket. He was going to look into the women tomorrow. He had the rest of today to enjoy himself.

Hawke pulled up to the Trembley barn as his phone buzzed. He parked, opened the door for Dog to jump out, and answered.

"Dr. Vance, what did you learn?"

"That this is your day off. You are going to die young if you don't relax more."

His last physical with the doctor, she told him he was in better shape than men twenty years younger. At least that was what his blood pressure, heart rate, and blood work said. He didn't tell her his joints were getting stiffer each year. "You told me I had nothing to worry about eight months ago. Are you changing your diagnosis?" He said it with humor in his voice.

She laughed. "No. I understand all you have is work, but you really should find something relaxing to do on your days off."

"I'm going hiking this afternoon." He grinned. Everyone at work called him crazy because he'd come back from patrolling the high country on his horse and head out the next day with his horse to ride a different mountain for relaxation.

"I guess if that's what makes you happy. I called because I received the victim's dental records. The missing teeth were in the same area, according to the x-rays, where there should have been a dental bridge."

"Do caps pop off in high heat?" He'd have to ask if anyone found the porcelain caps.

"These didn't. A bridge is fastened to two teeth on either side of the gap. Those teeth would have been ground down with enough tooth left to attach a cap to hold the bridge. The four missing teeth were all ragged. As if they were broken either by force or by pliers."

Hawke rubbed a hand on his jaw. The idea of either made his teeth and jawbone ache. "The deceased isn't the man whose dental records you have?"

"As far as I can tell, correct. It could be several weeks before we get any DNA confirmation."

"Let's keep this between you and law enforcement. There are a lot of angry people who are happy James Pruss is dead. Best to leave it that way until we catch him." Hawke had had an inkling James wasn't the victim after talking to the people he worked with. The man had stolen money from the business, and who knew how much he'd pocketed from the stolen parts, and he'd told his mother she'd never see him again when he headed to the muzzleloader competition. He'd planned to disappear. But who helped him? A woman in the stolen Ford Escape?

He slid out of his vehicle, absently patted Jack, Horse, and Polka Dot on the heads as he headed to his apartment over the arena. He'd write up his report and email it to Sergeant Spruel. Then he could go for a ride and try to figure out who the dead person really was and how he'd fit Pruss's dental records all but the bridge?

Chapter Thirteen

Hawke, riding Polka Dot, with Dog leading their way across Herb's hay field, settled deeper into the saddle. The young horse was proving more and more to be what he needed to take over the mountain trips when Jack grew too old. They'd jumped a covey of quail, a cottontail, and a deer that had bedded down by the creek as they made their way to the field. The gelding had stopped and stared but hadn't flinched, shied, or carried-on. While he didn't care for the name, the horse was much calmer and clearer headed than Boy. He was glad Darlene had talked him into trading the flighty blanket appaloosa for this calmer leopard appaloosa. She'd wanted the fancier looking gelding for one of her riders who was looking for a project horse.

His phone buzzed. Dot's ear tipped back, but the horse didn't miss a step.

Hawke barely pulled back on the reins and the animals stopped.

"Hawke," he answered the call.

"Spruel. It's your day off, what are you doing sending me additions to your report?"

"It's a beautiful day and I'm out riding my new horse. So yes, it is my day off." Hawke knew his superior didn't call to chew him out for working.

"Good. Glad you're doing something fun. Interesting, the findings from Dr. Vance."

"Yes. I told her not to tell anyone. I've encountered too many people who were too pleased the man is dead. Best to leave him that way until we find him. I would say he's the one who committed the homicide. I just have to figure out who the victim is and who helped Pruss plan his disappearance."

"You think he had an accomplice?" Spruel asked.

"The woman in the stolen Ford Escape. Has anyone found the vehicle ditched anywhere?" Hawke asked.

"I'll put out for law enforcement to be on the lookout for the vehicle. Shoberg obtained the warrant. He's collecting records from the car dealership as we speak."

Hawke grinned. "He's going to need hazard pay for that job. I can guarantee Mrs. Pruss did not part with it easily, even with a warrant." He squeezed his legs, and Dot began walking. "I'll come in tomorrow morning and help look through the records."

"No, you won't. It's your day off."

"I can come in tomorrow and take Thursday off." Hawke didn't like having two days in a row off work. Unless he planned to visit his mother or spend the night on the mountain.

Spruel sighed. "Fine. But you better take Thursday

off. You know how picky the governor is getting about overtime."

"Yeah. See you tomorrow." Hawke ended the call and urged Dot into a smooth lope. There was nothing better as the sun was setting, than to go for a ride.

Tuesday morning, Hawke was dressed, his chores finished, and on his way to the Rusty Nail before sitting down at the office and going through the car dealership's bank records.

At the café, he sat at his usual stool at the counter.

"Heard you caught a poacher out at Dale's place," one of the locals said to him after he'd ordered his usual breakfast from Justine.

Hawke spun on the stool and studied Darnell. "I did."

The man dropped his gaze a moment. "Dale said it was someone from out of the valley."

Hawke nodded and picked up his coffee cup.

Darnell picked up his fork and went to work on the pancakes on his plate.

While he enjoyed the food at this café and catching gossip that helped him with his job, he never gave away anything. He would have expected people to ask him about the homicide rather than the poacher.

Justine cleared her throat.

Hawke faced the counter and the breakfast his friend had placed in front of him.

"You're in your uniform. I thought you had today off?" Justine wiped at the counter beside him.

"Since when do you keep track of when I work and when I don't?" It irritated him that she even brought it up. It was none of her business when he worked.

"Dani stopped in here before she went back to the lodge. She mentioned you had a couple days off, that's all. You don't have to get your hackles up." She spun around and marched into the kitchen.

Hawke shook his head. He was happy the two women had found friends in one another, but he hated that they both meant something to him. Justine was a friend, kind of like a sister. Dani was the one that made his body feel like a teenager again. He should get used to the two talking about him, but he hated knowing there were two people, besides his mother, who now worried.

The eggs, French toast, and bacon didn't taste as good today. He finished quickly and left money under the edge of his plate.

He drove the short distance to the State Police Office in Winslow and went straight to Sergeant Spruel's office. "You have those bank records for me to look at?"

The sergeant glanced up, took off his reading glasses, and leaned back in his chair. "Come in and have a seat."

Hawke did, not sure where this was going.

"Detective Donner has been pulled over to the Willamette Valley to help with an officer involved homicide. Shoberg said he'd take over the investigation into the car fire if you helped him." Spruel leaned forward. "But you can't neglect your patrolling either. Shoberg is lead."

Inside, Hawke was grinning. He'd planned to spend as much time on this case as possible. Just like when he found tracks to follow in the wild, when he had evidence that didn't add up, he had to keep digging to find the answers. "Sir, I can do both."

"Let's see you do. You have three hours to go over the dealership records and then you need to go patrol Sled Springs for turkey hunters." Spruel put his glasses back on, thumbed through a pile of folders, and picked out a file, handing it to him.

Hawke knew when he was being dismissed. He left the office, walked over to his desk, placed the file in front of the computer monitor, and logged onto the computer. While everything was booting up, he grabbed a cup of coffee and returned to his desk.

Opening the folder, he began scanning what appeared to be the income and payments of the car dealership. He rubbed a hand across his face and stared at the numbers. He needed Cindy here to explain things to him.

He found the number for Wallowa Valley Car Sales and dialed the number on the phone on his desk.

"Wallowa Valley Car Sales, this is Cindy speaking. How may I direct your call?"

"Cindy, this is Trooper Hawke. I'd like you to come to the Winslow State Police Office and help me decipher the records Trooper Shoberg picked up yesterday with the warrant."

There was a long pause. "Will this help find out who killed James?"

"Yes." He didn't mind the small white lie. They were going to find out where James went and who he killed in his place.

"I'll tell Mrs. Pruss I have to run some errands. I can be there in twenty minutes."

"Thank you." He ended the call and opened up the case file. He hadn't caught up to Red Beard, Wylie

Lambert, yet. Reading through Shoberg and Novak's notes, he didn't find any mention of Wylie or a phone number for the man.

He entered the name Wylie Lambert into the DMV and up popped a photo and an address. The man lived in La Grande. He went on another site and came up with information as to his marital status – single, he was in his forties, worked as a computer consultant and he had two phone numbers connected to his name. Hawke wrote both numbers down.

His desk phone buzzed.

Picking it up he said, "Hawke."

"Hawke, there's a Mrs. Albee to see you," Marsha, the Fish and Wildlife receptionist said.

"I'll come get her." He replaced the phone. He forgot to tell the bookkeeper to come in the back way. He made his way through the connecting door and into the F & W side of the building, walking by offices with wildlife biologists and volunteers working.

"I'm sorry, I didn't realize State Police and the Fish and Wildlife were two different things," Cindy apologized.

"It's on me. I should have told you to come to the back." He nodded to the receptionist. "Thanks, Marsha."

She smiled and waved them off.

Hawke led the bookkeeper down the hall and into the quieter side of the building.

"Wow, this is a difference of night and day between the two sides," Cindy said, stopping inside the open area where the troopers all had desks along the wall.

"Yeah, we like the quiet." Hawke pulled a chair up

beside his. "I can't figure out what's what on these records. It will go faster if the person who puts them together explained things to me."

"Sure. But don't let Mrs. Pruss know I'm here. She was mad I handed the books over, even though there was a warrant."

Hawke stared at the woman who was opening up the folder holding all the photocopied pages. "Does she have something to hide?"

Cindy looked him square in the eyes. "That she fudged on taxes, she turned a blind eye on the stolen auto parts because it made money, and that her son had slowly skimmed two hundred thousand out of their profits over the last two years."

Hawke whistled. "That's a lot of money. Was he a gambler or drug user?"

"No. As far as I can tell, he got it all as cash. It wasn't directed to any other accounts." She shrugged. "If he had done that then it could have been recouped."

"Who, besides you and Mrs. Pruss, know about the missing money?" Hawke wondered if Burke had figured it out.

"As far as I know, just the two of us, and now, you."

"Can you show me who was paid for the stolen parts?"

They poured over the books until Sergeant Spruel interrupted. "I told you be out on patrol by now."

"Sorry. Cindy Albee, the Pruss bookkeeper, has been explaining the money ins and outs of the car dealership," Hawke said, closing the file they'd been highlighting and going through.

"Miss—"

"Mrs. I'm Mrs. Albee." The woman stood. "I need to get back to work. Mrs. Pruss will threaten to fire me, again."

"How often does she do that?" Hawke asked.

"Every time she doesn't like something I show or tell her in the books." She smiled. "But because I know all of that, she can't fire me."

Hawke laughed. "You know how to keep a job. Keep your mouth shut."

"Exactly, but I couldn't let the missing money go after hearing about James' death." She peered at the sergeant then at Hawke. "With James dead, someone else became very rich."

That thought swam around in Hawke's head as he led the woman to the front of the building and walked back to close his computer.

Sergeant Spruel was reading the file they'd highlighted. "What was she talking about, someone else becoming rich?"

"The alleged fire victim, James Pruss, was stealing money from his family business in cash. It seemed when someone would come in and pay cash for a car, or a payment, or service, he pocketed the money but wrote it down as paid. It wasn't until Cindy started making numbers match up that she'd realized there wasn't as much money in the accounts as the receipts said there should be. At first, she thought it was Mrs. Pruss trying to escape paying taxes on the cash deals, but then she realized Mrs. Pruss was also looking into the missing money."

"Do you think, James finally had it with his mom, used someone to help him fake his death, and then left the country with the cash?"

"That's what it's looking like. But let's keep it between us." He picked up his cap. "I need to go patrol. Talk to you tomorrow."

Chapter Fourteen

On his way to Sled Springs, Hawke left messages at both the numbers he had for Wylie Lambert.

He knew the only reason the sergeant wanted him to check out here for turkey hunters was to make sure no one was encroaching on the Wenaha elk feeding area. This was the time of year when shed hunters tried to get into the restricted area to find the shed antlers of the big bull elk that wintered in the safe zone of the feeding area. However, that area was posted off limits to the public.

It was a sanctuary of sorts for the elk.

Hawke drove to the area, checking the roads into the reserve for fresh vehicle tracks or footprints. Up the road a half mile beyond the sanctuary, an out-of-state vehicle was parked. Hawke wrote down the license then called in a check of the plate. It came back belonging to a man who was known for going on private land to gather antlers.

Having a feeling he'd find the man in the restricted feeding area, Hawke parked his vehicle, locked it, and followed the man's tracks.

An hour later, he came upon the man, packing three nice half racks of shed antlers.

"Mr. Bowen, you are in a restricted area," Hawke said, when the man looked up and saw him.

"I'm on public land." The man was equal in weight to Hawke and a couple inches shorter. He spread his legs as if taking a stand and glared. Bowen was going to try and badger his way out of this.

Hawke sighed. "Mr. Bowen, you need to drop the antlers and come with me."

"I don't either. This is public land. I read you can be in this area from April first to December thirty-first. I can collect sheds on public land." He hugged the antlers as if he were afraid Hawke was going to jerked them out of his arms.

"Sir, this is the restricted feeding area of the Wenaha Wildlife Area. I followed your tracks. You crossed the fence right next to a sign that said you were crossing into a restricted area." Hawke stuck his thumbs in the front of his duty belt and studied the man. "If you drop the antlers and come with me, I'll give you a warning. If you insist on trying to tell me you can be here and don't drop the antlers, I'll cite you for trespassing and gathering illegal antlers." He shrugged. "It's your choice."

The man swore and dropped the antlers.

"I'm glad you're a sensible man," Hawke said, escorting the man back the way they'd come.

"Does anyone ever take the sheds out of the restricted area? You know, so the rest of us can have a chance at them." The man asked as Hawke stopped at their vehicles.

"I've never asked. You can write a letter to the Wallowa County Fish and Wildlife and ask them." Hawke unlocked his door and slid behind the wheel. He backed up to let the other man drive out, then wrote the encounter down in his logbook.

Since he was in the area, he decided to have a chat with the business owners in Troy. Maybe one of them got a look at the woman driving the stolen car. He backtracked to Troy and parked in front of the Wenaha Bar and Grill.

It was 2:10. As if realizing the time triggered his gut, his stomach grumbled. Food and gathering information- a good combo. He locked his vehicle and entered the bar and grill.

Stepping through the door, he could see most of the establishment. Knotty pine tables and chairs and a counter were to the left. To the right was a slim selection of grocery items. Across the room was a small hallway with a sign that said Restrooms.

He sat down at the counter and a man in is fifties appeared through an opening from the kitchen. "What can I get you, Trooper?"

"A burger, fries, and iced tea." Hawke didn't even look at the menu.

"I'll have that out in a jiffy." The man disappeared into the kitchen and returned a few minutes later with his drink.

"I would guess in a place this small you'd notice if there was anyone new hanging around," Hawke said.

The man studied him. "You have a question to ask?"

"I'm wondering if there's been a new blue Ford Escape in the area lately?" Hawke sipped his tea. He worked hard at not making a face. It was made from a mix. It had a distinct taste he didn't like.

"One buzzed through here a couple times last week after dark."

"How did you happen to see it?" Hawke wondered at how fast the man had replied. He didn't even have to think.

"Week nights around here this time of year are slow. I tend to sit out on the porch and hope someone local comes by and chats. The rig you're talking about went through here the same time both nights. A woman was driving, there was a man in the passenger seat."

"Did you get a good look at the people?" Hawke wondered why they came up here two nights in a row in a vehicle from the dealership. Had James taken it and then picked up the woman? But why was she driving?

"No, there wasn't any light on in the car and as you can see, we don't have street lights. Just saw the silhouette of a woman in the driver's seat and the man in the passenger side." He glanced over his shoulder into the kitchen. "I'll get your food."

Hawke nodded. He was trying to figure out why there were two trips. He could see maybe one, where they brought the gas can and hid it in the bushes, but why two?

And if Burke noticed the odometer reading on Thursday, how did the woman get the car on Friday if Pruss was the one taking the car off the lot?

The man returned with his burger and fries. "You here asking questions because of the body that burned at Grizz Flat?"

"Yes. Did you see anything unusual, other than the couple in the car?" Hawke picked up the burger and took a bite. Juicy and tasty.

"Hadley, up the road, said he saw lights bobbing through the trees behind his place that night."

Hawke pulled out his logbook. "What's Hadley's last name?"

"Rundell. He's up the road about two miles on the right. Up Eden Lane."

Hawke wrote down the last name. Eden Lane was southeast of Grizz Flat. The woman must have driven to a spot on Eden Lane and waited for Pruss.

"Thanks. Can I get your name and a to-go container?" He took one more bite of his burger while the man said he was Ben Bowie and reached under the counter. The owner set a Styrofoam container beside Hawke's basket of food.

Hawke dumped the food in the box, paid for his meal, and headed to his truck. As he drove to Eden Lane, he gobbled down the rest of the burger and most of the fries. He found Hadley Rundell's place and drove up to the house.

Two dogs ran from behind the house, barking.

Stepping out of his truck, Hawke gave a high pitch whistle that stopped the dogs barking and he could talk to them. "You've told everyone I'm here. No need to continue barking."

A man in his sixties stepped out onto the porch. "Can I help you, Trooper?"

"I was talking to Ben down at the bar and grill. He said you noticed lights in the direction of Grizz Flat on Friday night."

"I did. I saw the lights after I found a car sitting on

the road. No one in it and it was locked, like they were off hiking." The man pointed back down the road Hawke had driven up.

"Could you show me where the car was and where you saw the lights?"

The man nodded. "I'll get my hat."

Hawke waited just off the porch, patting the dogs on their heads.

Rundell appeared with a straw hat and clomped down the porch steps. "I was out looking for Griff, that reddish dog there." The man pointed to the dog that looked as if it had some kind of hound in it. "He hears something, starts sniffing the ground, and he takes off."

"Did he see or hear the person walking through the forest?"

"I don't know if that's why he took off or not. He's kind of finicky about what he chases."

Hawke held back a snicker at the man's comment. He'd never known a dog to be finicky about chasing anything.

They'd walked back down the road about two hundred yards when the man stopped and pointed to the ground. "This is where the car was sitting."

Hawke scanned the ground and discovered barely visible tire tracks. He pulled out his phone and crouched to take a photo of the least faded print. If they could prove this was the missing Ford Escape they could prove…what, he wasn't sure. But he had a feeling the dead body wasn't James Pruss. Why would teeth be knocked out that should have been caps? Why was a car from the dealership used? It only added up to Pruss staging his own death. Why? And who was the real victim if that were true?

He rose. “Which direction did you see the light?”

Rundell walked across the road and into the trees. “I was about here, when I saw the light. I’d already seen the car and figured whoever had parked and hiked were coming back.”

“Did you get a look at the person?”

“I did not. Didn’t think it was any of my business. Then I heard about the person burned up at Grizz Flat and I’d wished I’d been more nosey.”

Me too, Hawke thought. It would have helped him piece things together. “Thank you for your help. I’m going to wander around toward Grizz Flat.”

“Want company?” the man asked, nodding toward his dogs.

“No, I’ll be fine.” Hawke set out slow and methodical, searching the ground for footprints.

He knew where the car was parked and where the camping area was in relation to that. The ground had lots of wildlife activity. Deer, various small creatures, turkeys, and he’d discovered a cougar track.

Halfway between his two coordinates, he finally discovered what looked like a woman’s or small man’s hiking boot and an even harder to make out moccasin print. The prints were leading from the camping area to the car. She hadn’t been at the rendezvous. Everyone he’d encountered at the camping area had on moccasins or period footwear. The man could easily be Pruss. As the president, he would have been wearing period clothing as well.

Now that he had a trail, as faint as it was, he followed it to the brush where he and Dani had found the gas can. That definitely connected the car with the fire and homicide. After that, the woman’s hiking boot disappeared. Had she waited by the bush for the killer to return with the gas can?

Biscuit and Hardtack were lucky they hadn't investigated the sound Biscuit had heard. They could have both been victims. Hawke was certain the sound Biscuit heard wasn't a turkey but the couple stashing the gas can.

He walked from the bush down to the camping area. As he broke out of the trees and stood slightly elevated above the camp area, he studied the layout, remembering where each person's tent had been. Did the president of the club always camp by the storage container? If Swift Arrow had looked up, toward the hill, she might have seen the two hurrying away from the murder.

Her gaze had been lower. She'd witnessed someone by the victim's tent.

Hawke opened his logbook and glanced at the sequence in which he saw and spoke to people. The only person he still hadn't contacted that might have had a run-in with Pruss was Red Beard, Wylie Lambert. Was he the body that had been in the Jeep? And who had packed up the man's camp if he was dead?

Chapter Fifteen

Dog ran out to greet Hawke when he returned to his place after dark. “Hey, boy. Did you have a good day? I could have used your help.” He rubbed the dog’s ears before walking over to the stall.

Three heads hung over the gate, waiting for a pat and some grain. He never got tired of coming home to Dog, the horses, and the mule. They were always happy to see him and eager to please.

“It’s a beautiful night. You should all be out in the run staring up at the stars.” He rubbed their foreheads and walked over to the feed storage room. Dog rushed in as soon as the door opened. The animal liked to catch the rodents unaware.

Hawke put grain in three plastic troughs and hung them on the top of the wooden gate. The crunching and shifting of feet as they ate always brought Hawke a sense of restfulness. He enjoyed taking care of animals. He’d had few as a child. His uncle had horses and that was where he'd learned all he knew about the animal that took care of his ancestors. Both his Nez Perce and Cayuse descendants had been known for their knowledge of good horses. His uncle told stories of races his forefathers won and how they'd discovered breeding to make a faster horse and for color.

Hawke knew his cousins would keep on raising the horse that was so important to their people. Jack nuzzled his arm where it rested on the gate next to his feed trough.

Patting the animal's neck, Hawke's mind shifted from the animal to what he'd learned today.

A loud thunk jerked Hawke out of his thoughts before he'd had a chance to review. A feed trough had landed on the ground by his feet. Raising his gaze, he caught Horse with Jack's trough in his teeth, ready to drop it over the gate.

"Thanks for the help," Hawke said, as the animal released the empty plastic feeder.

He grabbed the feeder beside him, before the mule's big teeth grasped it, and bent, picking up the other troughs. "You just like making more work for me, don't you," he said, straightening and peering into the mule's not sorry gaze.

He put the troughs away and walked up the stairs to his apartment over the arena. After checking the scant array of food in his fridge and cupboards, he shed his uniform and put on a t-shirt and jeans. Looked like he'd be eating a peanut butter sandwich for dinner. One of these days, he should buy more food. He'd used up his canned food the last trip he'd made into the Eagle Cap Wilderness. His next day off he'd go shopping.

After making the sandwich, he filled Dog's dish

and sat down at the small table with one chair and opened his laptop. He found the file on the Grizz Flat fire and started reading everything that Shoberg had discovered today. Which turned out to be the white van with the license Juan gave Hawke had been stolen from a bakery in Portland three months ago.

The paper with the license Juan had handed him had looked more worn than three months ago. He made a note to ask Juan when he saw the van.

There had been no sign so far of a blue Ford Escape without a license being seen anywhere. He made a note to Shoberg. *A license could have been put on the vehicle. I'll get the VIN number from the dealership and numbers off of the parts last received.*

It appeared he'd be doing some detective work in the morning.

After taking care of the animals, Hawke slid into his patrol vehicle and radioed dispatch he was on duty headed for Alder. If anything came up between the time he left home and arrived at Olive's Café, he'd deal with it. Otherwise, he'd clock out to eat breakfast then clock in and cross the street to talk to Juan at the car dealership.

As if dispatch had been in his head, the radio crackled to life.

"A call came in of a reckless driver headed toward Alder from Winslow. Light blue nineteen-ninety-one Toyota pickup."

"Copy. Any idea the mile post?"

"Forty-seven."

"Copy." The vehicle was three miles behind him. He pulled over at the first wide spot and waited.

A small model pickup appeared, weaving all over the road, with a line of four vehicles behind it. As soon as the vehicle was abreast of him, nearly swiping the driver's side of his patrol vehicle, Hawke turned on the lights and the siren, as he peered at the driver.

Shaking his head, he pulled in front of the first car in the line behind the swerving vehicle and waited for Mrs. Van Hoosan to see his lights, hear the siren, and pull over.

After another half a mile, she pulled into the Smith's driveway. He pulled in behind her and the cars she'd been holding up all laid on their horns as they zoomed around them.

Hawke walked up to the driver's window and motioned for the woman, who was in her nineties, to roll it down.

"Officer, I was going the speed limit," she said in her crackly voice that told you she'd used her vocal cords more than the average ninety-something. He'd learned a previous time when the woman had been pulled over, she was a music teacher for thirty years and gave vocal lessons after she'd retired.

"Mrs. Van Hoosan, you were going the speed limit, but you were weaving all over the road, scaring the other drivers. Why are you driving? I thought after you were pulled over the last time, you were told not to drive." He opened the door as he talked to her.

"I had to get to Dr. Ashley's. Roscoe is scratching and itching so much, the poor thing can't sleep." Tears welled up in her faded brown eyes.

"I'm headed to Alder. If I drop you off at Dr. Ashley's, do you have someone who can come pick you up?" He helped her out of her car, took the keys, and locked the doors.

"I can call Merrilee." The woman nodded her head as he helped her shuffle to the passenger side of his vehicle.

"Merrilee? As in, the owner of the Rusty Nail?" He didn't see the crusty owner of the café dropping everything to come help out Mrs. Van Hoosan.

"Yes, Merrilee. She's my cousin." The woman said it as if that explained why the woman would come get her.

Hawke helped the woman up into his vehicle, closed the door, and dialed Justine.

"Hello, Hawke. Why are you calling me when I'm working?" Justine answered as if he'd just committed a mortal sin.

"Will Merrilee pick Mrs. Van Hoosan up if I leave her at Dr. Ashley's?" He was skeptical Merrilee ever did anything for anyone other than cook good food for money.

"Yes. She gets calls from her all the time and takes off out of here. Why?"

"I just picked her up weaving all over the road headed to Alder. She said Roscoe needed medicine from Dr. Ashley."

"That old cat should be dead by now." Justine laughed. "I'll tell Merrilee where to find Mrs. Van Hoosan."

"Thanks." Hawke climbed in behind the wheel. "You don't need to call Merrilee. I just did."

"Thank you, Officer." The woman was buckled up, sitting with her purse on her lap and her hands clasped over the top.

Hawke shook his head, started up his vehicle, and

continued to Alder.

"Dispatch. There's a car at mile post fifty-six that needs towed to the lot and impounded." He was going to make sure the elderly woman didn't cause a wreck.

"Copy."

"Do you know where Dr. Ashley's office is?" Mrs. Van Hoosan asked.

"Yes, Ma'am, I do." Hawke smiled at the woman and turned on the next road heading to an area with small acreages. The veterinarian had fifteen acres and a large barn that she practiced her veterinary services from.

He pulled up to the barn and the door with the word "Office" over it. Hawke walked around to the passenger door and helped the older woman out.

The office door opened, and Dr. Ashley stepped out. "Hawke, Mrs. Van Hoosan, what are the two of you doing here so early?"

Mrs. Van Hoosan began telling the doctor all about her Roscoe. When she stopped for a breath, Hawke said, "Merrilee will be here to pick her up shortly."

The vet nodded and led the older woman into the barn. That was what he liked about this county. Everyone looked out for one another. It reminded him of growing up on the reservation. Everyone was family even if you weren't related by birth or marriage.

Hawke returned to his vehicle and called dispatch. "I'll be off radio for an hour."

"Copy."

He headed to Olive's Café. Five minutes after loading Mrs. Van Hoosan into his vehicle, his stomach had started growling.

At the café, he parked in front of the building and

wandered in. He'd eaten in here a few times. The owner, Olive Good Fox, had opened the café six years ago and seemed to be doing well. He liked coming in every once in a while to see the new art on the walls. She supported the local artists by hanging their work around the café, with the artist's business cards and prices of the work.

"Hawke, you've been a stranger," Olive said, walking out from behind the counter and greeting him.

"I spend more time out on the dirt roads than in Alder," he said, sitting at a small table in the corner. The counter had all six stools filled. He didn't recognize anyone. Not like at the Rusty Nail.

"I heard you've been protecting the land." Olive always talked about the land and animals as if she were Native American, but she'd married into the culture. After her husband died in the military, she moved back to the county and opened the restaurant to support her two boys.

"I am always protecting the land." Hawke set the menu down. "I'll have scrambled eggs with ham and wheat toast, please."

She poured coffee into the cup in front of him. "I'll get that right out."

He studied the people in the café. The small groups around the tables seemed disinterested in him. But one of the men sitting at the counter, looked his direction every few seconds.

The man didn't look familiar. What was he so nervous about?

Olive returned to top off his coffee. He touched her arm where the man couldn't see and whispered, "Who's the guy on the far end of the counter?"

She didn't even turn to look. "He comes in once a month and meets up with James from the car dealership."

"Do you know his name?"

"No." She headed back to the kitchen, and the man stood. He shoved money across the counter and walked out. Hawke moved to the window. The man climbed up into a jacked-up Ford pickup. Hawke pulled out his logbook and jotted down the license plate.

Chapter Sixteen

Waiting for his food, Hawke texted the pickup license number to Shoberg. *He's been meeting with James Pruss.*

Before he'd finished off his hashbrowns, his phone buzzed. Shoberg.

"Hawke," he answered.

"That license number you sent was reported as stolen. A Chevy Camaro."

Hawke grunted. "It was on a jacked-up Ford pickup."

"I'm seeing a pattern here. Did you get a good look at the guy?"

"Yeah."

"I'll pull photos of all the people known to deal in stolen car parts. They'll be in a folder in the case document." Shoberg sounded distracted.

"I'm headed to the car dealership now to ask Juan a couple of questions and get some more information about the parts that Pruss purchased." Hawke didn't think the stolen parts he was taking off the criminal's hands had anything to do with his disappearance, but it never hurt to follow all trails when looking for the truth.

"Keep me informed. Even though we are seventy-five percent certain the victim isn't Pruss, I have to wait for the DNA to confirm before we can put out a BOLO on him."

Hawke agreed and ended the call. He walked across the street to the dealership.

Burke met him before he'd traveled halfway across the lot. "Have you learned anymore about James's death?"

"We're working on evidence," Hawke said, continuing into the building.

"Mrs. Pruss isn't in today. She said she couldn't deal with all the sympathy people were giving her." Burke said it as if the woman would melt from kind words.

"I'd like to talk to Juan and Charlie." Hawke pushed the door open and headed to the service department.

Cindy stepped out of her office. "Trooper! Have you learned any more?"

He shook his head and pushed through the door into the service area.

Charlie glanced up from where he was working under a hood. He put his wrench down and wiped his hands as he walked toward Hawke. "Anything new?"

"Maybe." Hawke scanned the area. "Where's Juan?"

The mechanic nodded toward the restroom.

"Does he ever work?" Hawke asked.

Charlie laughed. "He's been more nervous since James's death."

"Why do you figure that?" Hawke moseyed around the room as he talked. There were several alternators on a shelf not in boxes. They were shiny, but he noticed worn edges.

"I think Juan is worried that without James around to run interference, Mrs. Pruss will fire him." Charlie walked closer to Hawke. "Mrs. Pruss didn't want to hire him, but James said it looked good for the business to have more color in the personnel."

Hawke tipped his head toward the alternators. "These some of the stolen parts?"

Charlie's gaze drifted from Hawke to the alternators and back. "You've got good eyes. Most of the customers we do work for, don't even look at what goes in the vehicle."

"They're clean but I see the worn spots." He glanced up as Juan stepped out of the restroom.

The Hispanic mechanic caught sight of him and froze. That's when Hawke recognized the resemblance between him and the man who'd hurried out of Olive's.

"Juan, could I have a word with you?" Hawke walked toward the open garage door.

The man dropped his chin, staring at his feet as he walked over to Hawke.

"I believe a relative of yours was sitting in Olive's across the street waiting for James." Hawke studied the man. Juan's head couldn't droop any lower.

"After I was hired, James asked me if I knew anyone who could get us cheaper parts." He sighed and continued. "I said my cousin lived in the Tri-cities and he had a shop that tore salvage vehicles apart for the parts."

"Salvage vehicles?"

The man barely shook his head. "They don't make enough money from salvage parts. There are more new cars on the road now than the older models in the salvage yards. Stolen cars are brought to them."

"Did James know these were stolen parts and not used parts?" Hawke wanted to know how dishonest the supposed victim was.

"Yes. He laughed all the time about how his mother would have a heart attack if she knew they had been selling stolen parts." Juan peered into Hawke's eyes. "I did nothing but put my cousin in contact with James. Otherwise, I just did my job here."

"Knowing you were installing stolen parts and charging people for new parts."

Juan dropped his gaze. "Yes."

"Now tell me where you really got that license plate number from? It was a van reported stolen three months ago." Hawke pulled out his logbook, ready for the man's response.

"When I was visiting my cousin in Kenewick at New Year's, I saw it in his salvage yard. I figured it was stolen because it had the name of a Portland bakery on its side. But I didn't want to cause trouble."

"What did you plan to do with the information?" Hawke could see the man wanted to be honest and law-abiding but he also felt loyal to his family. Unfortunately, when there was an unlawful member of a family someone had to stop them. As he'd felt it his job to stop his wife's drug dealing brother. It not only got one drug dealer off the street, it cost him his marriage. There were consequences for following your own integrity.

"I have been battling that for months." Juan stubbed one toe into the concrete floor, not looking up at Hawke. "I would like my cousin to see the error of his ways, but I don't want to be the one to point a finger."

Hawke put a hand on the man's shoulder. "I'll keep your name out of it. Do you think your cousin might know what happened to James?"

Juan's head snapped up and he stared at Hawke. "You think Berto killed James?"

"I don't think so, but I need to look into all aspects of James's life to find out who did." Hawke tapped his pen on his logbook. "Can you give me a phone number and address for your cousin?"

Juan dug through the slit in the overalls and pulled out his phone. He scrolled and rattled off a number. "I would have to go home and look up his address."

Hawke handed him a card. "Call me when you get the chance to look up the address."

Juan shoved the card in his overalls with his phone.

Burke and Charlie stood over by a car up on a rack. Their backs were to Hawke as he walked up behind them.

"Excuse me."

They both jumped at his voice.

Burke whipped around first. "Didn't know you were still here."

Charlie was shoving something into his pocket.

"I have a couple more questions for you two. The other day you mentioned James liked the women. Who was his latest conquest?"

A big grin spread across Charlie's face. "The artist

that moved into the big place up along the lake, Edward Storm, his daughter."

Burke stared at Charlie. "She's barely out of high school?"

"I saw James and her going at it in one of the cars in the show room after hours." Charlie nodded.

Hawke gave the salesman credit, he appeared disgusted. "Anyone else?"

"Someone from his muzzleloader club, I think," Burke said. "Anyway, they started out talking about the rendezvous here at the lot and my daughter saw them having a cozy dinner at Rimrock Inn."

This caught Hawke's attention. He had a feeling the Muzzleloader club was where he'd get more information about the whereabouts of James than his place of business. The restaurant he mentioned was on the North Highway, going toward Grizz Flat. "That was before the Rendezvous?"

"Yeah. They were talking about competitions when I walked by."

"What day was this? Could I get your daughter's name and phone number?"

"I think Tuesday. The Rimrock isn't open for dinner on Mondays." He rattled off his daughter's name and phone number.

"Thank you," Hawke said, tucking his logbook into his pocket and heading to the open garage door.

"You think the lady with James killed him?" Burke called out.

Hawke just kept walking. James wasn't dead, but he could be holing up with the woman. He just had to figure out who it was.

His phone buzzed as he slid behind the steering

wheel.

"Hawke," he answered without looking at the name.

"This is Kristen Pruss. I called the Medical Examiner to see when they would release James's body and they said I had to talk to you."

Hawke leaned back in his seat. Shit! He'd forgotten the mother had talked about making arrangements for a funeral. Lying to the wife didn't feel right, but at the same time, he didn't need her getting caught up in their investigation trying to find her runaway husband.

"I've requested more tests be run to determine more about the cause of death. You want your husband's killer caught, don't you?" He wasn't lying about more tests. They had to find out who the victim really was.

A sigh whistled through the phone. "Yes. But I could use the insurance money to pay off debts."

"Debts? Yours or your husband's?"

"James, of course. He liked expensive things, thanks to his mother always telling him he needed to look better than anyone else." The distaste for her mother-in-law squawked in her voice like an angry bird.

"As soon as we can release the body, I'll let you know." Hawke ended the call and quickly texted Shoberg. *I have more information. Do you have time to meet?*

Hawke started his vehicle and his phone buzzed.

Can meet in Eagle in two hours.

I'll be at Al's Café.

Putting his vehicle in gear, Hawke pulled away from the curb and headed to the North Highway. He was this close, he might as well see if anyone remembered the couple and the blue Ford Escape at Rimrock Inn.

Chapter Seventeen

The large brown, red, and teal building sitting on the edge of Joseph Canyon had suffered through several winters judging by the flaking and fading paint. Hawke studied the teepees off to the side that were used for glamping. Glamour camping. A phrase that made him choke just thinking about it. The whole county had used his tribe, his ancestors, as bait to lure in tourists. This establishment was no different.

His ancestors had wintered in this deep, impressive canyon to get away from the cold higher country. When the settlers came along and named things, they named the great crack in the earth after the Nez Perce Chiefs who had led the Wallowa band. Old Joseph, whose Christian name was given to him when Reverend Spaulding baptized him in Lapwai. His Indian name was Wellamnootkin, a Cayuse word for the way the Nez Perce wore their chin length bangs bear greased up off their foreheads and rounded back, and his son,

Young Joseph or Hin-mah-too-yah-lat-kekt, Thunder Rolling Down a Mountain.

Hawke walked between the brightly painted teepees to stand at the edge of the canyon and peer down at Joseph Creek snaking along the bottom. He'd ridden horseback into the canyon on several occasions. One was for pleasure. It was one of the places in the county where he'd felt a deep connection to the earth and nature. One of his mother's friends had talked about constructing a sweat lodge in the canyon for The People to attend during a certain length of time. Staring into the chasm, watching Joseph Creek rushing by in the very bottom, he had an interest in seeing it happen and attending a sweat.

"Hey! Stay away from the edge!" called a male voice from behind him.

Hawke blinked, pulling himself to the present and why he'd ventured to this place. Facing the man, who he figured must be the owner, he said, "Trooper Hawke. Are you Mr. Moody?"

The man stopped in his tracks, his gaze taking in Hawke's uniform and duty belt. "Yeah, I'm Charles Moody. I don't usually yell at people. My dog, Dart, usually barks and warns me of people back here. But I haven't seen him in over a week. What can I do for you officer?"

"I was wondering if you remember a couple who ate here last Tuesday night?" Hawke pulled out his phone and brought up a photo of James Pruss.

Mr. Moody glanced at it. "That's James. Heard he died in a fire."

"Who was the woman he was with on Tuesday? And did you happen to get a look at the car they were in?"

The man crossed his arms. Not a good sign.

"James was a good customer. Why are you asking all these questions?"

Hawke stared at the man. "If he was a good customer, I'd think you'd want to help catch his killer."

The man mumbled and uncrossed his arms. "You don't think that woman he was with killed him, do you?"

"Whether she did or didn't, she might have information that could help us catch who did." Hawke pulled out his logbook. "Do you know her name?"

"No. But she doesn't live in the valley. From the bits of their conversation I heard, she's from somewhere else." The man shifted his feet. "I need to get back in and help my wife prep for dinner tonight."

"I'll come with you. Maybe she'll have some information I can use." Hawke fell in step beside the man as he walked to the back door of the establishment and entered through a kitchen door.

"Mae, there's a policeman here wants to speak to us," Mr. Moody called out as they entered. He faced Hawke. "She doesn't like anyone other than staff in the kitchen."

That was Hawke's opening. "Is Trudy Harris here today?"

This question seemed to shake the man more than any other he'd asked. "What's Trudy have to do with James's death?"

"Nothing other than she'd mentioned to her father she'd seen James here with a woman. I'd like to ask her about that." Hawke saw the man's tension ease a bit.

"Mae!" Moody shouted before, muttering, "I'll go

find both of them."

Hawke wondered that the man would leave him alone when Moody had said his wife didn't like anyone other than staff in the kitchen.

A woman older than Moody, wearing an apron and cook's hat, entered the kitchen. She started at the sight of Hawke. "What are you doing in my kitchen?"

"Your husband left me here to look for you and Trudy."

"What do you want with Trudy?" Her eyes narrowed.

The two were protective of the young woman. "I have questions about the other night when James Pruss and a woman had dinner here. I heard Trudy waited on them."

The woman's eyes widened briefly before she dropped her lashes low enough to cover any emotions that might flicker in her eyes.

Moody and a young woman entered the kitchen. "Trooper, this is Trudy Harris."

Hawke smiled at the woman. She smiled back, not a bit worried about his presence.

He stepped toward her. "Let's go sit in the dining room to talk."

She spun around and walked back through the doors.

"I'll visit with you two in a few minutes," Hawke said to the couple. He noticed they didn't even acknowledge each other.

In the dining room, Hawke sat at the table where Trudy already sat.

"My dad told you I saw James and a woman here, didn't he?" The woman seemed eager to tell what she knew.

"He did. What can you tell me about the woman and anything they might have said?" He placed his logbook on the table in front of him.

"James was his usual self. Acting like royalty. The woman laughed at him and told him he'd get more from people if he crawled down off his high horse." She thought a moment. "I liked her. Wondered what she was doing with him. Everyone in the county knows he beds women to get what he wants then leaves them. His poor wife. I don't know how she put up with him. I would have left him long ago."

"Did James call her by a name? Or did you hear where they were going?" Hawke needed to find out about the woman James was with when he made trips to the flat before the rendezvous. They had to have worked together to fake his death.

"I think he called her Dee or Di. I'm not sure. I didn't hang around the table listening. You could tell they'd been together a while. There was attraction, but they didn't cling."

"What did she look like?" Hawke didn't remember any of the women in the Wallupa Muzzleloader club with a first name that started with D.

"She was probably as tall as me…hard to tell, she had on these kickass boots with stiletto heels. Jeggings and a long flowy caftan over a skin tight black tank. Lots of jewelry. That's what got me about her telling him to come down off his high horse. She looked like an actress out on the town."

None of this described the woman. "Her hair, eyes, facial structure?"

"Reddish…no copper, curly hair. I didn't notice

her eyes, so they must have been brown or hazel. Blue or green always sticks out to me. Facial structure? Definitely Elle Fanning."

Hawke stared at her. "Elle Fanning? Is that a face shape?"

The young woman stared at him with her mouth open for half a second before snapping it shut and saying, "She's an actress. Pretty but not drop-dead gorgeous. Down to earth looking."

Hawke wrote down the characteristics the young woman rattled off and asked, "Did you happened to see the vehicle they were driving?"

"Yeah. It was a brand-new Ford Escape. I think blue. No license plate. Did he take it off the lot just for his date?" She scowled. "If Dad knew that he'd be furious. He's always saying James would ruin the business he and Mr. Pruss started."

"Your dad still believes the business is his?" Hawke had wondered at how easily the man had talked of stepping out of the partnership to be a salesman. Was he just biding his time to get his hands on the business again?

"He knows it isn't his, but most of the county knows he and Mr. Pruss started it. That makes him feel responsible for how the people are treated."

Hawke nodded. "Thank you for answering my questions." He glanced up at her. "Could you send the owners out here to talk with me?"

"Sure." She popped out of the chair and headed to the kitchen in the back.

Hawke tapped his pen on his logbook. He needed to find a woman named Dee or Di who had been connected to James.

The Moodys walked over to the table.

"Have a seat. What can either of you tell me about the woman James Pruss was in here with a week ago Tuesday?" He studied the two. Body language said they weren't a happy couple. The rings under the wife's eyes revealed she'd been crying.

"She had red hair, was good looking, fit," Mr. Moody said.

"I wouldn't know, I was in the kitchen cooking," Mrs. Moody answered.

Hawke didn't think it was a matter of she didn't know because she was cooking. She didn't know because she didn't want to know.

"Did you get the name of the woman?" Hawke asked the husband but kept his focus on the wife.

"No. James paid for the meal and they left." Mr. Moody didn't even look at his wife. He knew about his wife's connection to Pruss. He was putting a dig in that the man had left with a beautiful woman, not her.

"Did you see what he was driving and which direction they went?" Hawke finally shifted his attention to the man.

"They drove off in what looked like a vehicle from the lot. And they were headed north." Moody nodded as if that was it.

Hawke shifted his attention to the wife. "Did you see or hear anything between the two while they were here?"

She glared at him. "I was in the kitchen, where I always am during mealtime." She stood and strode to the kitchen door.

"You knew your wife was having an affair with James Pruss," Hawke said, studying the man.

Moody glared and shoved back from the table. "I don't know what you are talking about."

Hawke shook his head. "I've talked to a lot of men who had their wife's head turned by Pruss. Your wife has been crying and it's not over you. I could tell your marriage disintegrated a long time ago."

The man leaned forward. "How we live is none of your business."

"It is if it caused a man to die." Hawke stared at the man. "I think you know more either about the woman or where the two were going."

Moody ran a hand over his face. "Those two have been in here before. They would meet here. In two different cars. That was after Pruss told my wife she was too old for him to hang his hat on her bedpost." He laughed. "She's older than me, but at first I liked that. She was experienced. Or so I thought. But now…all she cares about is her cooking, until Pruss gave her the eye. Then she was dressing up, looking like the woman I'd married. Soon as he dumped her, she went back to worrying about her kitchen and nothing else."

"Did you get a look at the license plate on the woman's car when they met separately?" Hawke really didn't care about the marital problems, but he did care about catching the man who had used so many people, especially women.

"It had a Washington plate."

Red hair, Washington plate. Hawke needed to go back over his interviews at the Rendezvous.

Chapter Eighteen

Shoberg sat at a table in Al's Café eating a burger and drinking coffee, when Hawke arrived.

"Sorry, I'm late." Hawke sat down and caught Lacey Ramsey's attention. "Same." He pointed to Shoberg's plate.

"Why did you want to meet?" Shoberg wiped his mouth with a napkin and picked up his coffee cup.

"I don't think the stolen car parts had anything to do with mistaken identity. The wife called wanting to know when she could collect the body."

Shoberg set the cup down and peered at Hawke. "What did you say?"

"Told her we were still waiting on tests. That didn't she want to catch who killed him?"

"And?"

"She's hoping for the insurance money to pay off her 'late' husband's debts." Hawke leaned back as Lacey filled a cup with coffee. "Thanks."

"You're welcome." Lacey walked back to the counter with the coffee pot.

"Do you think she's in on his disappearance?" Shoberg tossed his napkin in the red basket his burger and fries came in.

"I don't think so. I don't think she'll miss him, but I don't think she helped him stage his death." Hawke leaned back as Bart, Lacey's husband and co-owner of the café, placed a burger basket in front of him.

"Anything else I can get you guys?" Bart asked.

"We're good. Thanks," Shoberg said.

"I was out at Rimrock Inn following a lead. Pruss and a redhead had dinner there on Tuesday night and were driving the missing car from the dealership. I think they are the two who drove out to Grizz flat and left the can of gas." Hawke picked up the burger and took a bite.

"Do you have more than a redhead to go on?" Shoberg asked.

"Washington plates." Hawke pulled out his logbook and plopped it on the table. He thumbed through it, eating fries. The name he was looking for was circled, just like he'd remembered. "There was a woman at the Rendezvous, Chessie. She was from Washington. I didn't get her real name but it should be in Novak's report. As soon as I get her name, I'll look up her address. We may need to ask the local P.D. to watch her house and see if Pruss is going in and out."

Shoberg nodded. "Once you get the address, I'll send them a photo of Pruss."

"There's one problem. I was told she's married. They may have to follow her to find out where Pruss is hiding." Hawke didn't like having someone else waste time on something that he thought might be, without facts. "Tomorrow's my day off. I'll go watch her and if I see Pruss, I'll call in the locals."

Shoberg stared at him. "You have to run that by someone higher up the ladder than me."

Hawke nodded. He'd take it to Spruel and see what his sergeant had to say about it.

"You know this means no pay and no way we'll back you up if it goes south," Spruel said, when Hawke told him about planning a trip to Pullman, Washington tomorrow to look for Pruss.

"I know I'm on my own. I'll take Dog and my own vehicle." Hawke had something else nagging him. He still hadn't heard from Wylie Lambert. "Would you see if you can get a county or state cop to check out Wylie Lambert's place. I've been trying to contact him for days and can't seem to connect." He rattled off the man's address for both his home and his work.

"That I can do. Be careful tomorrow. If your hunch is right, those two have killed to make Pruss disappear. They won't hesitate to do it again." Spruel stared at Hawke.

"I won't do anything stupid." Hawke left the sergeant's office and sat at his desk. He logged in and wrote out his reports for today before looking through Novak's notes to find Chessie's real name. Dre Holmes. Novak had been thorough. The deputy had taken down everyone's phone number and address. Hawke put the address into his map app on his phone and discovered he had a three hour drive. He'd get up at five and be to Dre Holmes' place by eight. Catch her heading to work or whatever she did on a Thursday.

He logged out and headed to his vehicle. Dog would be excited to go along for a ride. He'd been left behind a lot the last month. Hawke was looking forward to working the Snake River this year. After his weeks spent on the Idaho side following a killer last year, he was ready to enjoy the view from the river. He took Dog with him when they floated the river keeping tabs on anglers.

The Rusty Nail drew him into the parking lot like a fly to sugar. He not only wanted to grab something to eat for later, he wanted to find out if Mrs. Van Hoosan made it home safe.

The door jingled as he walked in. Head's turned. A few locals raised a hand or nodded as he walked to the counter.

"You here for a late lunch or early dinner?" Justine asked, looking as if she'd had a long day.

"I'd like to order a chicken fried dinner to go."

Justine wrote it on a ticket and stuck it up in the kitchen window. She faced him with a coffee pot in her hand. "Want some coffee while you wait?"

"Iced tea, please."

When she placed the drink in front of him, he asked, "Did Mrs. Van Hoosan get home okay?"

The waitress put a finger to her lips. "Don't let Merrilee know you're asking about Mrs. Van Hoosan. She's pissed at you for having the car impounded."

He frowned. "Why? It needs to be impounded so Mrs. Van Hoosan doesn't drive."

"I agree, but the way Merrilee sees it, you are costing her money."

"Money?"

"She doesn't want Mrs. Van Hoosan to drive either

but there's a fine for every day the car is impounded. That will cost Merrilee."

"Why? Mrs. Van Hoosan can get it out and someone can disable it so she can't drive it." Hawke didn't see how it could cost Merrilee anything.

"Merrilee pays all of Mrs. Van Hoosan's bills. Seems she had someone disable the car. They supposedly disconnected the steering."

Hawke stared at Justine. "That's why she was weaving all over the road worse than normal? She could have been killed or killed someone. Who was the Jackass that thought to disable the steering instead of taking off the distributor cap?" Anger started to bubble up in Hawke. The person could have caused multiple deaths by doing something so stupid.

"It was Merrilee's grandson, Jason." Justine raised her eyebrows.

"I suppose he is in Mrs. Van Hoosan's will?" Hawke was getting the picture. Jason had been in trouble since he was thirteen. Drugs, drinking, gambling. He was always broke and looking to make it big. He'd off Merrilee if the woman wouldn't kill him before he got her.

"Tell Merrilee—"

"Tell me what?" Merrilee walked out of the kitchen with a to-go box. She slapped the box down on the counter in front of him. "You could have just given me the keys to the car."

"I gave them to impound. It seemed like the safest thing to do. After hearing about the steering, it was. When you get it back, call me. I'll come pull the distributor cap. It won't go anywhere then." He handed a twenty to Justine, picked up his dinner, and left the restaurant.

Merrilee was tough. But it came from years of trying to make a living after her husband left her in debt over her head and bringing up four kids. He always paid more than his meal for Justine and Merrilee.

Driving home, he decided there wasn't any reason why he couldn't head to Washington tonight. He'd change, take care of the animals, let Herb and Darlene know he'd be gone, and take off. That would give him more time to watch the Holmes' residence and Mrs. Holmes.

Dog sat in the passenger seat staring at the road ahead of them. Even if Hawke had tried to get away, the animal wouldn't have let him. He was ready for a road trip. An hour after arriving home, he and Dog had loaded up and took off. Now they were slowly winding their way up the Washington side of Rattlesnake Grade between Alder and Clarkston, Washington.

The Flora turnoff had pulled at him as he'd passed, but he could do another look around the crime scene on his way home. By now there wouldn't be much to see. He already knew Pruss and his accomplice had walked to the car parked on Eden Lane.

His mind did a quick rewind. Novak had talked to Chessie, Dre Holmes, the night of the fire. When would she have had time to meet up with Pruss? And she hadn't driven off, he'd talked to her the following morning. Was this a wild goose chase? The footprints had been that of a woman and a man.

As he finished the climb to the top, Hawke wondered if he'd missed something. Everyone had linked Pruss with women. Could a smaller man have helped him escape? This jumped his thoughts to Wylie Lambert. What had people said about him? He'd have to wait until he stopped to check his logbook.

He slowed going down the hill into Asotin, through Lewiston, Idaho, and continuing across the Clearwater River, to head north to Pullman, Washington.

The neighborhood where the Holmes lived was a newer subdivision. The houses and yards were tidy. No more than two cars parked in driveways. A few driveways had basketball hoops. Definitely a family neighborhood.

If he sat in his truck for very long someone would either come out and ask what he was up to or they would call the police to come take a look. He drove by the Holmes's house and parked three blocks down.

Clicking the leash on Dog, he opened the door and they strolled back along the sidewalk toward his target. Street lamps were on. Houses were lit up inside. It was too early for everyone to be in bed. A man walked out to retrieve a garbage can.

"Nice evening," Hawke said.

"Yes, it is," replied the man, before dragging the refuse bin back to his garage.

Two houses before the Holmes residence, Hawke stared hard at the home he was interested in. He didn't want to be seen staring in the windows as he walked by. A man and woman were sitting at a dining room table. The man wasn't Pruss. The woman was Chessie. A bike was propped up against the corner of the garage. They had a child.

His gut said to knock on the door and ask her questions. His head said to do what he'd told Sergeant Spruel he would do. He continued two blocks past the house, walked to the other side of the street and headed back toward his truck. All the time scanning every home, every bush for someone lurking.

The more his mind ran through what he knew, he didn't see how this woman could have helped Pruss escape. She wasn't the redhead with him at Rimrock Inn. He remembered the name Trudy had given him for the face of the woman. He stopped and put the name into his search app on his phone. The face wasn't shaped like Dre Holmes. She was more angular.

Going with his gut, he returned to his truck, drove it to the Holmes residence, and parked in front.

"Stay," he told Dog, and walked up to the front door, pressing the doorbell before he changed his mind.

Chapter Nineteen

"Trooper Hawke? What brings you to Pullman?" Dre Holmes asked when she opened the door.

"I have questions." He glanced over her shoulder at the man standing in the living room doorway.

"Mark, this is the trooper who arrived when the accident happened at the Rendezvous." The woman stepped aside so Hawke could enter the house.

"Dre told me about the poor man drinking too much and driving his vehicle over a campfire." The man shuddered. "Heck of a way to go."

"I agree. I have some follow up questions. Do you mind if I talk to your wife alone?" Hawke asked.

"No. By all means. I'm sure you have loose ends to tie up." The man kissed the top of Dre's head. "I'll be in my office if you need me."

"Thanks, Mark." She watched her husband walk out of the room before motioning for Hawke to take a seat. "I'm surprised to see you. I told you all I knew."

Worry wrinkled the corners of her eyes.

Hawke drew in a breath, trying to decide what to tell the woman. They hadn't let anyone know it wasn't Pruss who died in the Jeep. However, he had a feeling this woman knew more about the man than anyone else, including his wife.

"During my investigation, I've uncovered that you were at the Rimrock Inn with the victim on several occasions."

She held up a hand, stopping him. "That was months ago. Not lately. I'd stopped seeing him about four months ago."

"According to the owners of Rimrock, and one of their employees, you were there last Tuesday with Pruss in a blue Ford Escape from the dealership." He studied the woman.

She shook her head. "No, I wasn't. I was here on Tuesday evening, getting my gear ready and helping my son with his homework. You can ask him and my husband."

Hawke leaned back. She peered into his eyes. She wasn't lying. "Can you think of another woman in Pruss's life who has red, no, they said copper, hair and the name Dee or Di?"

Dre leaned forward. "My husband doesn't know about my little fling." Her voice was barely above a whisper.

"You were pretty bold telling me all about it at Grizz Flat. If you want to keep it quiet, help me find the person who sounded a lot like you when she was described." Hawke continued to hold eye contact.

The woman settled back on the couch. "I don't know anyone with hair the color of mine. At least that he'd mentioned to me. His latest, or the ones he had when I called things off, were Seamstress Sue and some artist's daughter. I don't know what she looks like or what her name is. He called her his sprite."

Sprite-pixie. The actress he'd looked up had a face like a pixie. Had he conned Storm's daughter into helping him?

"Thank you. Another thing now that you've had more time to think about it. Any idea who would want the victim dead?" He knew it wasn't Pruss in the morgue, but maybe one of his enemies had ended up in the Jeep. It would give them a place to start looking.

"From the way the Wallupa club were talking, any of them. He was trying to change things too much. His business life…the man who was partners with his father. He never got over being left out when James's mother took over." She laughed. "Any number of husbands or boyfriends of women he'd used."

Hawke jotted all the information down in his logbook. "Thank you. If you can think of another woman, let me know."

She stood, studying him. "What does a woman have to do with his death?"

"You said yourself that many have been spurned by the victim." Hawke walked to the door, opened it, and walked out.

Dog sat in the driver's side of the pickup watching him.

Hawke slid in behind the steering wheel and put a hand on Dog's head. "Looks like we'll be heading home tonight. I don't think we'll find Pruss here."

He turned the key and put the vehicle in gear thinking about the information he'd gathered at

Rimrock Inn. They had to have known the redhead wasn't the same as he'd met at the restaurant before. These thoughts banged around inside his brain as he drove back to Alder.

Thursday was his day off. He'd called Spruel on his way back from Pullman to let him know there was no reason for anyone to watch the Holmes residence. That he now believed, either the Rimrock owners and employee had lied about a redhead being with Pruss or they hadn't paid enough attention to the woman to know who she was.

As he fed the horses and went about cleaning out the water trough, his mind couldn't let go of the fact they had to have lied to him. But why?

"I thought you weren't going to be here this morning," Darlene said, leading a mare up to the arena gate.

"What I planned to do, didn't pan out." Hawke walked over to the gate and leaned against it. "What do you know about the couple who own Rimrock Inn?"

"The Moodys? The name fits. Especially the wife. They moved here about four years ago. Added the teepees and upped the menu."

"Then they aren't from around here originally?" Hawke didn't see how they fit into the equation. They were relatively new to the area.

However, Trudy was the daughter of the man who felt he'd been gypped of his partnership in the car dealership. She had a better reason to set Pruss on fire than the Moodys.

"No. They haven't made many friends in the area. Why are you asking?" Darlene opened the gate and led the horse into the arena.

"Trying to figure out why they would be lying about who they saw with James Pruss several nights before the fire."

"You know they are lying?" She mounted the mare. The leather squeaked as she wiggled the saddle and settled the animal.

"The woman they said was with him, wasn't. She fit the description. Red hair a face like Elle Fanning—"

"Marcy, our granddaughter, said there is a young woman living at the lake who looks like the actress Elle Fanning." Darlene winked. "Small world."

"I think I know who she is talking about. Thanks." Hawke walked away from the arena as Darlene began walking the mare around.

Hawke pulled out his phone and called Shoberg.

"Shoberg,"

"Hawke. Have you heard anything about Wylie Lambert?"

"Negative. No one seems to know where he is."

"Then we need to get his dental and medical records. I believe he's our vic."

Shoberg laughed. "I thought you were taking today off."

"I am. I'm just calling and letting you know that I believe, for whatever reason, the owners and employee of the Rimrock Inn fed me half-truths and the woman who might have helped Pruss is Edward Storm's daughter. That is if she has copper hair."

"I was going to have a word with her today. Meet me in Prairie Creek at noon. We can interview her together. Gotta go." Shoberg dropped the call.

Hawke glanced at the time. Four hours until noon.

Dog stood by his pickup.

"Let's go for a hike."

Dog woofed and wagged his tail.

Hawke walked over to the vehicle, opened the door, and Dog hopped in.

A hike always helped him think clearly. Especially when he'd be checking out the area around the Storm residence.

Hawke and Dog sat on a log, not far from the large log house and a smaller version, he'd discovered was the artist's studio. Sipping water, while Dog lapped some from a portable dog water bottle, Hawke studied the house. They'd walked a mile both directions from the property and all over the property. These were the only two buildings where Pruss, if he was here, could hide.

A look in the smaller building had revealed clay, wire, tools, a couple of chairs, restroom, and a couch. There weren't any signs of someone living in the space.

His phone buzzed.

Shoberg had texted. *Out front. See your vehicle. Where are you?*

Coming. Hawke texted back and stood. "Come," he said to dog who had wandered over to a bush.

They walked around the house.

Shoberg stepped out of his vehicle. He glanced at the house and back at Hawke.

"I was taking a look around the area," he said, opening his pickup door for Dog to jump in.

"Did you find anything?" Shoberg waited beside his vehicle.

"No. The only other building is a studio. Doesn't

look like anyone has been living there." Hawke motioned for Shoberg to go first. He was the one on duty and in uniform.

They walked up to the door.

Shoberg clanged the large metal frog against the lily pad hanging on the side of the house beside the heavy wooden door.

"Coming!" called out a female voice.

The door opened. A young, copper-haired woman, standing barely five feet tall with a dainty face and large eyes smiled at them.

Hawke could see why someone would call her a sprite. She looked like an elf or a pixie seen in children's storybooks. Minus the pointed ears.

"I haven't done anything, officer," she said gleefully and backed up, allowing them in.

"Miss Diamond Storm?" Shoberg asked.

"Technically, yes. But I prefer to be called Di."

Hawke rehashed the remarks made by the Moodys and Trudy in his mind. He'd jumped to the conclusion it was Chessie, Dre Holmes, when it appeared this young woman had been Pruss's date.

"Miss Storm," Shoberg said as she led them into a large great room filled with huge wooden furniture and many bronze statues. "Where were you a week ago Tuesday?"

"I'm not sure what I did all day." She sat cross-legged on a big stuffed chair.

Hawke and Shoberg sat on the couch opposite her.

"Tuesday evening." Hawke started to say, 'Did you have a date?' and refrained. It didn't do to put words in a suspect's mouth. Though, with her size, she wouldn't have been much help to Pruss when it came to putting a body in the Jeep.

"Let me get my date book." She stood and walked out of the room.

Shoberg's leg started to bounce.

"She's not going anywhere," Hawke said to calm his friend.

"How do you know?"

"My pickup has been sitting in plain sight all morning, and she didn't show the least bit of surprise at our being at the door. She's been watching me. To run now would make her look guilty."

"Of what?" Miss Storm asked as she entered the room with a tray of drinks and a book.

"Of whatever would make you run," Hawke said.

She smiled at him, placed the tray on the table, and motioned with the book she'd plucked from the tray toward the tall glasses of what appeared to be iced tea. "Take one while I look in my date book."

Hawke grabbed two, handing one to Shoberg.

"Where's your father?" Hawke asked. He was surprised the man hadn't appeared since he wasn't in the studio.

"He's at an art show in Jackson Hole." She flipped another page. "Here. A week ago Tuesday, I have down I had dinner with James Pruss." Her eyes teared up. "I can't believe that only three days later he died in such a violent way."

"Did you and James have many dinner dates?" Shoberg asked, pulling out his logbook.

Miss Storm studied Shoberg. "What you are really asking is did I know he was married. Yes. He told me that before we started dating. You don't find very many men with good taste around here. I enjoyed his company."

"He was old enough to be your father," Shoberg said.

Hawke shot a glance at the trooper. Was he trying to get her riled up?

"He was four years younger than my father. But I've learned growing up in the world of art, age means nothing. What is in a person's heart and mind is all that matters."

Hawke studied her. She thought she had them captivated. He could see it in the gleam in her eye. She'd forgotten to appear grief stricken over Pruss. "Have you sent your condolences to James's wife?"

There it was, the switch to teary eyes and pouty lips. Clearly, she'd learned to turn her emotions on and off. So much for her romanticizing about art and age as if they meant anything to her.

With no one but Shoberg present to say anything, Hawke decided to cut to what they really wanted to know. "We know you and James used a car from the dealership to haul a can of gasoline to Grizz Flat on Tuesday night after your dinner at Rimrock Inn. And I believe you waited for him at Eden Lane Friday night after he knocked out Wylie Lambert's teeth and put him in the Jeep to make it look like he, James, had died in the fire." He stood up and walked around the room. "Where do you have him hid?"

The woman hadn't flinched while he talked.

She followed his movements with her eyes and raised a glass of iced tea to her lips.

"I don't hear you gasping that James isn't dead. Or denying you helped him." Hawke sat back down across from her. "Where is James?"

"I don't know what you're talking about. James died in the fire. I did go to Rimrock with him on Tuesday, and we drove one of his lot cars to the flat. He had some targets and things he wanted to put in the storage container. As for helping him Friday night…." She grinned like a coyote who'd just played a trick. "I was on a date with Mike Starr." She picked up a cell phone sitting on the table next to her. "I can give you his phone number."

Shoberg wrote down the number she rattled off.

Hawke didn't take his gaze from her. She was a user and a manipulator, just like Pruss. He couldn't see the man getting her to help him kill someone without having to give her half of the money he stole and then being blackmailed whenever it helped her out. No, she didn't help him the night he disappeared.

As Shoberg asked her a few more questions, he realized that she hadn't blinked when he'd said Pruss was still alive. She wasn't surprised he hadn't been the person in the burned vehicle. While she may not have helped him, she hadn't believed he had died, even if she had squeezed out a few tears for show.

Chapter Twenty

As they walked to their vehicles, Shoberg said, "Meet me at Olive's in Alder."

Hawke nodded. He had a feeling the trooper wanted to compare notes on the interview and reassess where this investigation was going.

As he pulled up to Olive's and parked, Shoberg sat in his vehicle talking on the phone.

Hawke exited his pickup and walked into the café. He'd get a table in the corner where they could talk. They were across the street from one or more of their suspects at the car dealership. He ordered an iced tea and wondered about the dealership car that was missing and hadn't been found yet. He knew that dealerships sent in the registration slips for cars that were purchased and the license plate was sent to the person who purchased the vehicle.

If Pruss kept the car, he must have registered it under the alias he'd planned to use or under the name of his accomplice. Hawke stared at the building across the street. There should be a record of the registration on that vehicle in the office.

Shoberg entered the café and sat in the seat across from him. "That was forensics." He ordered food and a drink when the waitress arrived at the table. When she'd walked away, he leaned closer. "Your hunch was correct. The medical and dental records on Wylie Lambert correspond to the body that burned in the Jeep."

While Hawke felt pride at having figured out who the victim was, he was still a long way off on finding Pruss, who he believed was Lambert's killer. "Will you keep that quiet for a bit longer until we can try to get Pruss to surface?"

Shoberg shook his head. "That's not my call. It's up to the Lieutenant."

Hawke nodded. He knew that but had hoped Shoberg might keep that bit of information away from his superior for a couple more days. "Then we need to find Pruss before he goes so deep we never find him." He tipped his head toward the dealership. "If he's still using the blue Escape, we may be able to get him." He went on to tell Shoberg his thoughts on the vehicle registration.

"Good idea. I'll get Vickers to sign a warrant for all their records." Shoberg pulled out his phone and walked outside.

The other trooper's food arrived. Hawke stole several fries before Shoberg returned. Maybe he should have ordered food too. He'd skipped lunch. Catching the attention of the waitress, he ordered a grilled cheese sandwich and fries. The woman looked up as he ordered and shook her head.

He swung his gaze to the door and caught the backside of Burke, the salesman, hurrying across the street back to the dealership. Hawke touched the woman's arm to stop her from walking away. "What's your name?"

She studied him. "Why?"

"Curious. You just signaled Burke not to come in here. Was it because of me and the other trooper?"

Shoberg walked back into the café.

The woman shot a glance his way and then back to Hawke. "I don't have anything to do with anything."

Hawke shoved the chair at the side of the table out. "Have a seat."

"I'm working."

"I know Olive, she won't mind."

Shoberg sat and sent Hawke a 'what's up' look.

The woman sat.

Hawke motioned for Shoberg to pull out his logbook. When the trooper had his pen poised over his logbook, Hawke asked again, "What's your name?"

"Michelle Harris."

"Burke is your husband. That's nice he can pop over here and visit with you when he wants." Hawke tried to sound encouraging when he really wanted to ask her a lot of questions at once.

"I've been working here since Olive opened. That way Trudy could have my car for school and now to drive to work. I ride in every day with Burke." Her tension seemed to ease as she spoke of her family.

"I imagine your family had to make many sacrifices when Burke lost the partnership of the car dealership to Pruss's wife and son." Hawke's stomach grumbled.

"I should put your order up," She started to stand.

"Put it up but come back. Please. We need to rule your husband out as a suspect in James's death." He knew that would bring her back.

"He didn't do it! I'll be right back." She hurried to the kitchen window, put up his order, and hurried back with a pitcher of iced tea. She refilled their glasses before setting the pitcher down and settling back in the chair. "I don't know why you would think my Burke would do such a terrible thing."

"Where was he last Friday night?" Hawke asked, not really believing the salesman had helped Pruss stage his disappearance by killing a man.

"We were at the Foley's playing cards. We go every other Friday night to their house and they come to ours the other Friday nights." She put her arms on the table and leaned forward. "If anyone killed James it would be either the men he purchased the stolen parts from or a husband of the women he messed around with."

"Can you give me any of the women's names?" Hawke noted Shoberg had been writing down all the woman said.

"There's Diamond something, though it would be her father who would want to kill James. Then a woman who lives in Eagle. I think she's part of the muzzleloader group. I've also heard he's been stringing several women from that organization along as well."

She wasn't helping him much. He knew all of the women she was talking about. "Anyone else?"

She shook her head, then stopped. "Burke said Cindy was spending a lot of evenings in the office after

Mrs. Pruss went home."

The bookkeeper would have access to the registration paperwork. Hawke wondered if she was James's accomplice. "Isn't she married?"

The woman wrinkled her nose. "Yes. Malcolm drinks too much."

Hawke glanced at Shoberg. They may have found their link if the registration papers turned up on the car.

The kitchen bell dinged and the woman popped up, hurried to the window, and returned with his food. "Will that be all?"

"Yes, thank you." Hawke picked up half of the sandwich and began eating.

"That warrant for the records should be ready at the courthouse," Shoberg said. "Stay here and finish your food. I'll go get it and come back."

Hawke waved a hand and continued eating.

Shoberg pulled into the Wallowa Valley Car Sales lot followed by a city and county car. He'd brought reinforcements for the seizure of records, it appeared. Hawke had been sitting at Burke's desk talking to him about how the business had been doing lately. It appeared James had baled along with $200,000 right before there was a large loan due to be paid. That was why Mrs. Pruss was so furious. Her best salesman was dead, to her knowledge, and she was missing money she needed.

Hawke had a feeling the young man had intentionally hurt his mother this way. Why, they'd never know until they caught him.

"What are you doing driving into my lot like I'm a criminal?" Mrs. Pruss asked, walking down the stairs from her upper level office.

Shoberg walked up to her, holding out the warrant. "We're here to collect your title and registrations slips for the last six months and all records of the cars that came in and were purchased in that time frame."

The woman's chin dropped, leaving her mouth open. She quickly snapped it shut and marched down the hall to the office where Cindy Albee worked.

Hawke followed the procession of uniformed law enforcement officers. He heard Burke breathing behind him. Hawke spun, putting out a hand. "If you have nothing to do with this, you might want to go back out there and tend to any customers."

The man glanced over his shoulder, shrugged, and headed back the way they'd come.

"Cindy, give these men all of the records mentioned in this warrant." Mrs. Pruss slapped the paper down on the woman's desk and headed for the door.

"Profitt, stay with Mrs. Pruss," Shoberg said.

The woman's face turned red as the Alder City Policeman fell into step behind her.

Hawke knew it was to make sure the woman didn't destroy any records that may have come from this office.

Cindy's hands shook as she picked up the paper and read the request. "Why do you want these records?" she asked.

"We can't disclose that information, but it has to do with the death at Grizz Flat," Shoberg said.

Hawke grinned. The trooper hadn't shown their hand with his reply. Cindy continued to stare at the paper.

"The records, please," Hawke said, quietly.

She glanced up, nodded, and walked over to a filing cabinet. "I just don't understand what six months of records has to do with his death." She pulled out files, piling them on a chair.

"Novak, go see if you can round up some boxes," Shoberg said.

The deputy left the office.

Hawke stepped in closer to the filing cabinet to see some of the labels. She had missed a file marked pending sales. He pointed to it. "That one, too."

Her face became ashy gray. Her hands shook as she grasped the file and placed it on the top of the pile.

Hawke made a note to check that file first.

Novak returned with two file boxes. He and Shoberg put the files in the boxes. Hawke plucked the one he wanted to look at, out of the pile and placed it on the top of the first full box.

"Are there any files upstairs that fall under this warrant?" Shoberg asked.

"There could be. I don't know what Mrs. Pruss may do with some of the files once I've filed them." Cindy sat down in her chair, her hands in her lap. She was guilty of something.

Hawke could sense it in her actions. He made a mental note to contact her outside of work and ask about her affair with James and if she'd helped him to disappear.

Chapter Twenty-one

It was Hawke's day off. He should have left the dealership and headed home, but he followed Trooper Shoberg and the files to the Winslow State Police Office.

"What are you doing here?" Sergeant Spruel asked as Hawke walked through the door to the inner offices.

"I want to check a file Shoberg subpoenaed from the car dealership." He walked into the conference room carrying the box with the file he wanted to look at. Shoberg followed him with the second box.

"Get me up to speed," the sergeant said.

While Shoberg told Spruel what had transpired, Hawke pulled out the top file in his box and flipped through the pages.

He grinned. "This was what she didn't want us to see." He held up the paperwork for a registration for the Escape.

"Who?" Spruel and Shoberg said at the same time.

"Cindy Albee, the bookkeeper at the dealership. She'd passed over this file until I pointed it out to her. She became more nervous when I did that. Her name is down as the one who purchased the blue Escape that is missing."

Spruel plucked the paper from Hawke's hand. "You think she's Pruss's accomplice?"

"We won't know until we ask her." Hawke glanced at Shoberg.

"I'll call and ask her to come down here for some questioning." Shoberg pulled out his phone.

"You might want a deputy to keep an eye on her. She might try to get away." Hawke had witnessed the woman's nerves and fear. If she knew where Pruss was hiding, she might run to him.

"That's a good idea. Wait to call her. Hawke, take your vehicle and see where she goes." Sergeant Spruel swung his gaze to Shoberg. "Hawke will call you when he has a visual and then you make the call."

Shoberg nodded, and Hawke headed for the door.

Cindy Albee walked out to her car, slid in, and sat for a moment.

Hawke watched this from across the street in his pickup, as he patted Dog on the head. "Where do you think she's going?"

Dog whined.

"Yeah, if she goes to Pruss, I'll call for backup."

The car pulled into the street. Hawke swung out of his parking space and followed. She turned left, headed toward Winslow.

She stayed within the speed limit all the way and pulled into the State Police and Fish and Wildlife parking lot.

He drove to the back, knowing she would be going in through the Fish and Wildlife side. Hawke rolled the windows down halfway so Dog wouldn't get hot and strode into the State Police side of the building and through to the Fish and Wildlife.

"I'll take her over," he said to the receptionist listening to Cindy Albee's flustered explanation of why she was there.

"Trooper Hawke, I'm glad to see you." The way the woman said it, he believed her.

"This way." He led Cindy through the doors into the State Police offices. Shoberg stood by the conference room door.

Hawke let the woman enter the room first. The boxes they'd subpoenaed sat on the table with folders spread out.

The woman stopped, drew in a deep breath, and walked over to a chair, sinking down on it as if her legs had given out.

"Do you know why we asked you to come here?" Shoberg asked, sitting on a chair at the corner of the table, and facing the woman.

"The registration form for the missing car." Her words were barely above a whisper.

"Yes. Why is your name on the registration for the car that we've been told was stolen?" Shoberg opened his logbook as Hawke sat on the edge of the table on the other side of the trooper.

She sighed heavily and her eyes glistened with tears. "Six months ago, James started paying attention to me. You know, like he did with the women who came in to buy cars. We've worked together for years and he's barely talked to me other than business. Then all of a sudden, he was hanging around my office, asking me to stay after everyone else had gone home." Her cheeks darkened. "Making me feel special. Two months ago, he asked me to send in the registration for that car with my name and address. He said, he was working on his mother to give it to me for being such an exemplary employee." She glared at Shoberg. "I should have known it was a trick. That woman wouldn't give anyone anything without something attached, preferably money."

Hawke studied the woman. She appeared to be another pawn in James Pruss's game. "When you realized what he'd done, why didn't you tell us?"

She glanced up at him. "Because I thought you might think I had something to do with his death."

Hawke and Shoberg exchanged glances. Did they dare let her know the man was alive?

He decided to ask a few questions first. "Had you seen him paying any special attention to a woman the weeks before his death? Or receiving calls where he'd want privacy?"

She started to shake her head, then stopped. "He did answer his phone twice and walk outside. When he talked to customers he always stayed where everyone could hear what he was saying. You know, kind of bragging, he had a buyer."

"What was his cell phone number?" Shoberg asked.

Cindy rattled it off from memory.

"Where were you on the Friday night of the fire?" Hawke asked.

"At home with my husband. Though he was so

drunk he wouldn't be able to tell you."

The sadness in the woman's eyes reminded Hawke of his mother's before his stepfather died in a car accident.

"Thank you for coming in and telling us the truth," Hawke said, standing and escorting the woman back to the Fish and Wildlife side of the building.

When he returned, Shoberg was on the phone requesting a warrant for Pruss's phone records.

Hawke turned on his computer and went to DMV records. Now that they had a name on the registration, he looked up the license plate number.

Shoberg rolled a chair over next to Hawke. "This Pruss went to a lot of work to make sure no one finds him."

"He's wanted for theft and murder." Hawke handed the number to Shoberg. "That's the license on the Escape."

"Go home. There isn't much of your day off left." Shoberg stood and headed to Spruel's office.

Hawke turned off his computer and left the building. The sun was lower in the horizon. He dropped onto the driver's seat and patted Dog's head. "Let's grab a chicken dinner to go from the Blue Elk."

Dog licked his lips.

Putting his vehicle in drive, his phone buzzed. He shoved it into park, reading the name. Dani.

"Hello," he answered.

"I'm at my place in Eagle. I had to fly out for supplies and fly a family of four into the lodge tomorrow." Dani took a breath. "You want to come by?"

"I'm leaving Winslow now and can be there in

twenty minutes." He grinned. This was a good way to end his day.

"See you then." Her words weren't anything to make his heart race, but they did.

He wondered for the thousandth time why this woman heated his blood.

Dani told Hawke to bring Dog up to the apartment she now rented year-around over an elderly couple's garage.

Dog walked around, sniffing, before he laid down on a rug in the kitchen.

"I'm surprised you made it here so fast and aren't in uniform."

Dani said, handing him a beer.

"It was my day off." He took the drink, sipped, and studied her. She had short cropped curls that framed her face, giving her a softer look. Her full dark brows that could show as much expression as her eyes, revealed she was confused.

"Day off? I thought those were Monday and Tuesday?"

He explained how he was following leads on the case they'd checked out at Grizz Flat.

"I see. You're in tracking mode, though you aren't really tracking." She led him into the living room, carrying a tray of cheese, crackers, and deli meats.

"You could say that. I do know that who everyone thinks burned up in the vehicle fire, isn't the person who was in the fire." He picked up a cracker, cheese, and meat.

Dani stared at him. "Someone else was killed to make it look like the murderer died?"

"Yeah." He bit into the food and crunched.

She stared at him. "How do you plan to find the man?"

Hawke swallowed the food in his mouth. "I'm working on it."

Narrowed eyes studied him. "How?"

"Asking questions, digging for the truth. I know a woman helped him. So far all the ones it should be have alibis."

"What do you mean by should be?" Dani curled her legs up under her on the couch and sipped her beer.

He liked that she was interested in his job. His ex-wife didn't like him talking about his day. Especially after he'd arrested her brother on drug charges.

He went on to tell her about all the women in the suspect's life and how each one with the most to gain by helping the suspect had an alibi.

"Who had the most to lose?" Dani asked.

"What do you mean by that?" Hawke studied her.

Dani picked at a string on the cuff of her pants. "Which woman had the most to lose if she didn't help him?"

"You mean like blackmail?" He hadn't thought of that angle. Pruss getting someone to help him out of duress.

"Was there a woman in his life who would help him to keep her affair with him a secret?"

His mind went to Seamstress Sue. Wendy Levens. She'd been shocked her daughter had known about her affair with Pruss. But her husband had acted as if he knew about it, too. "There's one woman, but I don't see how he could have blackmailed her. Her whole family seemed to know about the affair." But his mind kept spinning what Sourdough and Biscuit had said.

"What about the wife?" Dani grinned. "They always say the spouse is the first suspect. Maybe in this case, she helped her husband disappear, because…"

"She wanted to be rid of him and his mother," Hawke said the words as they came to him.

"She didn't light the wrong man on fire thinking it was her husband?" Dani sipped her beer.

"That's a possibility, but she would have had to have been working with someone. She would have known it wasn't her husband if she'd put him in the Jeep and drove it over the campfire."

This triggered a thought. Perhaps she'd paid Wylie Lambert to clobber her husband and set him on fire, and the tables turned on Wylie, and Pruss set him on fire.

"You are making me think along different lines. This is good." He smiled at Dani and she grinned back.

He'd have to check out Wendy Levens and Kristen Pruss in the morning.

Chapter Twenty-two

Arriving at the Trembley's barn and his apartment around 7 am, Hawke fed the horses and mule before he and Dog dashed up the stairs to the apartment. Dog wanted fed and Hawke needed to change and get to work. When he'd arrived at Dani's, he hadn't planned on spending the night. But they'd switched the conversation from the fire to how they both grew up and before he knew it, he'd had three beers and it was midnight. It seemed like crawling into bed with Dani was the responsible thing to do rather than drive home tired and having consumed the beer, even if it had been consumed over many hours.

He and Dog left the apartment as Herb walked into the barn.

"Seen your truck was back. Wasn't here earlier. You do something fun on your day off?" The older man had a sparkle in his eyes.

"Maybe. I'm late for work." Hawke walked past

Herb.

"If by work you mean looking for the killer of James Pruss you might want to listen a minute." The reprimand in the man's voice stopped Hawke's feet.

He'd never treated his landlords with anything other than respect. But he hadn't wanted the man to know he'd spent the night with Dani. Even though he and Dani were well past the age of anyone really caring, Hawke didn't like everyone knowing his personal business.

Hawke pivoted, facing the man. "Sorry. Just don't like to be late."

"You were asking about the Moodys. Darlene heard at the fair committee meeting that they haven't been getting along very well. Mae Moody was fooling around with someone younger than her and so has Charles. There's talk that one has asked the other to buy them out." Herb leaned against a stall gate.

"Do you know which one wants out?" Hawke wondered if Mrs. Moody wanted to move on and join James Pruss.

"The missus wants to buy out the husband. Seems she wants to stay and run the place." Herb pushed away from the gate.

That didn't fit in with what Hawke was just thinking. "Any idea who the husband was fooling around with?"

"Rumor is it's someone who works there." Herb raised his eyebrows.

"Trudy Harris." He'd seen the way the two looked to one another before answering his questions. He didn't see where they would help James. "Thanks." He started to leave and turned back around. "Sorry I was so abrupt earlier. Just things on my mind."

Herb grinned. "Don't you mean someone?" He laughed and walked into the barn.

Hawke shook his head, grinning. Herb and Darlene took pride in digging into his business.

In his vehicle, he called dispatch to let them know he was on duty, and he headed to the main road.

Wendy Levens, Seamstress Sue, had been on his mind since leaving Dani's house. In fact, he'd swung by the Levens residence on his way home. It had been dark. He didn't know when the family rose for work and school, but it had seemed odd for it to be so dark.

Entering Eagle, he turned down a side street and parked in the Levens's driveway. It appeared just as dark and deserted as earlier. By now the family should be stirring. Biscuit would have school, and Jake would need to get to work.

He walked up to the front door and knocked. Not a sound came from inside. He scanned the street. A curtain swooshed on the house across from this one. Hawke knocked harder. Nothing.

A man walked out of the house next door and opened his pickup door.

"Hey!" Hawke called out to get the man's attention.

The man stopped and looked around. His eyebrows rose at the sight of Hawke in his uniform. "Yeah?"

Hawke walked over to the man and stopped. "Have you seen the Levens today?"

The man stared at his neighbor's house. "I haven't seen them since they came back from their muzzleloader weekend at Grizz Flat."

"They came back from that and left again?" Hawke

wondered where the family had disappeared. The whole family wouldn't be meeting up with James Pruss.

"Yeah. But I saw Sara, the daughter, here a couple days ago." The man scratched his head. "Are they in trouble?"

"No. I just wanted to ask them some more questions about the fire at the Rendezvous."

The man lit up. "That was something, wasn't it? James Pruss burning like that. I know quite a few people in this county that aren't too sad about it. He cheated everyone he sold a car to. Smooth talker that he was."

Hawke asked the man for his name, entered it in his logbook, and nodded toward the house across the street. "Who lives over there?"

The man followed the tilt of his hat. "Old lady Stevens. She keeps her nose in everyone's business. You can bet she'll know where Jake and Wendy are."

"Thanks." Hawke closed his logbook and headed across the street. The door of the small cottage style house opened as he stepped onto the porch.

"Come in, Officer," The older woman said, opening the door wider.

"Mrs. Stevens—"

"Miss. And not Ms. either. I never married and I never burned my bra." The woman shut the door and led him into the small living room. It looked like a photo he'd seen of a parlor in a house in the 1800s.

"All of the furniture are family heirlooms." She sat in a straight-backed cushioned chair with carved wooden base, arms, and back, caressing the smooth shiny arms with her hands.

"It all looks well-kept," he said, wondering if she

would take offense to him calling it antiques. He didn't want on the woman's bad side. He wanted her to willingly give him information.

"I have maintained all of the furniture in its original glory." The pride in the woman's words proved how much she loved the inanimate objects.

"When was the last time you saw the Levens family?" he asked, pulling his logbook out of his pocket.

"Together, Saturday night when they came back from Grizz Flat. Wasn't that fire awful! I can't think of a worse way to die." She shuddered and pulled the sweater she was wearing tighter around her.

"When was the last time you saw each one separately?" Hawke studied the woman as her faded brown eyes watched him.

"Why are you interested in them?" she asked.

"I have more questions for them about the incident at the Rendezvous, and I see they are not at home."

She gave a curt nod. "I don't know when Wendy left. Her car was missing Monday morning when I got up."

"What make and color is her car?" Hawke could look up all the license plates, but knowing which car belonged to which family member would be easier.

"Silver Honda. Older. I can't remember the model. Jake drives a pickup. Sara has her permit, no license. But I've watched her take her mom's car late at night." The woman's eyes glinted with merriment.

"Then it could have been Sara took the car and the parents went looking for her?" Hawke wondered if the girl had gone looking for Hardtack.

"No. I saw Sara later that day and Wednesday. She

came to the house to get more clothes. She's staying with a friend." Miss Stevens stood. "Would you like a cup of coffee?"

"If it's no trouble."

"None at all. I already have a pot made." The woman left the room.

Hawke scanned the photos on the walls and tables. The woman had many photos with different men, women, and families. He wondered at her living alone when he'd noticed she had spunk.

"Here you go. I forgot to ask if you used cream or sugar." She placed two mugs of coffee on the side table between their two chairs.

"Black."

She smiled. "I never understood why people drink coffee only to put in half a cup of cream or milk and a quarter cup of sugar." She settled back in the chair.

"Do you know the name of the friend where Sara is staying?" Hawke sipped the coffee. It was good. Strong but not too strong. Just what he needed this morning.

"Jill. I think Jackson. Just go to the Eagle High School and ask to see her." The woman sipped her coffee.

"And Jake? When did you see him leave?" Hawke wondered why the husband would take off after a woman who obviously didn't want to be with him. Then he remembered the boys. "And the boys? Where are they?"

"Jake and those two hooligans left Tuesday morning in Jake's pickup."

Hawke stared at the woman. "Are the boys school age?"

"Yes. I figure he took them to his sister in

Pendleton and went looking for Wendy." She sipped her coffee and added. "Sara is pretty strong willed. I'm sure she refused to leave her friends and school."

Hawke nodded. "Do you know the name of the aunt?"

"Only Aunt Clara. Nothing else. Go talk to Sara. She'll be able to get you the information." She sipped her coffee and peered at him over the cup. The glint in her eyes and slight tip of the corners of her mouth, implied she knew more than she was telling him.

"Do you have any ideas what happened?"

"I know Wendy has been unhappy for a long time. Before those two boys were born." She held up a finger. "I'm not sure those boys are Jake's."

"She likes to fool around with other men?" Hawke asked. He hadn't thought the woman was that loose. He'd believed her story of James Pruss seducing her. Had it been the other way around?

"Not a lot of men. Choice men. When men show up to 'try on' their reenactment clothing, I noticed the ones who can barely afford the costumes are only there for fifteen to thirty minutes. The ones with money…they can be there up to an hour. And back several times for 'fittings.'"

"Like James Pruss?" Hawke volunteered.

The woman's ears turned scarlet. "That man had no shame! He'd strut into that house and an hour later come out tucking in his shirt and grinning like a dog who satisfied his hunger with a big beef steak."

"Did Jake know about Wendy's long meetings with certain men?" The man had admitted he knew about Pruss. Had he known about all the others? Could the woman who had seemed so meek when he'd interviewed her, been playing him? Perhaps she had been blackmailing all the men with money. But how had she been in two places at once the night of the fire? She couldn't have driven Pruss away and then been at the camp when they started interviewing people. Or could she?

"How would you describe Wendy Levens?" he asked, knowing this woman had given him all truthful answers to this point.

"Physically or character?"

"I've met her. Character traits."

"Unhappy in her marriage. Likes nice things. Not maternal. Hates this county." She raised an eyebrow. "I think she left for good."

That was what Hawke was thinking as well. She may have found her way out with James Pruss.

Chapter Twenty-three

The Eagle High School was in a two-story block building. He walked through the double door and up to the office window. A large sign beside the window asked all guests to please check in with the secretary.

An older woman with blue tips on her white curls looked up from her keyboard and smiled. She rolled her chair over to the window. “May I help you, Trooper…” she glanced at his name tag, “Hawke?”

“I’d like to speak to Sara Levens, please.”

“Oh my! I hope nothing terrible has happened to her family.” The woman batted her lashes behind thick glasses.

“No. I just need to ask her some questions about the Grizz Flat fire.”

“Oh, yes! She was there. At the Rendezvous with her family. One moment, please.” She picked up a phone, pressed a button, and waited. “Mr. Crawford, could you please send Sara Levens to the office.” A pause. “Nothing’s wrong. Thank you.” The woman spun her chair towards the window. “She’ll be right here.”

“Thank you.” He moved away from the window and waited.

Five minutes later, Sara walked down the hall toward him. “What are you doing here?” she asked.

“Looking for you.” He glanced at the secretary, listening to their conversation. He smiled at her. “I’ll take Sara outside to talk to her.”

“Is this about the fire?” Sara asked, leading the way out the front doors of the building.

“Yes and no.” Hawke pointed to a bench beside the walkway up to the doors.

Sara sat. Her gaze settled on her feet.

“I stopped by your house to talk to your parents and they weren’t there. Any idea where I can find them?” He’d start with that and work his way to what he knew.

“No.” She scuffed the toe of her shoe back and forth across the cement. “We woke up Monday morning and mom was gone. She’d packed all her good clothes and left in her car while we were all sleeping. Dad was pissed. He shouted and threw things for an hour. When he said we were all going to Aunt Clara’s while he looked for her, I told him I wasn’t going. I called Jill and she said I could stay with her family. Dad and the boys left Tuesday. You can call Aunt Clara.” She rattled off the full name and a phone number that Hawke added to his logbook.

“Do you know why she left?” The girl had proven during his interview of her and her mother that she knew more than the mother thought she did.

"She's been unhappy for a while. Dad just ignored her. Acted like everything was fine. But it wasn't. She quit doing anything unless it was making costumes or going to the Rendezvous and shoots. It was like she wanted to be anywhere but in the real world." Sara looked up. "There were days she'd look at me and I could tell she wished I wasn't here."

Hawke had seen too many dysfunctional families like this in his years on the job. "I'm sure your mom just needs some help. Do you know where she might have gone?"

"She liked the coast. The beaches, water. But she always talked about going someplace tropical." Sara looked hopeful. "Do you think she just took a trip to a tropical island and will come back in a week or two?"

"Could be. If you hear from her or your dad, let me know." He handed the girl his card.

"Yeah. Sure."

He left her sitting on the bench as he walked back to his vehicle. Once inside, he called Aunt Clara.

"Hello?"

"Mrs. Felding, I'm Oregon State Trooper Hawke. I just talked to your niece, Sara, and she gave me your name and phone number."

"Is she okay? I couldn't believe Jake was stupid enough to leave a teenage girl alone by herself." The woman was obviously not happy with her brother.

"She's fine. She's staying with a friend and attending school. Can you tell me if Jake is there?" He didn't need the husband charging around trying to find his wife.

"He dropped the boys and said he was going after Wendy. Though why, I'll never know. Over the years, he's told me about the men she's slept with and how she ignores her own children."

"Did he say where he thought she might be going?" Hawke had to intercept the man before he saw James Pruss was still alive and murdered him.

"He said she always went to the coast when she was in one of her moods. He headed there right after dropping off the boys." She paused. "He won't do something stupid, will he?"

"He's your brother, what do you think?"

She sighed. "He's forgiven her every time she's had an affair. I don't see why he wouldn't forgive her if she came home."

"Did he mention any specific town on the coast?"

"He said around Newport." Her voice sounded tired. "If you can find him before he does something stupid, I would appreciate it."

"We'll do our best." Hawke ended the call and headed for Winslow. He needed to get the State Police and local police in the Newport area looking for the Levens's vehicles. That would be the easiest way to find them.

The A.P.B. on the Levens's vehicles was issued. Hawke also added the license of the blue Escape that was missing. He didn't think it would be a coincidence if that car was found in the vicinity of Wendy Levens's Honda.

He pulled out his logbook and added everything he'd learn to the file. Kristen Pruss had known about all of her husband's philandering. Had she really not cared? He thought about Dani's comments the night before about blackmail. Had she blackmailed her husband about one of his affairs? Who would he have been fooling around with that he would want to keep it quiet?

Maybe a look at the women he'd sold cars to in the last six months to a year might shed some light.

He rolled his chair away from the desk and stood.

Sergeant Spruel walked out of his office. "Any luck finding the Levenses?"

"It's too early. Are the boxes from the dealership still here or did Shoberg take them back?"

"There here, but he planned to take them back this afternoon." Spruel studied him. "You want to go through them again?"

"Just want to see who some of Pruss's clients were." Hawke wandered to the breakroom. "And you can let Shoberg know I'll return the files."

Spruel nodded.

Hawke continued into the breakroom and flipped through the files, looking for the sales lists for the last six months. The county had a small population and not everyone could afford a new car. The file was thicker than he'd expected.

Placing the file on the breakroom table, he filled a cup of coffee and sat down to read.

Right on top of the list was a cash sale of a pickup to Wylie Lambert. The victim. Hawke sat back in his chair. Why would Lambert come here to purchase a vehicle when there were three dealerships in La Grande? He scanned the paperwork. The pickup didn't look any cheaper in price than if he'd bought locally. Cash? Lambert would have had to save a lot to afford a brand-new pickup and pay outright.

Hawke pulled out his phone and dialed Shoberg.

"Shoberg," he answered.

"This is Hawke. Have you gone through Wylie Lambert's place yet?"

"The victim's? No. When you were wondering about his not being around, a city policeman checked out his place and said it looked like no one was home, but we haven't gone through it. You wanted it kept quiet that he was the victim." Shoberg's muffled voice said something to someone else. "I'm in the middle of a vehicle accident. Can I call you back?"

"I'm heading to Lambert's place. Give me a call when you break loose." Hawke ended the call and photocopied the sales receipt before putting the paper back in the folder.

He left the breakroom, walking by the sergeant's door.

"Hey!"

Hawke backed up and looked in the door.

"I thought you were taking the boxes back to Wallowa Valley Car Sales? You could do that on your way to check turkey hunters out north." His superior stared at him over glasses halfway down his nose.

"While going through the records I saw a receipt for a new pickup sold to the victim by Pruss. Thought I'd go take a look around Lambert's place." Hawke knew he should be doing more patrolling and less investigating, but once he got on the trail of tracks or evidence, he was like a dog trying to pick every bit of flesh and sinew off a bone.

Spruel frowned. "Can't Shoberg do that?"

"He won't know what to look for."

"He would if you told him." The man removed his glasses and stared at Hawke.

He sighed. "I'm not sure what I'm looking for. Something to prove, I don't know what, but maybe why Pruss killed him and made it look like he died." A memory of the investigation of the fire flashed through his mind. "Someone took down Lambert's camp and drove his vehicle away. I want to see if it's at his house. If not, that may be the vehicle we should be looking for."

Spruel waved his hand. "Go. You aren't going to be any good to us until you get the pieces of this homicide laid out in order."

"Thank you. I'll patrol tomorrow." Hawke hurried out of the building before Spruel changed his mind.

In his vehicle, he called in his destination to dispatch and drove out of Winslow on his way to Minam Canyon and La Grande.

Chapter Twenty-four

An hour later, Hawke stood in front of Lambert's home. Newspapers were piled up on the front porch. He knew Lambert wasn't married and apparently didn't have anyone living with him either. There was a large shop out back. He headed there since he wanted to wait for Shoberg to arrive with a key to search the house.

There wasn't a new Chevy pickup in front of the house. Maybe it was stored in the shop. Hawke tried the doorknob. It turned. Surprised the shop hadn't been locked up, he shoved the door open and stepped inside. Only a few slants of sunlight through small windows up high gave any light to the dark interior.

He felt along the door frame and found a light switch. Powerful lights came on, illuminating the pile of cardboard boxes and two metal work benches piled with electronic parts and wires.

Hawke scanned the area. No vehicles. Only what looked like computer components that needed to be put together. He'd read the man's occupation was a computer consultant. Did he build computer systems for clients?

A tall metal file cabinet sat at the end of one of the workbenches. Hawke walked over and pulled out a drawer. If all of this was expensive computer parts, why hadn't the door been locked?

He thumbed through the files and found one labeled Pruss. Had the dealership used Lambert's expertise?

Flipping open the file, he read, put it down on the workbench and pulled out his phone. This wasn't invoices for a job. These were transcripts of phone conversations. Now he knew why Lambert was killed.

"Hawke!" Shoberg called.

"In the shop!" Hawke shouted back, as he replaced all the papers and set the folder to the side to see if the man had been forging fake identification for anyone else.

Shoberg entered the building as Hawke replaced a file that was legitimate work invoices and information that he assumed had to do with the computer work Lambert did for the client.

"What are you doing in here?" Shoberg walked up to the workbench, eyeing the stack of cardboard boxes.

"I found out why Lambert is dead and who Pruss has become." Hawke held up the folder.

"That easily?" Shoberg grabbed the file and flipped through the pages. "You think Pruss knew Lambert had recorded their conversations?"

"I don't think so. This building was unlocked. He could have walked in and looked through the files if he'd had an inkling the man was going to blackmail him. I think Pruss killed Lambert to keep his new identity quiet." Hawke started for the door. "Let's take a look inside."

"We have what we need already," Shoberg said, carrying the file with him.

"Maybe. I want to learn more about Lambert. And where is his truck? I want to find the paperwork from the sale of the truck. It wasn't in the file cabinet." Hawke walked to the back door of the house. "Do you have a key?"

"No, the key they found at the crime scene was too disformed. He owned the house, and I couldn't find a next of kin who had a key. "We'll have to break in."

Hawke studied the door latch and pulled out his wallet. He rarely used his credit card for purchases but it came in handy at times like this. He inserted the card between the door and jamb angling it toward the latch bolt's side with the slant. Easing the card between the slant and striker plate, he put pressure on the door and eased the bolt loose. The door opened.

"I'm glad you're on our side," Shoberg said as they walked into the house.

Hawke had learned how to get into a locked house when he was in high school. It was out of necessity when his mother had been at work and his drunken stepfather had fallen asleep after locking the doors to the house. He'd come home from a football or basketball game and find the house all locked up. It was easier to let himself in by picking the lock than waking his stepfather and being punished for rousing the beast.

Stepping into the kitchen, Hawke was impressed with its cleanliness. There wasn't a smell of stale food and other than a faint skiff of dust on everything, the house was as clean as Darlene Trembley's.

They crossed the room and stepped into the living room. Again, the place looked unlived in. Everything in its place. Hawke noted the coasters on the side tables and fancy frilly handiwork under the lamps on the tables.

"A woman has been living here," he said.

Shoberg stared at him. "The man isn't married."

"Then he had a girlfriend. Why hasn't she come forward?" Hawke moved through the room to the hallway. He stopped at the half bath. It had a fancy towel on the back of the toilet, fancy soaps in a soap dish on the counter. He continued to the bedroom. An afghan of vibrant colors hung over the back of a chair. Fancy stitched handiwork covered the top of the dresser and the two nightstands. "Yep. A woman has had a hand in decorating this place."

He crossed to the closet and opened the doors. All he saw were men's clothing. He moved the garments looking for something a woman would wear. Nothing. A plastic contraption hung from the closet pole. It had compartments in it for shoes. He pulled out all the men's sneakers, slippers, and a pair of boots that were wedged in. Then he ran his hand into each compartment. The third one down on the right, he felt something. It was a sparkly flower that would go on a woman's piece of clothing. A belt or shoe perhaps. He showed it to Shoberg. "There's been a woman living here who cleaned out everything either before the Rendezvous or right after."

"I don't see any re-enactment clothing or any muzzle loading gear." Hawke walked to the dresser. "Why don't you take a look around for that. I'll see if I can find anything else the woman left behind."

Opening the top dresser drawer, a floral scent filled the air. No man he knew of would have flowery smells in his dresser. It was the work of a woman. He pulled out each pile of underwear, socks, and t-shirts. Hawke found a clasp that might have come off of women's underclothes. He pulled out an evidence bag from his backpack and dropped the clasp in.

The next drawer held sweatshirts, shirts, and shorts. Following how he'd looked through the first drawer, he found a woman's sock. The kind that only covered the foot. It was in a ball in the back corner of the drawer. That was bagged.

The third drawer held jeans. He pulled each pair out and checked the pockets. This drawer came up empty for any women's items.

The bottom drawer held neatly folded leather clothing. He'd found the re-enactment clothing. Or at least some of the clothing. There were two pairs of pants and one white shirt. The label on the shirt was Seamstress Sue. Wendy Levens. Had Lambert been one of her lovers or just a customer?

He took photos of the contents and the label.

"I found where he stored his muzzle loading equipment," Shoberg said, from out in the hall.

Hawke stood and walked to the door. What had appeared to be a door to a linen closet turned out to be the door to a room with three muzzleloaders, a keg of powder, balls and other paraphernalia that would outfit a mountain man in the 1800s.

"How did you discover this?" Hawke stood in the room, taking photos.

"When I couldn't find anything in the spare room

or in the garage, I came back in and started opening all the doors." Shoberg stood by the door.

"Did you see a new Chevy pickup in the garage?" Hawke wondered if whoever picked up Lambert's camp had also taken the vehicle.

"There's a silver Honda."

Hawke stopped taking photos and rattled off the license number of Wendy Levens's Honda.

Shoberg left and returned. "That's the one. How did Wendy's car end up in this garage?"

Putting his phone away, Hawke walked out of the room. How had the woman kept her affair with Lambert a secret from her family? Where was she? Did she know that Lambert was dead and not Pruss?

"Now we have two fugitives. James Pruss and Wendy Levens. You question the neighbors about a woman living with Lambert. I have someone else to interview." He hated to go back to the school and ask Sara more questions, but she was the only one around who might have a clue about Lambert and her mother. Unless…

Hawke pulled up in front of Miss Stevens house. The curtain fluttered and the door opened.

"Trooper Hawke, did you find Sara? Was the child okay?"

"Hello, Miss Stevens. Yes, I talked to Sara, she's fine." He followed the woman as she turned and walked into the living room.

"I'm glad she's okay. The two boys were always into trouble, but Sara was always nice to me." She sat in the straight-backed chair and motioned for Hawke to take a seat.

"What can you tell me about Mrs. Levens's activity the last month?" He studied the woman.

Her eyes narrowed and her lips pinched a little before she cleared her throat and said, "Do you mean her gentlemen callers?"

"I've been led to believe she was aloof or uninterested in her life and family but found excitement with other men."

The woman snorted and apologized. "That wasn't ladylike." She stood. "Let me get some coffee for us. Talking about Wendy's men is going to take a spell and dry my mouth."

Hawke grinned and nodded as the woman walked out of the room. His phone buzzed.

Shoberg sent a text. *Neighbors say the pickup arrived on Sunday as they'd expected knowing Wylie had gone to the Rendezvous. Noticed it missing on Tuesday morning.*

Thanks. Hawke replied.

Miss Stevens entered the room with two steaming mugs of coffee. "I remembered you like yours black." She smiled and set a cup on a coaster on the side table near him.

She settled onto the chair with the cup in her hands. "I can't tell you if she had any one in particular that she saw more often. There was the young man from the car dealership. The one I heard is dead. He came a lot the last couple of weeks. He'd carry in buckskin clothing but he'd stay much longer than any adjustments needed on the clothing." She sipped her coffee.

"What about the times when Mrs. Levens would be gone for several days? Did anyone in the family say anything about where she was?" Hawke didn't want to come out and ask if she'd seen the new pickup or a man with red hair and beard.

"I've lived across the street from them ever since they moved in. The first time she took off, poor Jake was beside himself. I think Sara was only three at the time. Then they got used to coming home from school and work and finding Wendy gone. Sara would come over here and stay with me until her dad came home. Then after the boys, I noticed the men showing up during the day. Different men. Many never carried anything in or out." She raised her cup to her lips then lowered it. "There was one man came once, not that long ago. He had a brand-new pickup. He revved it as he pulled up to the house. That's what made me look. He got out, and Wendy didn't look happy when she met him at the door. That was the only time I saw him. The pickup sat in front of the house for several hours before I noticed it was gone."

"What did the man look like?" Hawke stamped down his interest so the woman didn't just blurt something out to satisfy him.

"I didn't see his face, only the back and side of him. He was about Wendy's height, broad shoulders, and it looked like he had a nicely cropped red beard."

Hawke nodded. "What color was the pickup?"

"Red. I thought it looked like a big shiny apple."

That fit the description of Lambert's pickup and the man. Why hadn't Wendy wanted Lambert to come to her house? Was it because that was where she'd disappear to when she'd leave her family? But why stay married and unhappy if she had someone else she could go to? This homicide felt like it was going in circles.

"Thank you for the information." Hawke set his

empty mug on the side table and stood.

"Do you have any idea where Wendy is?" the woman asked.

Hawke shrugged. "She could be anywhere."

"I take it she's not with the man in the new pickup?"

"No. That I know for sure."

Miss Stevens stared at him. "You've talked to him?"

"No. But he has been identified. Thank you for the coffee." He walked to the door before the woman asked any more questions he couldn't answer.

Out at his vehicle he checked the notes he wrote, while the woman was talking, before he called Sergeant Spruel.

"We need to put an A.P.B. out on…" he read off the license and information on the pickup Lambert had purchased. "And pull the one on Mrs. Levens's Honda. It was in Lambert's garage."

"Did you learn anything else?" Spruel asked.

"It appears Mrs. Levens and the victim were acquaintances. I think she'd leave her family here and go stay with him when the mood came over her. Lambert made fake identification for Pruss. That's probably why he ended up dead. I wonder if he decided to blackmail the man after he was paid, but we haven't found a trail of any money—" It hit him. "That's why Lambert had the new pickup. I bet Pruss gave it to him for the ID. I'm headed to talk to Cindy Albee. See if she knows anything. She was in on the fake registration of the blue Escape."

"You will patrol for turkey hunters tomorrow?"

"Yes. I'll be out north first light tomorrow."

Chapter Twenty-five

The dealership was getting ready to close when Hawke parked in front of the building. Burke walked out the door, not as cocky as the first day they'd met.

"When are you going to let Kristen bury her husband?" Burke asked without any preamble.

"When forensics is through with the body." Hawke had to hold his tongue to not say, 'when the man was dead.' "Is Cindy still here?"

"Yeah. You've been talking to her a lot lately. Does she have anything to do with James's death?"

"No, she has access to all the records." Hawke walked into the building and straight to the woman's office. He knocked once and walked in.

"I'll talk to you later," she said, placing the receiver back on the phone. "What do you want, Trooper Hawke." Another hostile employee.

"What do you know about the Chevy pickup James gave to Wiley Lambert?" He was tired of people only giving him half the information.

"I don't know what you're talking about." The words said one thing and her flaming cheeks another.

"You know about the pickup James gave Lambert for services rendered. To hide a money trail to the person who made his fake ID, he gave the man a new pickup. I saw the cash sales receipt. I'd say that your books are missing the forty thousand the receipt said Lambert paid for the vehicle. You had to know. You balance the books." Hawke sat in the chair in front of her desk and opened his logbook. "Did you confront James about the discrepancy?"

Her face had paled as he spoke. "What do you mean fake ID?"

"What was James's explanation for giving Wylie Lambert the pickup?" He dodged her question.

"He said it was going to charity. It would be auctioned off for some charity for Union County and Wylie was picking it up for them." She swung around to her file cabinet, pulled the door open and huffed. Swinging back around, she said, "You have all of my files concerning the vehicles in the last six months."

"If Wylie was picking it up for charity, why is it registered to him? And I found a cash sales receipt for the vehicle." Hawke watched as the woman's hands shook.

"James told me it was to be marked as a charity donation. I don't know anything about it being registered to Wylie. But it explains more of the discrepancies in the books." The woman deflated against the chair back. "I'm going to lose this job, and never find another one in this county, when Mrs. Pruss finds out."

"If she brings in an outside accountant to look at the books she's going to find out. You might want to let her know on your own." He felt a bit sorry for the woman who had been caught between Pruss and his mother. Doing things for the son, thinking he cared for her and now being left as the scapegoat for all of his actions of tearing down the business his mother had built up.

"Did James ever take you someplace that he said was his favorite place?" He was grasping at straws hoping to find the man.

She shook her head. "He didn't take me anywhere. Because we're both married, we just, you know, dated here at the dealership."

Hawke rose. "Thank you for your time." He walked to the door and faced her. "Will the discrepancies in the books ruin Mrs. Pruss and the dealership?"

Cindy nodded. "We'll all be out of jobs unless someone comes along and takes this off Mrs. Pruss's hands."

Early Saturday morning, Hawke was driving out north to check on turkey hunters in the Sled Springs area. His mind kept rolling everything they'd learned so far about Pruss, Lambert, Mrs. Levens, and other people close to James Pruss. He was missing something.

Pruss had to have told someone about his plan to disappear. The one that made sense was the person covering up his misappropriation of money from the dealership. But Cindy Albee had looked upset and worried. Was it a ruse? Would she get fired and disappear, joining Pruss wherever he was?

He passed by Flora, drove through farm ground and headed out the road to Lost Prairie. It wasn't public land, but the land owners welcomed hunters to keep the turkey populations down. A Dodge pickup barreled down the road toward him, stopping with their grills inches apart.

Before Hawke could get out, the passenger door flew open and a young man in his twenties ran up to his window.

Hawke rolled the window down. "What's—"

"There's a car out in the trees. Smelled like there might be a body in it. We were headin' out to get a signal to call the police." The man was clearly upset.

"Tell your driver to turn around and take me to the spot. After I get your statements, I'll call it in."

The man nodded and ran back to the truck. The vehicle turned around, pluming dust from the back tires and took off faster than Hawke cared to go. If there was a dead person, they couldn't do any more if they arrived in fifteen minutes or an hour.

Following the vehicle, Hawke contacted dispatch to let them know he had a possible body.

The truck stopped on the right side of the road and the two men hopped out, striding toward his pickup.

"It's through there. We'll have to walk from here." The driver of the vehicle said.

Hawke stepped out, opened his back door and grabbed his pack, shoved several bottles of water into the pack, and shouldered it.

The two men were dancing back and forth on their feet as if the ground under their shoes was hot lava. "You need to hurry," the passenger said.

"If there is a body and as you said, 'it smelled like something dead' there is no hurry. We can't help them now." He pulled out his logbook. "What are your names and what are you doing out here?"

They stated their names and said they were hunting turkeys. Hawke asked to see their hunting licenses and tags.

"You don't need to be checking us out, you need to be checking out the car," the driver said.

"I came out here to check turkey hunters." Hawke finished writing everything down.

He studied the area along the road. There didn't seem to be any tracks indicating a vehicle had left the road. "How did you find it?"

"We were walking along a path the turkeys made," the driver said.

Hawke waved toward the trees. "I'll follow you."

The buckbrush tugged at his pant legs as the smell of pine grew with the heat of the sun. A turkey gobbled off in the distance. The hunters both stopped and listened, as if zeroing in on the location of the bird. The last few years the turkey population in this area had been growing. It was no wonder the two had come here to hunt.

The second Hawke spotted blue between the trees, his gut clenched. Was this the Escape they'd been looking for?

"Okay. I have it from here. Don't hunt in this area for the rest of the day. There will be law enforcement coming and going. Wouldn't want one of you to accidentally shoot an officer."

"Don't we get to see what we found?" the driver asked.

He studied the two who stood staring at the blue vehicle in the distance. “You can read about it in the paper. Go on.” He handed them each a bottle of water and walked toward the vehicle.

Working his way closer, the putrefaction of the body told him it had been here more than a couple of days. The gases and decomp of the body filled the air with a smell that caused him to swallow continuously to keep from vomiting.

Holding his hand over his nose and mouth, he walked up to the car. The skin had a green hue and maggots squirmed in the eye sockets. He backed away to give his lungs a chance to draw in fresher air.

Why had the car ended up hidden in the trees? He had a hunch the man was Pruss. The woman who picked him up, must have…what? Had she killed him and left him here? Did she get her hands on the money? How did she get away?

The one thing he knew for sure, whoever did this couldn’t have been someone at the Rendezvous. They wouldn’t have been able to drive here and get back to the campground in time for the interviews. Especially Wendy Levens. Her husband said she was there at seven when he went looking for Sara. And Sara didn’t say anything about her mother being gone when everyone was putting out the fire.

Studying the body through the open door, he noted the victim didn’t have a seat belt on. The body was curled and slumped sideways toward the driver’s side.

Hawke pulled the camera out of his pack and took photos. He’d have the whole place well documented by the time the M.E. and the retrieval team arrived.

<◇><◇><◇>

Hawke sat on a rock fifty yards from the car, looking through the suitcase he'd found in the back of the vehicle. The clothes were all casual. Jeans, polo shirts, underwear, socks, and toiletries. Nothing that would give him any help discovering if it was James Pruss.

"Hawke! You here?" called Shoberg.

"Yeah. Keep coming." He stood and walked toward the sound of several people scraping through the underbrush.

He'd backtracked through the trees looking for the vehicle's tracks. The car had left the Lost Prairie Road a quarter of a mile past where he'd parked his vehicle and then dodged trees to get to the spot where it was.

He spotted the group of seven between the trees. Shoberg, Deputy Corcoran, Dr. Vance, two state forensics officers, and Bonnie and Roxie, ambulance EMTs.

"Couldn't you have found a body closer to the road?" Roxie teased, lugging the front end of the wire gurney basket.

"I didn't find it, two turkey hunters did." Hawke caught Shoberg's gaze. "I think it's Pruss."

"You're kidding. The guy who burned up last week at Grizz Flat?" Corcoran asked.

"He didn't burn up. He ended up here." Hawke led them to the vehicle.

"That's the car we've been looking for," Shoberg said. "As long as it took us to get rounded up and here, did you get all the photos and evidence?"

"All but looking for a wallet on the body. I didn't want to mess with it before Dr. Vance had a look."

"That's a good thing. You could have had a mess

on your hands." Dr. Vance pulled a face mask out of her pocket, settled it on her face, and pulled latex gloves on before moving closer to the vehicle.

They all stood back while she stepped behind the open car door and examined the body. When she returned to where they stood, she held out a wet, nasty wallet.

Shoberg donned gloves and took it from her.

The forensic specialists started collecting evidence from the car as Bonnie and Roxie watched and waited.

"When you put the body into the bag, use towels to grab the limbs. He's falling apart," Dr. Vance told the EMTs.

The license inside the wallet was the name of the identification Lambert had made for Pruss. It seemed they had found the man they'd been searching for, and he'd been dead since he'd murdered Lambert.

Chapter Twenty-six

Hawke followed Shoberg, Dr. Vance, and the ambulance back to Alder. The forensic specialists were still combing through the car for evidence when everyone else left. He and Shoberg headed for the State Police headquarters in Winslow. They both had reports to write up. Hawke also had photos and fingerprints to enter into the computer.

Spruel met him as he walked through the door. "I sent you out to check turkey hunters and you find the body of the man we've spent a week looking for."

Hawke shrugged. "I guess I'm just lucky."

Shoberg had followed him into the building. The trooper laughed. "You call finding a week-old body lucky?"

"We know what happened to Pruss and that someone killed him for the money he embezzled from his mother." Hawke turned on his computer, walked into the breakroom for a cup of coffee, then sat in the chair at his desk. Digging through his pack, he pulled out the camera, flipped open the lid, and pulled out the SD card.

"You want help uploading those to the investigation?" Shoberg asked.

"No. I want to look at them again. I hope Dr. Vance can discover the manner of death. That might help us narrow down the list of suspects." Hawke sighed and slid the SD card into his computer and watched the photos appear one by one.

Shoberg sat down at the computer next to Hawke. "Who do you have on your list?"

"Too many." Hawke clicked on a photo of the inside of the vehicle. "See how the driver's seat is more forward. Someone shorter than the victim drove the car. That fits with my witness seeing a woman park the car on Eden Lane."

Shoberg studied the photo. "That means all your suspects are women."

"Yeah. But one sticks out as knowing everything. The money, the car, all the things he did to undermine his mother."

Shoberg stood. "I'll go talk to Cindy Albee at the dealership."

Hawke stopped him. "Just keep an eye on her until I get there." He hadn't gotten a feeling when talking to her that she was a cold-blooded killer, but she was the only person he could think of who knew everything and who Pruss would have trusted to help him hide. "I want to reread everything she's said and see if we can catch her in lies."

"I'll wait and let you know if she leaves work."

Another photo popped up. He'd found a wadded-up piece of waxed paper on the floor of the passenger side. The paper was in an evidence bag headed to the state forensic lab in Pendleton with the specialists. Why would there be wax paper in the car? The only use he knew for the paper was in between layers of cookies or candy. He'd received a box of goodies from Darlene every Christmas. The layers had the waxy paper in between.

The body didn't look like there had been foul play, but in its condition, it was hard to tell. He also wondered at how the mouth had been open, as if calling for help. What could have made him call for help? The car doors, even if locked, could have been opened from the inside. There wasn't any evidence he'd been suffocated with fumes from the running car. He'd checked the fuel gauge and there had been plenty of gas to get them to Washington or Idaho to hide. Something had to have incapacitated him to keep him from getting out of the car while he'd died and his body to be left in the vehicle while the killer walked away.

He pulled out his phone and dialed Dr. Vance.

"Hello," she answered.

"I know we just found the body and you have patients to see before you do the autopsy, but did you see anything from your preliminary examination that showed how he was killed?"

"The skull didn't appear to have blunt force trauma. The neck was too decayed to tell if strangulation occurred. I won't know that until I can take a look at the hyoid bone. There didn't appear to be any blood loss, but there was evidence that he may have vomited at some point. And the way his mouth was open…"

"What would cause that?" Hawke hoped she would say what he was thinking.

"He possibly ingested something that didn't set well with his stomach or—"

Hawke jumped in, "Was poisoned?"

"Poison? Possibly. What makes you think that?" The doctor sounded truly interested.

"Just a hunch. We'll know for sure when the state lab finishes going through the evidence I sent. I just wanted you to have an open mind if there was a way to test for it."

"I can ask for the toxicology to test for poisons. Any in particular?"

"I'll let you know as soon as the lab gets me the results."

"I will keep an open mind while doing the autopsy and a closed nose." The doctor signed off chuckling.

Hawke had liked Dr. Vance the moment he'd met the newly accredited Medical Examiner at her first trip to a fatal accident.

He finished uploading the photos and then started entering the information about the turkey hunters and how he'd been stopped by them and led to the car.

There had to be another person involved. How had Mrs. Albee, or whoever drove Pruss into the trees, returned home? Someone had to have been waiting or called for a ride. How would a woman explain being out on Lost Prairie Road at night alone without a vehicle? And wouldn't whoever picked her up have wondered about it after hearing about the fire at the campground?

He made a mental note of his questions and finished adding to the report. After that he pulled up all the interviews with Cindy Albee. She said she was home with her husband the night of the fire. Hawke had yet to meet her husband. The Albee's lived between Winslow and Alder. He'd stop by there on his way to the car dealership.

The Albee farm was small and cluttered. Pretty much as Hawke had expected knowing Mr. Albee was a drunk. Cindy worked all day and late at night at the car dealership, she would only have Sunday to work at the farm. He had a feeling she put in the long hours on purpose.

Hawke walked up to the front door of a small, older, one-story farmhouse with a porch stretching across the front. He knocked.

Several dogs barked inside.

"Shut up!" a male voice yelled.

Hawke waited. No one came to the door. He knocked again.

The barking commenced.

"Shut up!" bellowed the man.

This time Hawke continued knocking until an unshaven man in a dirty t-shirt and jeans opened the door.

"What do you want?" Mr. Albee asked in an irritated tone.

"I'm Trooper Hawke. I'd like to ask you some questions about your wife." Hawke took a step into the house, making the man back up.

Three various breeds of cattle dog all growled.

"I'm a friend," Hawke said in a low, conversational tone.

The three stopped growling, but watched him

intently.

"What do you want to know about Cindy?" The man had been taken by surprise.

"A week ago Friday night, were you and she here together all night?" Hawke pulled out his logbook.

The man shoved his hand over his unshaved face and tugged on an ear. "I don't know. What's today?"

It was obvious the man couldn't help him establish if his wife was home or not.

"Has your wife been coming home at her usual time?"

Mr. Albee stared at him. "What do you mean? She's always here to make my dinner."

Hawke had a feeling being constantly drunk, the man had no sense of time. She could put dinner on the table at seven in the morning and he'd think it was seven at night.

"Thank you for your time," Hawke turned to leave and noticed a photo on the wall. "When was that picture taken?" He pointed at Cindy standing in front of the Rimrock Inn along with the owners and Harris family.

"I don't know, some family gathering." The man plopped down on the couch and picked up a half empty bottle of whiskey.

"Family gathering? Is Cindy related to the Harrises?"

"They're her aunt, uncle, and cousin. She lived with them after her parents died." Mr. Albee waved a hand. "She thinks the world of them. More of them than me."

Hawke had a feeling James had pulled the wrong person into his disappearing act. He disappeared all right, soul and all.

Chapter Twenty- seven

Shoberg sat in his vehicle along the street to the dealership. Hawke parked behind him, exited his pickup, and settled into the passenger seat of Shoberg's cruiser.

"Cindy Albee's vehicle is parked in the usual spot. I haven't seen her, but Burke Harris has walked around the lot a couple of times. Only once was it to talk with a perspective buyer."

"I just learned Burke is Cindy's uncle, but more like a father." Hawke had a file with all the information he'd gathered on the woman and how she was connected to people who would be interested in the Pruss family losing the car dealership. He'd printed it out at the Sheriff's Office after visiting Mr. Albee.

"Really? Why hasn't someone told us this before?" Shoberg stared at him with a glint of anger in his eyes.

"I'm pretty sure the Harrises didn't want us to know given the fact Burke is pretty sore over not being a partner. Why Cindy hasn't said anything… I don't know. But we're going to find out." Hawke opened the cruiser's passenger door and stood.

Shoberg exited the vehicle at the same time.

They walked across the lot side by side.

Hawke shoved open the showroom door.

"Can I help you with anything?" Burke Harris asked, blocking their way.

Shoberg stepped around one side of the man and Hawke the other. When they opened the office door, Cindy Albee glanced up. Her face paled, and she shoved her chair back as if to rise.

Hawke could see in her eyes she wanted to flee, but had nowhere to go. They were blocking her only exit.

"Sit back down, we have some questions for you," Hawke said, calmly, and friendlier than he was feeling.

The woman sat, dropping her hands into her lap and out of their sight. He didn't think she had any type of weapon to worry about, but it was telling that she didn't want them to see her agitation.

Shoberg pulled a chair up to the desk.

Hawke sat in the chair that was already there. He set the file on the edge of her desk and opened it. "Why didn't you tell us that Burke is your uncle?"

Her face scrunched up, and her eyes lost the fear as they stared at him. "I didn't think it had anything to do with this whole mess."

He studied her. She seemed genuinely confused by the question. "You didn't think your helping James steal from his mother, a woman your uncle feels stole his partnership in the business from him, wouldn't make you look guilty of helping your uncle gain control of the dealership?"

She glanced at Shoberg, then Hawke. "I still don't understand. I know that Uncle Burke has been angry over not being a partner, but he's done well as a salesman and had less headaches than if he ran the business." She shook her head. "I didn't tell Uncle Burke about what I did for James." Her cheeks flushed. "If he knew I'd been fooling around with James or helping him, he would have had me fired. He told me when I took this job that he would consider it thumbing my nose at him if I let James sweet talk me." She shook her head. "I would never hurt him by telling him what I've done for James."

Hawke studied her. She seemed to be telling the truth. But someone had to have helped James. "What about Trudy? Have you ever told her? You know cousin to cousin about what you have been doing for James."

She started to shake her head and stopped. "I think I mentioned to her that James was being friendly. She told me not to think he would treat me any different than he did all the other women he smiled at." Cindy pulled her hands off her lap and picked up a pen. "I thought maybe she'd been one of his conquests, but when I asked, she said, thankfully, no." She peered at Hawke. "I don't know what she meant by that, but I took it to mean she knew someone who had fallen for him."

"You did," Shoberg said.

Her cheeks flushed a deep red. "I didn't fall for him, but rather let him use me rather than go home to my husband." She stared at her hands. "I'm not proud to say it, but that is the truth."

Once again, Hawke was struck by how many

people stayed in loveless or dysfunctional marriages when all they had to do was divorce the person who was causing them the grief.

"Who else would have known about the registration for the missing car, the pickup he gave to Lambert, and the missing money?" Hawke had a feeling while the woman may not have known the complete plan, and obviously didn't know that Pruss hadn't been the victim in the fire, she knew more than she realized.

"His mother could have known. She could have come in here and looked through the books and the files at any time when I wasn't in the room. Mrs. Pruss often stayed after hours, claiming she had paperwork to catch up on."

Hawke studied her. "Would she have been around when James purchased stolen parts?" If he remembered correctly, the owner of the dealership had feigned outrage at the notion they sold or used stolen parts.

"She could have been. I don't really know. I think he did that after dark." Cindy glanced toward the door. "She liked to shift numbers around to make it look like the business wasn't as successful as it was. You know, for the IRS. When I first saw the missing money, you know, that James took, I thought it was something she'd done. I went to her to ask, and though she was outraged at first that I thought she'd stolen that money from her own business, I could tell she wasn't happy with the discovery. She asked James to come to her office as we were all leaving that night."

Hawke wouldn't rule out the mother, but as angry as she was with her son for stealing from her, he couldn't see her killing him. She was too proud of her offspring to do that. Even if she'd not closed down the business after hearing of his fake death.

He shot out of his chair. The reason the pickup hadn't been scrutinized by her and she hadn't been harassing them to find her son's killer was because she knew he didn't die in the fire.

Shoberg stared up at him. "Hawke, what's up?"

"We need to go talk to Mrs. Pruss." Hawke headed for the door. He stopped with his hand on the doorknob. "Don't tell anyone, even your family, what we talked about."

Cindy Albee nodded.

Walking down the hall, Hawke said, "Mrs. Pruss hasn't insisted we find her son's killer. Why do you think that is?"

Shoberg slowed two steps then caught up. "Because she doesn't believe he's dead."

Hawke grinned at his co-worker. "She helped him disappear. Why?"

"I think that's a good question to ask Mrs. Pruss."

They'd climbed the stairs as they talked and stopped outside the door to her office. Hawke knocked.

"Come in," the woman called out.

Hawke and Shoberg stepped in the room, and she focused on them.

"Troopers, what can I help you with?" She didn't sound as if she really wanted to help.

"We were wondering if you know a Steven Alderman?" Hawke asked, mentioning the fake identification they'd found with the body in the car.

Her eyes widened briefly before she glanced down at the desk. "No, I don't think I know that name."

"You're sure?" Shoberg asked.

Her small eyes narrowed on him, and she snapped, "If I say I don't, I don't."

"We discovered that James traded a pickup from this dealership to Wylie Lambert in exchange for new identification. Over a week ago, he knocked Lambert unconscious, put him in his Jeep, and lit it on fire." Hawke paused to see if this was shocking the woman. It wasn't. Her lips remained in a clenched straight line, and she glared at him. "He had an accomplice waiting for him on Eden Lane. However, that accomplice didn't want to live the rest of their life with James. But they did want the money he'd stolen from you." While it wasn't confirmed the body he'd found in the car was James, he was going to go with his gut. "Yesterday, I found the blue Ford Escape that is missing from this dealership. There was a body in it that had been deceased for eight days. The identification we found with it was Steven Alderman."

As he'd continued the woman's lips had started to part. Now they quivered. "James is really dead?" she whispered.

"I'm sure the Medical Examiner will confirm it later today," Shoberg said. "You knew he hadn't died in the fire. You can be tried as an accomplice to the murder of Wylie Lambert."

She shook her head. "I didn't know he was planning to actually put a person in the vehicle. He said he would make it look like he was dead. He was in debt for gambling and wanted to disappear. I told him to take the car and do whatever he needed to do to get a new life. Then he was to call me when he settled somewhere. Let me know he was safe." A tear trickled down her cheek. "He was always so sure of himself. I didn't think anything would happen to him."

"Do you know who he trusted enough to meet him after the fire?" Hawke asked.

She shook her head. "He wouldn't tell me. He said it was better that way."

"Do you have any idea who it could have been?" Shoberg asked.

"I know it wasn't his wife or that simpering Cindy. It would have had to have been someone that completely fooled him. Someone just as conniving as himself." She said the last as if it was a good attribute.

"Can you think of anyone he's been fooling around with that fits that scenario?" Hawke asked.

"That artist's daughter and there was a woman he met at Rendezvous that he said he couldn't fool about anything."

"Do you remember her name?" Hawke wondered who it could have been. If he'd been told this the night of the fire, he would have said Chessie, but she couldn't have driven to Lost Prairie Road with James and made it back to the campground on foot and been there when Novak interviewed people. And there was still the matter of who drove Wylie Lambert's belongings back to his place.

"I didn't care to know any of the women's names in my son's life. They came and went like indigestion."

Hawke stepped out into the loft area.

Shoberg followed. "We know where to find the 'artist's daughter'," he said.

"We do. I doubt she was the one, but it doesn't hurt to follow up that lead." Hawke stared out into the growing dusk of evening. "But let's talk to her tomorrow. I want to think on this some more."

“Meet you at Olive’s at nine in the morning? We can go on to the lake together.” Shoberg descended the stairs with Hawke behind him.

As they’d stood in the woman’s office, he’d felt like there was something he should ask and he couldn’t put a finger on what it was. She knew her son was skipping out on a gambling debt…that was it. Who did he owe money? And why would they give up if he left and not go after Mrs. Pruss for what was owed?

“I just thought of something. I’ll see you in the morning,” he said to Shoberg as a foot hit the bottom of the stairs. He did an about face and headed back up.

Chapter Twenty-eight

Mrs. Pruss startled when Hawke opened her door without knocking. "What do you want?"

"Who did your son owe money?" He wasn't going to even try to be tactful. The woman was blunt, and he could be in return.

"It was a gambling debt."

"What kind of debt? Who did he owe?"

"He bet on sports and played poker. I'm not sure who he owed. He just said he had to disappear."

"Didn't you worry whoever he owed would catch up to him or he'd just rack up more debt wherever he went?" Hawke had never understood the addiction to gambling. He worked hard to make and keep his money. He didn't believe in throwing it away.

"As long as I didn't lose the car dealership, he could do what he wished." She glared at him.

"But the car dealership is what was up to pay his debt, wasn't it? That's why you agreed to his pretend death. With him dead, he no longer has a connection to the dealership and you don't have to pay whoever was collecting." He switched tactics. "I heard you had a loan coming due and not enough money to pay. Is that true? Or did you make it up thinking you were going to lose the dealership to your son's addiction to gambling?"

She sucked in air through her clenched teeth and stared daggers at him. "Who said I had a loan coming due? That loose-lipped Cindy? She can't keep anything to herself."

"So you do have a loan coming due? You could lose your dealership from two different directions. Was it your idea for James to die or his?"

This time a gut-wrenching cry escaped her angry, controlled demeanor. "It was my idea. Had I known he would really die, I would have told him to let whoever it was take the dealership, and we'd let them deal with the loan." Tears ran down her angular cheekbones. "Get out. Let me grieve in peace."

He slipped out of her office and took the steps two at a time down to the bottom.

Burke stood between him and the door. "What were you talking to Vivian about for so long? And what did you say that upset Cindy?"

Hawke studied the man, deciding if telling him would help or hinder the investigation. He was still a person of interest because he could have wanted the dealership to go under. Hawke decided to start with an easy question. One that could have come up in his investigation of James's death.

"Do you know who James owed a gambling debt?"

The man shook his head. "I knew he gambled and

figured that was where the money was going."

"What do you mean, figured that was where the money was going?" Up to this point Burke hadn't said anything about knowing there was missing money. Cindy said she hadn't said anything.

Burke waved a hand. "We usually have six or seven new models in this showroom. There have been only four since the middle of last year. Look at the lot. It was packed with cars before. Now we're down to half the inventory. I knew something was happening. Vivian and James just said the factories weren't producing as many vehicles due to the economy. I could see what was happening. That prodigal son of hers was ruining everything she's worked for."

"And you have worked for," Hawke said.

"I'm retiring next month. I'm tired of being her monkey. Michelle and I are going on a long vacation to some place tropical and when we get back, we'll decide what to do from there." Burke glanced up at the loft and owner's office. "I need to give her my two-week notice but haven't had the heart since James's death."

"She doesn't know you are retiring?" Hawke wondered what the woman would do without any salesmen. It would be a job opening for someone who was out of work.

"I'd mentioned it a few times to James, who was more than happy to see me leave. I thought he'd say something to his mother, but she hasn't acted like he'd said anything to her."

"Without salesmen, will she hire more?" Hawke knew while at times the prices on the vehicles seemed a bit high, this was more convenient for people than going to Lewiston, La Grande, or farther for a new vehicle.

"I don't know what she's going to do." He sighed. "And frankly, I don't care. I gave up trying to become a partner in this business when Jim died."

Hawke nodded and walked out of the showroom and over to his vehicle. His stomach growled. Eat at Olive's or go home to a peanut butter and jam sandwich. While he was ready to find a solitary place to think about everything in this case, his stomach was voting for a good meal to fuel his brain.

He walked across the street to Olive's. The proprietor and her niece were the only employees in the café. Two men sat at the counter and two tables had elderly couples eating what appeared to be dessert.

"Hawke, you have been in here in the last week more than we see you in a year," Olive said, walking over to the table he'd picked near a window.

"I seem to be making a lot of trips to the dealership lately." Hawke flipped over his cup for her to fill.

Olive sighed and hung her head. "It is a shame that such a young life was lost. And in such a senseless way."

He knew she meant the fire the week before. Hawke nodded. "Did you know James very well?" Hawke took the menu she held out to him.

"He'd come in at least once a day and get coffee or something to eat. That was why I had my older waitresses wait on him. He was always embarrassing the younger ones. Especially, the teenagers. He would say inappropriate things to them."

This interested Hawke. "Did Cindy Albee ever work for you?"

"No. But her cousin Trudy did." Olive put a hand

on her hip. "She was one of the few young women who would give James back as much as he gave."

"She liked him?" Hawke hadn't gotten that vibe from her. She'd acted hostile. As if she hadn't cared for James at all. As if he were an enemy.

"No. She liked riling him up. I heard her tell her mom one day, he'd get what he deserved." Olive tapped her order pad. "What'll you have?"

"The fish and chips, only hold the fries and give me a salad." He'd been feeling sluggish lately. He was sure it was due to all the fat and carbs he'd been eating and not enough outdoor activity. At his age, if he slowed down, they'd give him a desk job or suggest retirement. He wanted neither.

Olive wandered back to the kitchen.

He pulled out his logbook and entered what he'd learned from Burke and Olive. Could Trudy be the woman who had bested James? Made him think she was interested in him and helped him then killed him and took his money? If the car dealership was having such money troubles, he had a notion Mrs. Pruss would start checking out every woman her son had been involved with the last six months to see if they had her money. That was once the grief subsided and she realized what had happened.

He had to admit the woman had looked defeated. Perhaps she was tired and ready to retire and do more pleasant things.

Sunday morning after breakfast at Olive's, Hawke and Shoberg headed to Diamond Storm's house at Wallowa Lake. They parked and exited Shoberg's cruiser as the front door opened.

A tall, slender man with long, thinning, gray hair stepped out onto the porch in paint spattered lounge pants that hung from his hip bones and no shirt or shoes.

"Mr. Storm?" Shoberg asked as they walked up to the man.

"Yes. What do you two want so early in the morning?" The man bent, plucking a newspaper from the ground by the door.

"We'd like to visit with your daughter." Shoberg motioned toward the open door.

"I'm sure she's still in bed. She came home around two in the morning. I was out in my studio when she came out to let me know she was home." Mr. Storm walked through the door and they followed.

Bringing up the rear, Hawke closed the door behind him.

"Want some coffee while you wait for her to show?" the man asked.

"Thank you," Shoberg said.

Hawke nodded. It would give them a chance to see what the father thought of James Pruss.

"I'll go tell her she has company and then bring in the coffee." The man left them standing in the middle of a tall entryway.

One pole stood in the middle like the mast of a ship. At the ceiling smaller logs splayed out from the top like poles on a teepee. Hawke wasn't sure that was what the structure was to represent, but it gave him a feeling of peace and familiarity he seldom felt in rich people's homes.

"How long do you think they'll leave us standing here?" Shoberg asked.

"Until they are ready to talk." Hawke was glad he had patience. He knew that to catch your prey you had to remain calm and show no anxiety.

Five minutes went by and the slap of the man's bare feet grew close down the hall.

"Come this way. I set out coffee in the dining room. Di will meet you there." Mr. Storm waved them down the hall to a door on the right.

A long wooden table took up the middle of the room. At one end sat four pottery mugs and a glass coffee pot. As well as a matching small pitcher of cream or milk and sugar bowl. Had the items been made of anything but pottery, Hawke wouldn't have noticed them. But he recognized the style of one of the potters from the reservation.

His presumptions of the artist were slowly tilting toward a man he might enjoy visiting with as opposed to a man hiding his daughter from the police. But he would wait for the visit until after the James Pruss and Wylie Lambert homicides were solved.

"Help yourself to coffee," Mr. Storm said, sitting down and filling a cup for himself. "Why are you two interested in talking to Di? Did she witness an altercation last night?"

"We wanted to talk to her about a friend of hers. James Pruss," Hawke said, filling a mug with the dark, robust smelling coffee.

"James? I thought he died in an accident. Fire or something, wasn't it?" The man seemed to know very little. "Di said something about it when I returned from an art show. Sad news. He had a bit of an ego but Di thought he was entertaining."

"You didn't know him well?" Hawke asked.

"No. He came by a couple times to pick up Di. We didn't talk much. He was always in a hurry to get going. I don't understand how people keep from going crazy when they are racing from one thing to another." He sipped his coffee. "And that man raced from woman to woman as if he thought it was his job to populate the whole world."

Shoberg spit coffee.

Hawk grinned at the artist. "I did hear he was a bit of a strutting turkey. You knew how he lived and you let him take your daughter out? She is a bit young for him."

The artist waved his hand. "She's like her mother with a mind of her own and a wild side. I'm hoping it will run its course and she'll settle down with a good man. One who makes her happy."

"I will always be happy because I have the best Daddy." Diamond walked into the room, wearing a flowing robe type garment and hugged her father around the shoulders before taking a seat opposite Hawke and Shoberg. "Daddy said you wanted to talk to me?"

The woman didn't look like she'd been up till two in the morning. Her eyes sparkled and there weren't any bags or dark circles under her eyes.

"We wondered if you could tell us more about the last time you saw James Pruss," Shoberg said, pulling out his logbook.

"Specifically, the trip you made to the campground," Hawke added.

She glanced from one to the other of them before she said, "We had dinner at Rimrock Inn, then drove down to the campground where James took what looked like a gas can out of the back of the car and a duffle bag and packed them up the hill behind the storage container."

"Did you ask him what the gas was for?" Hawke wondered that the bright woman hadn't figured it out by now.

"At the time he said it was for a bonfire the last night and he didn't want it in the storage container because the fumes could cause a fire. Sounded reasonable to me at the time." She raised her coffee cup to her lips and sipped, staring at them over the rim.

"And the duffel bag? Did he say what was in that?" Hawke asked.

"No. I figured it was a target or something. It didn't matter. We had a nice dinner, nice drive, and came home."

"Did he get any phone calls while you were together?" Shoberg asked.

Which made Hawke wonder why they hadn't seen the man's phone records when Shoberg had requested them. He made a mental note to check on those.

"The phone rang three times. Once when we were at dinner. He ignored it. Another time when we were driving back to Alder, he ignored it, again. But when it rang right as he was dropping me off, he answered it before I closed my door."

"How did he answer it?" Hawke wondered at his refusing to answer two other calls but that one he did.

"'Hi Chess.' Then I closed the door."

Chapter Twenty-nine

Chessie, Dre Holmes, had said she and James were just friends and they'd broken off their relationship. Why was she calling him the week of his fake and real death? Hawke quickly thanked the woman for getting up and talking to them. He practically pulled Shoberg out of the house.

"What did she say that got you so worked up?" Shoberg asked.

"Chess. That would be Chessie, short for Winchester. A woman who was at the Rendezvous and admitted to being one of James's lovers but said they were now just friends. She hadn't seemed too shook up over his death when we thought he was the fire victim." He cursed under his breath. "We need to see Pruss's phone records and learn more about Dre Holmes."

As they drove back to Olive's, Hawke came up with a plan of action. "I'm going to call Pruss's best friend and a member of the Wallupa Muzzleloaders and see if he can get the club members all together for me to talk to. I don't remember what group Chessie belongs to. We'll need to look up Novak's notes on the people he interviewed and find out the group. I want to talk to them, too."

"What do you hope to learn by gathering the two groups together?" Shoberg parked his vehicle next to Hawke's in Olive's Café parking lot.

"Get locations of people before, during, and after the fire. I can't for the life of me figure out how the blue car arrived at Eden Lane if my theory is correct that Chessie was the one who met James at the car and killed him. Perhaps that will come to me as I talk to people. In the meantime, gather all you can on Dre and her husband, Mark. She said he didn't know about her affair with Pruss, but he was too cool when I went there to interview her. Left us alone. Didn't walk in on us. As if he knew everything."

"He wasn't curious about why you were asking his wife questions?" Shoberg asked.

"No. I thought it was odd at the time, but then she is a strong personality. I figured she might rule the home. Now I'm wondering if it's because he trusted her to not say something incriminating."

"I'll go see what I can dig up about them from the Washington State Police." Shoberg drove away as Hawke climbed up into his truck.

His first call was to Grizzly, Adam Jolly, James's best friend and brother-in-law.

"Hello!" Adam shouted.

Hawke heard machinery in the background. "This is Trooper Hawke. I need to talk to you!" He shouted into the phone.

A whir and the sound lowered a few decibels.

"Let me walk away from the tractor," Adam responded.

Hawke waited, listening to the sound of weighted footfalls on metal steps and the crunch of dried vegetation under foot. The crunch went on for about a minute while the tractor sound grew quieter and quieter.

"Trooper Hawke, what are you calling about?" Adam asked.

"I have a couple of questions. Do you know if James was still having an affair with Chessie?"

"Chessie? What does that have to do with his murder?" The man sounded curious and a bit hopeful.

"I'm just trying to find out if things I've been told are true. Were they still seeing each other?"

Adam blew out a breath. "I honestly don't know. He had told me the two of them had split because her husband found out and she didn't want to risk her marriage. And you know James. He preferred his women to be tied to someone else so he didn't have to worry about them wanting him to leave Kristen."

Hawke stared at the street in front of him. "You're her brother. How could you let her remain married to such a man?" If his sister was married to a man who cheated on her all the time, he'd make sure she divorced him and got every penny she could out of him. Not that his sister was interested in marriage. She was a career woman. At least that's what she told his mother when she asked about grandchildren.

"I know. I've been a lousy brother, but Kristen didn't want a divorce. She loved him, flaws and all."

"What muzzleloader group does Chessie belong to?" He'd get back to the reason he'd called. Or one of the reasons.

"The Whitman Muzzleloaders in Washington. Why are you interested in her? Did she have something to do with James's death?"

"I don't know. I just have more questions for her. I also wanted to know if you knew who James gambled with? As in he owed the person a lot of money." Hawke didn't want Adam asking Chessie questions that would let her know they were on to her. If she indeed was the person who killed Pruss. And he wondered if she helped kill Lambert.

"James played poker with a group of us, but he didn't owe anyone more than usual."

"What do you mean more than usual? Didn't he pay up after every game?" Hawke wondered that they allowed the man to continue playing if he never had the money to back up his bets.

"We all come to the game with a certain amount of money. If you lose more than you brought, you have to pay it off the next time before the game starts. If you don't pay up and show you have enough to play, you aren't allowed to play and have to leave. He always paid up, except for the last game the week before he died."

"Who did he owe after that game?" Hawke also needed a list of the people he played with.

"He owed Burke Harris a couple hundred. Jake Levens a hundred. And me fifty. I knew his tells and knew when he'd bluff. I didn't want to take his money, so I'd fold." Adam was a gentle giant.

"How did Burke Harris get into your poker game?" Hawke didn't think it was a coincidence that the man who wanted to take over the car dealership had been gambling with Pruss.

"James brought him one night when Gravedigger couldn't make it. Then he started coming regular."

"Who else were regulars?"

"James, Jake, Gravedigger, Burke, me and Buckskin Bob. It started out as only members of the muzzleloader group, then Burke started coming."

Hawke wondered why the salesman hadn't mentioned that.

"Could you gather all the Wallupa Muzzleloaders together for me to talk to them this afternoon?"

"It's kind of short notice. Not sure I'll be able to contact all of them." Adam didn't sound enthused to call.

"I'd really appreciate it if you could. I have some questions about the events the night of the fire. It would help to have you all together to help each other remember what you saw and heard."

"If it will help find out who killed James, I'm sure they'll come."

Hawke figured it was more curiosity that would bring them to the meeting than caring who killed James.

"Where do you want to meet?" Adam asked.

"Grizz Flat at three. That should give everyone enough time to get there." Hawke ended the call. He started up his vehicle and headed out the north highway. He could do a little game warden work on his way to meet up with the Wallupa Muzzleloaders.

After giving out three hunting citations and a speeding ticket on the north highway, Hawke drove down into Grizz Flat at 2:45. He was surprised to see half a dozen vehicles already assembled. He recognized most of the group. The Levens were missing and Kristen Pruss.

Adam stepped forward as if he were the spokesperson. "This is all that could make it on short notice."

Hawke nodded. "I'm glad you were willing to help us find James Pruss's killer."

No one flinched, but they looked around at one another.

"Do you suspect one of us?" Buckskin Bob asked. "You know, like in the television show when they gather all the suspects in one place."

"No, I am ninety-five percent sure none of you took James's life."

The group let out a sigh and relaxed.

"What I need to know is who you remember seeing that night, from after dinner on." He sat on the bumper of his vehicle and pulled out his logbook. "We'll do this one at a time, but if someone mentions something, and you have more to add, please do. I'm trying to piece together events to discover who was missing."

"We have all been talking about how no one saw Red Beard after he marched over to Sure Shot's tent," an older woman, Hawke hadn't met before, said.

"And you are?"

"Bull's-eye Betty. Betty Durnell. I live in Promise."

"Thank you." Hawke smiled at the woman. "I can tell you, that I know where Red Beard was. Since you started, where were you camped?"

The woman mentioned she was on the edge of the Wallupa group and next to a group from the tri-cities.

"Who did you see after dinner that night?" Hawke

asked.

She reported seeing mostly people from the tri-cities and then her group when the fire broke out.

Hawke raised his hand with the pen in it. "How many of you were on the bucket detail?"

Everyone but Betty raised their hands. They, except for Buckskin Bob, were all twenty years or more younger than Betty and Bob.

"Did anyone from other groups help with the buckets of water?"

"Smithy and Swift Arrow," Dead-eye Duke said.

Scanning the group, he noticed heads nodding. "What about Hardtack?"

Adam spoke up. "He was there, beside Sourdough. They were up behind me."

"Did anyone see any other people from other muzzleloader groups in the area of your camp space?" Hawke didn't want to ask specifically if they had seen Chessie. It was apparent that the other groups had left the fire to the group where it had started.

They all shook their heads.

Hawke decided to try something else. "I find it hard to believe no one saw the Jeep being pushed over the fire."

Several gazes lowered to their feet, others stared at him.

"Any idea why no one saw the Jeep moving?" He scanned the group.

"Most of us were getting ready for bed," Adam said.

Peering at the few who had lowered their gazes, he asked, "Those of you who looked at your feet when I asked the question. Where were you?"

"I'd passed out," Dead-eye Duke said. "Me and Powder Keg had been drinking since the day's activities ended."

Another member he'd barely met, a young man, said, "I was making out with someone in another group."

Smokepole shrugged. "I thought the Jeep getting burned up served James right. I would have said something if I'd known he was in it."

Chapter Thirty

Adam grabbed Smokepole by the front of his shirt. "You saw the Jeep roll and didn't say anything! You could have saved James's life!"

Hawke stepped in between the two. "Not James's life, Red Beard's."

A collective gasp was followed by the far-off gobble of a turkey.

"That wasn't James in the Jeep?" Buckskin Bob asked.

"No. It was Wylie Lambert, Red Beard." Hawke went on to explain the evidence that pointed to James killing Lambert and planning to disappear.

"What do you mean planning? He did." The anger on Adam's face showed the man wasn't happy with the treachery his friend had committed.

"No. I found James's body on Lost Prairie Road Saturday. He'd been dead for a week. Whoever helped him fake his death, killed him and took the money

James had stolen from the car dealership." Hawke knew there was a chance this information could get back to Dre Holmes, but he hoped it would help these people, who lived in the area, think about what they had seen while leaving the area.

"Who packed up Red Beard's camp and drove off in his pickup?" Buckskin Bob asked.

Hawke grinned. "That's what I would like to find out. Did anyone see who was at his camp after the fire?"

Everyone glanced at one another.

"We were the last ones to leave the area. I didn't go by where he was camped until nearly everyone had cleared out," Adam said.

The rest nodded.

"Can you think of anyone he hung out with at the Rendezvous? Or who he was camped beside? Maybe they saw something." Hawke leveled his gaze on each face.

Smokepole finally said, "You could ask Seamstress Sue. That's the only person I ever seen in Red Beard's camp."

"Why aren't she and Sourdough here?" Dead-eye Duke asked.

"Jake said he wasn't in the area to make the meeting," Adam replied. His gaze landed on Hawke.

Giving the man a slight nod, that that was enough to say, Hawke asked, "How friendly were Seamstress Sue and Red Beard?" He already knew the answer but wondered if the woman had known that James had killed her lover.

Betty put her hands up like an exaggerated shrug. "I thought she was interested in Sure Shot, not Red

Beard."

Several others nodded.

"I see. Okay. If any of you think of anything, give me a call." Hawke handed out his card with his cell phone number on it.

Adam took the card and said, "Are you saying that James killed Red Beard, put him in the Jeep, and then set it on fire?" Disbelief rang in his voice.

"Yes, making it look like he'd died. His mother said it had to do with a gambling debt he owed. From what you told me over the phone he gambled at cards. She said sports. Did you know about that?" Hawke watched the others get into their vehicles and drive off.

"I know he liked to go to sports bars and bet on games. But I didn't think he bet more than he could afford to lose. That was the one thing about James you could count on. He never got out of control with anything. If he did once, he didn't do it again."

Hawke couldn't believe how loyal Adam was to the dead man. Even now when he could be telling Hawke all the dirt he knew on the man who did his sister wrong, he was loyal as a Labrador.

"Where can I find Hardtack?" he asked, to get on with the investigation. Hawke had the information on contacting the young man from his own interview, but he was curious about how much Adam knew about him.

"He's part of the Grand Ronde group, like Red Beard."

"Does he live in Union County?" Hawke asked.

"I guess. That's where most of the Grand Ronde muzzleloaders live." Adam shifted from foot to foot. "Any chance I can get back to plowing?"

"Yeah, go ahead." Hawke had a thought. "Would

you be able to show me about where Chessie's tent was set up?"

"You didn't ask anyone else about her. Why do you keep asking me?" The big man's cheeks grew rosy. Did he have a crush on the woman?

"Frankly, I was hoping one of them could have said they saw her around the Jeep or fire, but no one mentioned her."

"Is that good or bad? I mean for her."

"I don't know. Where was she camped?" Hawke motioned toward the end of the flat he remembered walking to when he spoke with the woman the morning after the fire. He wondered what time Novak spoke to her. He'd have to look at the deputy's notes.

They walked over to a spot that was the closest to the main road with lots of trees between.

"You can go now," Hawke said, heading to the trees, checking the ground for any type of trail. Not seeing anything, he looked up and figured out what would be the fastest way through the trees. Hiking through the brush, he caught sight of a piece of red cloth hanging from some buckbrush. Opening up a small evidence bag he'd pulled from his pocket, Hawke broke the tip of the branch off, dropping the cloth and tip into the envelope.

Scanning the ground, he discovered a slight indention that could have come from a hiking boot. Hawke pulled out his phone and took a photo of it. The sunlight dappling the ground made looking for another impression more difficult. He walked the direction the heel in the indention pointed and found another, better print. Snapping a photo of that, he glanced forward and spotted more prints. The prints led him to a curve in the road leading into Grizz Flat.

Once Hawke was back in his vehicle, he glanced back through his logbook and dialed Hardtack, Mason Pryor.

"If this is a telemarketer, you can go kiss my ass."

"This is Trooper Hawke."

"Oh, sorry. Your name didn't come up." The young man apologized.

"I've learned you were camped near Red Beard at the Rendezvous. Can you tell me when you saw him last?"

"That's the thing. I don't remember seeing him after he went to have it out with Sure Shot. Then in the morning when I woke up, his camp and truck were gone. I've tried to call him a couple times since we came back to see why he left so early and he doesn't answer. Did he kill Sure Shot? Is that why he took off?"

"No, he didn't kill Sure Shot. Did you see anyone else hanging around his camp?"

"Biscuit's mom went in his tent the first night we were there." He snorted. "Her telling Biscuit to leave me alone then her going to men's tents kind of pissed me off."

"Did you tell Biscuit about her mom and Red Beard?" Hawke wondered if that wasn't part of why the two women were angry with each other.

"Naw. She was upset enough about seeing James fooling around with Chessie when she knew her mom and Sure Shot had been seeing each other."

Hawke sat up straighter. "Sara saw Chessie with Sure Shot? When was this?"

"I'm not sure. That's part of what we were talking

about when we saw the fire. Her mad at her mom for being fooled by Sure Shot, and that Sure Shot was messing around with Chessie while his wife was busy with the little kids games." There was a pause. "I also saw Chessie go in Red Beard's tent late that night. She got around more than Biscuit's mom."

"Any idea of the time?" Hawke wondered why Chessie would be going into that tent unless she was there to pick up the camp.

"It was after you'd talked to all of us. I tried to see Biscuit but her dad was coming back to the tent so I headed to my camp. I didn't get to see her before they left. Do you have any idea why Biscuit hasn't been returning my calls?"

Hawke had a pretty good idea. "Her family is spread out right now. Keep trying. And thanks for the information." He ended the call and started up his vehicle. Dusk was settling across the flat. He wouldn't have daylight to look for tracks of whatever vehicle brought Chessie's accomplice back to the campground to pack up Lambert's camp and drive off in his pickup before the rest of the camp started moving out.

Once he was at the top of the grade out of the Grande Ronde River canyon, Hawke called Shoberg.

"Shoberg."

"Hey, what did you find out about Dre and Mark Holmes?" Hawke asked, picking up a cold cup of coffee and drinking.

"She is a computer analysist and he is a college professor. Dre belongs to a muzzleloader club and Mark is a cross-country bicyclist. Their son has been in and out of the hospital since he was born. Some congenital heart condition. They have large medical bills. I couldn't see where they'd paid any of them off."

Hawke let the information sink in. If they were smart, they wouldn't pay off the bills in a big payment. "Can you find out what businesses Dre has worked for? If her husband was a cross-country bicyclist. There could have been a bike stashed where the body and car were left. Mr. Holmes could have easily ridden back to the campground, put the bike in the pickup, and loaded all of Lambert's gear on top of it before driving out of there in his truck."

"That's plausible, but how are you going to prove it?" Shoberg asked.

"With good tracking skills and a few stories."

Chapter Thirty-one

Officially, it was Hawke's day off. He had plans to take Dog and hike the area on Lost Prairie Road where the turkey hunters discovered the car and body. There had to be something that could be used to prove the Holmes had been involved in the death of Wylie Lambert and caused the death of James Pruss. The only way to get the proof needed to bring them in for questioning was to go back to the scene of the crime.

He fed the horses and his mule, cleaned out their water trough, and packed a lunch. As he descended the stairs from his apartment, Darlene entered the barn.

"You've been industrious on your day off," she said, knowing that he usually took his time feeding and messing with the horses when he didn't have to go to work.

"Dog and I are going on a hike."

The animal yipped and made a tight circle as if chasing his tail, but instead his nose was pointed at

Hawke. Dog loved hiking and riding in the pickup. Both of which he would do today.

"I see. Well, you two boys stay out of trouble." She walked over to the feed storage room. "I have a couple people coming to look at Boy today. I think you were right about him not being a good trail horse. But he does like working in an arena. He's going to make a nice show horse."

"I'm glad you were able to find out what he likes. It sure wasn't going in the mountains with me." Hawke walked over and scrubbed the palm of his hand up and down the middle of Polka Dot's head. "This guy is turning into another Jack. He gets along with Dog and is eager to go up the mountain trails."

"I'm glad he is working out for you." She grinned. "Have you changed his name?"

Hawke laughed. "Are you kidding. If I don't call him Polka Dot, I'll have an upset girl to deal with. And besides, if I call him Polka Dot, maybe Kitree will quit calling Dog Prince Charming."

Darlene laughed. "That girl is something else. Have fun on your hike."

"We will. Come on, Dog." He and Dog headed to the pickup.

Once they were on the road, Hawke called Shoberg.

"It's your day off and mine," the other trooper answered.

"Dog and I are going hiking on Lost Prairie Road. Just wanted someone to know." Hawke knew it was doubtful he'd run into anyone. "Did you have someone in Washington ask the neighbors if both the Holmes were gone during the Rendezvous? If they do go somewhere, who watches their son?"

"I have someone working on that angle today. And the phone records for Pruss's and Lambert's cell phones came in. I'll take a look at them on Wednesday. I'm off today and tomorrow."

It might be his day off, but once Hawke finished his hike, he planned to go to the office and look over the phone records. "Thanks for the information." He ended the call and continued to Alder and out the north highway.

Dog stood with his front feet on the armrest of the passenger door as they drove through the small community of Flora. Hawke had lowered the window when they turned off the north highway and started down the road to Flora. His speed was slow enough Dog could sniff and not have the wind take his breath away.

Rolling onto Lost Prairie Road, Hawke slowed even more. He studied the trees, bushes, and grass along the east side of the road all the way to the spot where the law enforcement vehicles, tow truck, and ambulance had dug up the side of the road.

He grunted. All that dug up dirt and gravel and flattened vegetation wasn't going to help him find anything. He parked in the middle of the tracks on the side of the road.

Grabbing the daypack he'd prepared, he opened the door.

Dog knew they were at the start of their hike. He leaped out the door, over Hawke and the pack.

"Don't take off, we have to work together," Hawke said.

Dog stopped and looked at him with a tilted head.

"Come on, let's go up the road to where I think the car was driven in." Dog fell in step beside Hawke as they continued up the road to the now barely visible tracks of the car that had been hidden in the trees.

Scanning the ground twenty feet in both directions, he didn't see anything that looked out of the ordinary. No thin tire tracks behind trees or bushes, or fading footprints.

He followed the car tracks into the spot where the car had rested. The vehicle had been taken to the forensic lab in Pendleton. If they were lucky there would be something found in the car to help get the truth from Mr. and Mrs. Holmes.

Pulling out his phone, Hawke scrolled through the photos he took of this crime scene before everyone else arrived. He scrolled from photo to photo. Something didn't look right. He scrolled back to the photo that had caught his attention. On the ground in front of the open car door it appeared as if the ground had been disturbed. Not by footsteps but by… He found the spot that he'd taken the photo of and studied the grass and dirt in the area.

The ground had been disturbed to hide footprints. He found more swept dirt, and bent or broken pieces of grass, headed south through the trees. After about ten yards the slight indention of a hiking boot appeared. Whoever had left the car gave up hiding their tracks at this point. He followed the boot prints through the trees to a wide spot in the road. A clearer print was hidden under the edge of a bush, where it was apparent the person had waited for a ride.

Hawke took a photo of the print. It looked familiar. He'd check it with the other prints he'd photographed later. If the person waited for very long, they may have left some evidence. He dropped to his knees and began a thorough search of the ground from behind the bush to the edge of the road. He collected a few things that nature hadn't put there. A small triangle of plastic, likely from the corner of a food wrapper. A rock-hard wad of gum. Two shotgun cartridge casings that he doubted had anything to do with the murder and all to do with turkey hunting.

He stood up and walked slowly back into the bushes and trees searching every bush and scanning for more tracks. Behind a pine tree, with a two-foot girth, he found a set of prints with the heels deeper than when the person walked.

A grin spread across his face. The spacing and weight distribution confirmed what he'd expected. It was a woman. She'd squatted behind the tree to take a pee. He pulled out a large evidence bag, and using a stick, shoved all the pine cones, needles, and leaves within a foot of the boot prints, into the bag. If an animal hadn't come along and tried to cover the woman's scent, they might have viable DNA to use.

"Dog, we did all we can do here." Hawke stood. But if this had been Chessie, there was no way she could have waited here and been back to the camp when Novak started questioning people. However, there were the tracks from the road down to her camp.

He walked back to the pickup mulling over the time frame of the events as he knew them. If Chessie had helped kill Lambert and hiked to the car with Pruss, how had the car turned up on Eden Lane? And who picked her up and brought her back to Grizz Flat?

All he had were more questions. Time to head to

Winslow and have an on-duty trooper take the evidence he'd gathered to Pendleton. Then he'd look over the phone records. Maybe that would clarify his thinking.

Driving by the Rimrock Inn, he wondered where Mr. Moody would go after his wife bought him out. Where would she get the money? She was one of the women who had been used by James Pruss.

Four miles later, he pulled into the Joseph Canyon Viewpoint. A small parking area with a restroom that overlooked the deep, steep-sided canyon where his ancestors wintered. Down on the banks of Joseph Creek his great, great grandparents had braved the winters in the lower elevations of the canyon with less snow, leaving dead grass for the horses and cattle and water and food for the people.

It had been a while since he'd stopped here and said a few words to his ancestors. They were the reason he'd applied for this job over fifteen years ago.

Hawke stood at the wall that kept people from going out too far and falling down into the nearly 2000 feet deep canyon. Under his breath, he murmured, "I am here to keep our land and animals safe. It is my gift to you, my fathers."

Dog walked over and peed on the rock wall. Hawke grunted his approval and they climbed back into the pickup. Pulling out of the wayside, he turned north, retracing the road they'd just traveled down. At the Rimrock Inn, he rolled the windows down halfway and headed to the front entrance.

The door was locked. He glanced at the sign. Closed Tuesday and Wednesday. This was Monday. He walked around to the back, where he'd entered the business in an official capacity the week before.

Mrs. Moody walked out of a small greenhouse. She glanced up and hurried forward. She'd covered half the distance when she must have recognized him. Her steps faltered and she slowed. "How may I help you, trooper?" she asked when she stood on the back steps of the building.

"I was hoping to get some lunch. It's my day off. My dog and I were out hiking." He pulled his Stetson off his head and motioned to the door behind her. "Would you like me to get that. Your hands look full."

"Thank you, yes."

He opened the door, and she walked in.

He followed. "The front door was locked, but it said you were open today on the sign."

The woman put the lettuce in the kitchen sink. "We are open. I must have forgotten to unlock the door this morning." She waved to the door into the dining area. "Go on in and pick a table. I'll be in to take your order in a few minutes."

He studied her, trying to decide if he should ask if she was now the waitress, too, but refrained and went into the dining room.

The tables were set up the same as before, but he noted they looked more elegant than the last time he'd been here. Menus sat at each place on the table. He picked a table outside on the back porch. There was enough sun filtering onto the porch to be comfortable. And he appreciated eating in the open air any time.

"There you are. I thought you'd left," Mrs. Moody arrived with a glass of water and an order pad.

"Are you working by yourself? Where's Mr. Moody?" Hawke sipped the water she'd brought with her.

"I bought my husband out. He left over the weekend. What will you have?"

"A cheeseburger and chips." He set the glass of water down. "What about Trudy? Shouldn't she be working?"

"She quit last week. I believe it was the day after you were here. I have an advertisement in the paper and word of mouth that I'm looking for help. I'll get this right out." She disappeared back into the building.

Hawke pulled out his phone. He texted Sergeant Spruel.

Get backgrounds on Trudy Harris and Charles Moody. They have both disappeared.

Spruel replied, *I thought you were working on the Holmes as being our suspects?*

It never hurts to keep an open mind.

Footsteps approached. Hawke tucked his phone away. It vibrated in his pocket, but he waited until Mrs. Moody had set his food in front of him and left before he pulled it back out.

Why are you texting me this on your day off?

I took a hike around the second crime scene. I have evidence I'll be bringing by in an hour.

Copy.

He had a feeling Sergeant Spruel would have a few words with him when he showed up at the office in an hour.

Hawke bit into the burger and had to admit it was the best burger he'd tasted other than ones cooked on a grill. He saved a quarter of the sandwich to give to dog. He left a twenty beside his plate and exited off the porch and around the side of the building.

This double homicide had become more

complicated with each piece of evidence he dug up. He'd sure like to get reports from the forensic lab and the autopsy on both bodies to be able to start putting some of his theories together.

Chapter Thirty-two

At the State Police Office in Winslow, Hawke let Dog out to pee on the bushes behind the building before they entered. He carried his daypack with the evidence he would pass on to a trooper headed out of the county, if there was one.

As he'd expected, Sergeant Spruel met him at the door. "This is your day off. You should be riding your horse or relaxing."

"Dog and I went for a hike."

Dog woofed and walked over to Hawke's desk and lay down.

"Your hike was at an active crime scene. That's not relaxing." Spruel had followed him over to his desk. "What evidence do you have?"

Hawke told his superior of the tracks he'd followed and the evidence he wanted sent to Pendleton.

"If you want it there today, you'll have to take it. Be a good reason to have dinner with your mom."

Spruel raised one eyebrow.

Hawke nodded. "I'll let her know I'll be there for dinner and then I want to take a look at the phone records Shoberg said came in."

"Just remember, you aren't on the clock." Spruel headed to his office.

The man worried too much about overtime. Hawke was happy for his check once a month, but when it came to following tracks and evidence, he had a compulsion and couldn't let a thing like working on his day off stop his thought process.

He logged onto his computer and pulled up the files for the phone records. The printer whirred to life as he printed out the records from both victims. The scent of fresh brewed coffee wafted by his nose. He glanced up and watched Tad Ullman, another trooper in this area, walk out of the breakroom.

"Hawke, what are you doing here?" Ullman asked, walking over to his desk and slapping his logbook down.

"Checking out a few things. You make enough coffee for me to steal a cup?" He rose out of his chair.

"Sure. Aren't you supposed to be off today?" Ullman glanced toward the sergeant's office.

"I am. A file came in I wanted to read."

The sergeant's voice boomed out into the main office. "I know we're facing budget cuts."

"Second thought, I'll skip the coffee, grab my printouts, and go." Hawke knew when his sitting in the office on his day off wasn't good. He never put in the hours he worked on his day off and Spruel was constantly trying to get him to take sick days. Which he rarely used, because he didn't get sick and rarely was hurt bad enough to not be able to work.

"Good thinking," Ullman said.

Hawke grabbed the printouts, gave a soft whistle to Dog, and they headed out of the building. He waffled between going to the Rusty Nail to read the papers in his hand or just heading to Pendleton, handing over the evidence, and read the reports at his mom's. Of course, she'd be as insistent it is his day off as his sergeant.

He sighed and opened the door to his vehicle. Dog hopped in, taking his spot in the passenger seat. Hawke put the daypack back between them, shoving the papers behind the pack, and started the pickup. He'd head to Pendleton and get this evidence into the hands of people who could possibly come up with answers.

Hawke stayed on Interstate 84 headed west when he came to Pendleton. The new forensic lab was on the west side of town on Airport Road. Right next to the O.S.P. building. He turned right off the freeway, driving through a small industrial area, and up to the large open lot surrounding the lab and State Police building. The new lab stuck out like a bum wearing a tuxedo. The building was new, with a front full of shiny windows, while the lot looked as if it could use a renovation.

He parked.

"Stay, I'll be right back." Picking up his daypack, he patted Dog on the head and exited the vehicle.

Walking up to the new facility for the first time, he was impressed. He entered and walked up to the secretary standing behind a glass window.

"May I help you?" the woman asked.

Hawke pulled the chain around his neck out from

under his shirt, showing his badge. "I have evidence for your people to take a look at."

"I'll call up a lab tech to log it in."

A young woman with short, straight, black hair and green eyes appeared from the hall behind them. "You have items for us?" she asked.

Hawke handed them over. "These are for case one-zero-zero-seven-two-nine."

The woman nodded. "I've been working on that evidence and the other one from Wallowa County, one-zero-zero-seven-two-eight."

He smiled. "Then you're the person I'd like to talk to. I'd like to hear what you've learned so far."

"I sent a report out this morning." She studied him.

"I want to hear the report from you and ask some questions."

She had all the evidence bags in her hands. "Then follow me." She pivoted and strode down the hallway, flashed a card that swished open a door, and said over her shoulder, "I was just finishing up the report on seven-two-eight."

They walked down the long hall and into a room filled with the type of gadgets he'd avoided in high school chemistry.

The woman placed the bags on a cleared table by the wall. "By the way, I'm Bella."

"Trooper Hawke."

"Your name was on most of the evidence I've been working on. You sure you aren't part of the forensic team?" Her green eyes danced with good humor.

"I have a good eye for what is out of the normal."

Bella plopped down in the chair behind a computer and desk. "Take a seat," she offered not looking up from her computer.

Hawke found a folding chair leaning against the wall. He opened it and sat down.

"The victim's DNA has determined he was Wylie Lambert. We also determined his head and body had been rammed against the corner of a metal storage container—you sent us photos that helped us determine that was the indention in the skull and bruising in the muscles in the back." She clicked the computer mouse. "The blow incapacitated him, but it was the smoke in his lungs that killed him." She clicked again. "The other evidence that came from that case—the burned Jeep was arson. Gasoline was the accelerant. There was enough pattern to the burn and residual gasoline in the seats to show the vehicle had been doused and lit. The gas can had one partial print. We're still working on that. The tread of the hiking boot, fits a generic brand. They could have been purchased at any store that handles the brand. We do believe they are a women's boot because of the narrowness."

Hawke took all of this in. The woman's boot fit with where he was going with his theory. "Can you tell if the partial fingerprint might be a woman's?"

The analyst shook her head. "With what we have, it's really hard to tell. If we can find something to match it with, we can do that."

"I know it's early, but do you have anything on case one-zero-zero-seven-two-nine?"

She did multiple clicks, tapped some keys on the keyboard, and nodded.

"The body in the car. There was something interesting on the car seat. Driver's side. Grease. Not mechanical grease, cooking grease."

Before he could say anything, she continued, "The body was going into decomp. However, because the M.D. asked for a full toxicology to include poisons, we were able to establish strychnine was the cause of death. He'd ingested what we think—from the chemicals we could salvage from the stomach—that it was hidden in a dessert, possibly cookies or cake because stomach contents weren't complex. We looked for strychnine because the waxed paper sent as evidence had residue of powdered sugar laced with strychnine." She glanced up and smiled. "Good call to think to send that along."

Hawke grinned back at her. "Thanks. Any chance you know what kind of dessert the victim ate?"

"Something rolled in powdered sugar?"

He laughed.

"That's about all we have other than the seat was moved forward for someone shorter than the victim."

"Any prints on the buttons to move the seat?"

"Sorry. No prints on the car anywhere. I'd say the killer wore gloves. Possibly latex gloves. There weren't any fibers found in the car. Leather doesn't tend to leave fiber as easily. We did find one long hair. No root, so it can't be matched to any DNA."

"What color is the hair?"

"It was died red, had a copper hue, but the hair under the coloring is dark blonde." The woman touched her black as a cat hair. "Just as this color came from a box, so did the color of this person's hair."

"That means I can place a woman at both crime scenes." Hawke wondered if Chessie's hair was naturally copper and if Diamond's was natural or a box color. Diamond helping Pruss made sense, but why would she kill him? Her hair in the car could be explained that she had driven it the night the Moodys and Trudy Harris saw the two together. The night they delivered the gas can. Had the young woman mentioned that to prove she had nothing to do with the arson or to give a reason for her prints to be on the can and her hair in the car?

"Whether they are the same two women…that will be determined by possibly more evidence?"

"Yes. I brought in more from the crime scene for one-zero-zero-seven-two-nine." He played with his Stetson he'd been holding since entering the building. "Any chance you can get DNA from urine on a pinecone?"

The woman grinned. "It's slight unless there is some blood in the urine or bladder infection. But we'll need something to match it to."

Hawke nodded. "I'll get DNA samples from the women I suspect tomorrow."

Bella stood and held out her hand. "Pleasure working with you Trooper Hawke. We'll get on what you brought in today and await any DNA samples to match it with."

"Thanks."

She led him back down the hall and out the door that required her pass to open.

Hawke stepped out into the parking lot as the sun was setting. His mom was going to wonder what was taking him so long. Climbing into the pickup, Dog whined and wiggled.

"Yeah, we're going to Mom's. You can run around her backyard, and I'll get a good meal."

Chapter Thirty-three

"What do you mean, you have to head back tonight?" his mother asked when Hawke scooted back from the table and mentioned getting home.

"Mom, I have to work tomorrow."

She narrowed her eyes. "Aren't you working today? You made the trip to Pendleton to drop off evidence."

He sighed. "Today is my day off. I'm driving my pickup, not my work vehicle. I have Dog with me."

"I see. When will you be back this way?" She picked up the bowls of food.

Hawke stood, grabbing the dirty plates and silverware. He didn't like leaving when his mom was mad at him. She'd been so happy to see him when he'd arrived that he felt bad about not having arrived sooner, so they could have spent more time visiting. Even if she mainly talked about the kids she watched and their parents. People he only knew by names, except for a couple he'd met on previous visits.

When the table was cleared and the dirty dishes sitting beside the sink, he turned his mom toward him. He peered down in her thin face, becoming more and more etched with time. "Mom, I promise to come see you soon. I have someone I want you to meet." He knew bringing up a woman in his life would brighten her mood.

A light of hope blinked on in her eyes. "A woman?"

"Yes. Her name is Dani Singer. We've been dating a while now. I'd like you two to meet."

"Where does she come from?" His mom grasped his hand and sat the two of them back at the table.

"She's half Nez Perce. But she didn't grow up on a reservation, she attended the Air Force Academy and is a pilot."

She leaned back, her mouth open and her eyes wide.

"Mom, she's just like the rest of us, only doing more searching of her roots." Which was true. Over the last few months, Dani had started asking Hawke more questions about their ancestors who had lived in Wallowa County before the Whites invaded. He planned to take her to the next Powwow in Eagle.

"She sounds like a smart woman." Mom patted his cheek. "I'm glad you found someone."

"Thank you." He put a hand over her hand and sighed. "I really need to go."

She nodded. "As long as you promise to bring this Dani Singer soon."

"I will. But this is the start of her busy season at Charlie's Hunting Lodge."

A finger went in the air. "She is the person who flew you to New Mexico last year."

"Yes, she is."

Mom frowned. "Have you been dating that long and just now told me?"

"No. We weren't dating then. We were just starting to tolerate each other." He grinned when she started laughing.

"This is a woman I want to meet."

"Good. I want you to meet her." Hawke walked to the back door and whistled for Dog. The animal bounded from the far side of the fenced-in yard and slid across the kitchen linoleum.

"Thank you for dinner."

"You're welcome." She hugged him around the middle. "Come back soon."

"I will." He walked out of the house, knowing he hadn't lied to his mom, but knowing it would be a while before he and Dani could make a trip over. It was the beginning of the busy time of year for the hunting lodge. Not that there was much hunting through the summer, but it was becoming more of a vacation destination since she'd inherited it from her Uncle Charlie.

Hawke arrived at the Winslow O.S.P. building early the following morning. He'd discovered both victims had been calling back and forth, no doubt, setting up the fake identification and payoff. The number Lambert called the most was the landline at the Levens house. Apparently, he knew that the only one home during the day was Wendy, making it safe for him to call her. And it was less likely for her husband to catch her calling Lambert since landline phones didn't show the calls a person made during the day like a cell phone.

There were four numbers that Pruss called frequently. One was Wendy Levens. But those calls had become less frequent after Pruss and Lambert started calling back and forth. He knew the easiest way to find out who the other three were would be to call them himself. Which he planned to do at the office. That way he could write up a warrant for the female who checked off all the criteria for his suspect.

Before calling the numbers, Hawke caught Sergeant Spruel up to date on what he'd learned the day before and wrote up the notes on his trip to the crime scene and his trip to the Forensic lab so Shoberg would have all of that when he clocked back in on Wednesday.

Scrolling through the report, he realized one of the phone numbers belonged to Chessie, Dre Holmes, one of the women on his suspect list. He didn't need to call her, but he did need to know what the Washington State Trooper who'd questioned her neighbors found out. He looked up the trooper's region and called their dispatch asking for Trooper Brossy to give him a call and leaving his cell number.

Next, he picked up his office phone and dialed one of the numbers.

"Rimrock Inn, we are closed on Tuesdays and Wednesdays. If you leave a name and number, we'll get right back to you."

A recording.

"Beep!"

He replaced the phone and studied the incoming

and outgoing calls with that number. More calls were made to Pruss than from him. The ones to him started out late at night and slowly moved to during the day. The ones from him were at night and they slowly became less and less until they stopped, but the calls to him continued. That was a sign of a desperate, lovelorn woman. Mae Moody was still on his list, though he didn't see how she could have been in the woods hiking around, when she would have been cooking at the Inn.

He picked up the phone to dial the next number and his cell phone rang. "Trooper Hawke."

"This is Trooper Brossy from Washington. I was told you wanted me to call." The woman's voice sounded young.

"Yes. You are down as the officer who spoke with Mr. and Mrs. Holmes's neighbors. I wanted to know what you'd learned." Hawke poised his pen over his logbook.

"I can send you an email with my report unless you'd rather hear it orally." The young woman said the last as if she thought he didn't know how to work a computer.

"Does your written report tell how the people acted as you talked to them?"

There was silence, then, "No. Just the facts."

"Then tell me orally, if you have the time." He wanted to know as much about the people giving the statements as he did the information they gave.

"Just a minute, I'll bring up my report."

Within seconds, she started, "The neighbors west of the Holmes said the couple were thoughtful, took good care of their son, and were avid outdoors people. They seemed to genuinely like the Holmes family."

"Did they say what was wrong with the boy?" Hawke had the report that it was a heart defect, but wanted to know if the couple were hiding that from anyone.

"He was born with something wrong with his heart. They said he's had several surgeries, the last one about six months ago. The neighborhood had a yard and bake sale to help the Holmes with bills." She let out a sigh. "Everyone I talked to thought the world of the couple and their son."

"Who watches the boy when the couple is away?"

"Ms. Fenty. She lives a couple doors to the east of them. She's studying to be a nurse. Again, she had nothing but good things to say—"

Hawke cut her off. "Did she say if she watched the boy the dates we are interested in?"

"She did. From Thursday to Saturday. She said Mr. Holmes picked up his son at eight Saturday morning."

This was news that could be used to get them to talk. "Good. Anything else interesting?"

"They're about to lose their home, according to a neighbor who works at the bank they use."

"Which bank is that?" He wrote down the name and branch of the bank. "Thanks. This helps."

Hawke ended the conversation and stood. He walked into Spruel's office and told him what he'd learned about the Holmes.

"But can you place them in the car with Pruss when he died? And what about the money? If they got their hands on the two-hundred-thousand wouldn't they have caught up their house payments?"

"Those are questions I'd like to ask the couple. That is if you can get the lieutenant to give me permission to join the Washington police in questioning the two. I know all the evidence against them firsthand." Hawke didn't want the couple to have helped with the death of Lambert and caused the death of Pruss, but he also knew how parents would go to extreme lengths to take care of their children.

"I'll put a call into Titus. But you need to get out and do your job." Spruel picked up the phone on his desk.

Hawke walked over to his desk, picked up the phone, and called the fourth number that showed up frequently on Pruss's cell phone record.

"This is Diamond, leave a message."

All the women he had figured could be in on the disappearance were the most frequent calls by James Pruss.

Chapter Thirty-four

Patrolling the favorite turkey hunting areas in the county, Hawke's mind wasn't on the hunters. He was running all that he knew so far about the two deaths through his head. They needed DNA samples and fingerprints from the three women, no four, if they ever found Wendy Levens. Could she have killed Pruss and taken off with the money?

He was thinking more along the line, Wendy knew who killed Lambert and had run to not be the next killed. She wouldn't know that Pruss was dead. She'd disappeared before the body was found.

The dispatch radio crackled and came to life. "Collision between mileposts thirty-eight and thirty-nine, Minam Grade."

"Hawke, ten away."

"Copy."

He'd meandered down Promise Road, thinking about the homicides. Now he pressed down on the accelerator, making the vehicle fishtail on the gravel road. He was only five minutes from Highway 82, the road that snaked along the Minam canyon.

The tires grabbed traction as he burst out onto the asphalt of the highway. He turned right and flicked his lights on. There wasn't any oncoming traffic. That meant the road was blocked by the collision. Hopefully, the people traveling the road would be smart and not try to go around or push their way through.

He spotted the accident as he slowly maneuvered by the five vehicles parked on the outgoing lane.

It appeared a semi misjudged the thirty mile per hour corner and a car coming the other direction hit the back tires of the trailer. Flashing lights on the other side of the wreck was either another law enforcement officer or the tow truck had already arrived.

Parking with his lights flashing, Hawke walked up to the open driver's door of the semi. The cab was empty. He hurried to the car. A man around seventy sat behind the wheel, his forehead bleeding and looking dazed.

"Sir, can you hear me?" Hawke asked.

The man's eyes tracked to his face. "I hear you. What happened?"

Hawke studied the man. It was evident, he was in shock and could have a concussion. "Just sit tight. The EMTs will be here shortly. They'll take good care of you." He wondered where the truck driver had gone.

Checking the traffic in the other direction, he spotted a Union County Deputy. That was the car with the lights flashing. Hawke walked over to him. "What are you doing down in the canyon?"

The deputy looked up from the statement he was

taking. A grin spread across his face. "Hawke, mi amigo. Haven't seen you in ages."

Hawke patted his friend on the back. Deputy Sanchez had been with a search and rescue that Hawke had participated in a couple years ago. "What happened?"

"I got a call about a semi driving erratically through Elgin. When I figured out it came this way, I thought I'd see if maybe the driver pulled over somewhere, but I heard the call about the accident and," he pointed to the semi, "that is my truck."

"Where's the driver?" Hawke wondered what drugs the driver had in his system that he would ditch his vehicle after hitting someone.

"According to the people in the first two cars, he is bobbing down the river." The deputy grinned.

"And freezing his balls off." Hawke stared downstream. "Did you call it in?"

"Yeah, unless he made it to the bank, which is unlikely given the run-off filling the river, they should be able to net him at Minam." Sanchez nodded to the cars on his side. "I'll hang out until the tow truck comes."

"I have an injured civilian on this side. I'll get the statements from the cars on my side." Hawke put a hand on the deputy's shoulder and squeezed. "It is good seeing you. Too bad it wasn't over a beer."

"Next time you're in Union, look me up."

"I will." Hawke checked on the injured man before stepping up to the first car and taking the driver and passenger's statements.

"How long do you think it will take to get the road cleared?" the driver asked.

"I'm guessing a couple hours. You'd be better off to go back home and try this again tomorrow." Hawke knew it could take over an hour for a tow truck to arrive. Then they would have to assess the situation. The car could be moved and that would give one lane for traffic to pass, but he figured the truck wouldn't get moved until around dark.

The ambulance drove by his vehicle and up to the car.

Roxy, one of Hawke's favorite EMTs, stepped out of the ambulance. "Is this the only one with injuries?"

"That we know of. The truck driver jumped in the river." Hawke couldn't keep the mirth out of his voice.

She scowled. "A person could die of hypothermia if they are in that snow melt for too long."

"I know. I shouldn't find it funny. I guess the guy didn't have any common sense."

An hour later, Hawke was relieved by a county deputy to keep the traffic flowing on the one lane.

"Hawke, off duty," he radioed dispatch. His day on the job was over and he'd not heard back from Spruel whether or not he could be in on the interview with the Holmes. If nothing else, he needed the woman's DNA and—Damn! That's what had been bothering him. While he believed the couple had killed Pruss, he'd also come to the conclusion the husband had driven the car to the trees and rode his bicycle back. The evidence he'd found had shown a woman had driven the car and waited for her accomplice. That didn't fit with the scenario he'd built on the guilt of the husband and wife.

He stopped in Eagle at Al's Café. He'd get some dinner and head home.

"Hawke, you don't usually show up for dinner," Lacie said when he walked through the door.

"I was called to the wreck on Minam." The tables were full. He took one of the few places left at the counter.

She waved her arm. "Half of these people came here to wait for the road to open."

A woman walked over to him. "Do you know if the road has opened up to get to Elgin?"

"One lane is open. There's a deputy there directing traffic."

"Thank you." She hurried over to her table and soon the three were out the door.

"I'll have iced tea, a burger, and a salad." Hawke placed his hat on his knee.

"I'll get right on it." Lacie placed his order on a clip in the window between the dining area and kitchen and went to get his drink.

His phone buzzed. Spruel.

"Hawke," he answered.

"Spruel. I talked to Titus. He wants to know if you think there is enough evidence to bring the Holmes in as suspects or are we still in the questioning phase of the investigation?"

Hawke told his superior about his doubts now. "The logistics don't work out for Mrs. Holmes to have driven Pruss away in the blue car. And it was definitely a woman who left him in the trees. But I'd still like to visit with the couple at their home. Keep them from thinking we suspect them of anything. While I don't think they killed Pruss, they were both gone and the tracks from her camp to the road… I want to know why those are there."

"I'll relay this to Titus and see what he says. The board says you are off tomorrow. Do you want to visit the Holmes on Thursday?"

"No. Tomorrow."

"You know you can't get paid for working on your day off."

"It's not about the pay. It's about finding the truth. I won't be able to stay away from the case anyway. I might as well go talk to them."

"What time do you want to meet a city policeman at the Holmes residence?"

"Noon. It is my day off. I'm going to sleep in."

Hawke and Dog parked in front of the Holmes residence behind a city cruiser. He stepped out at the same time as a woman officer who looked to be about thirty, but possibly forty.

"Officer Rawlings," she said, offering her hand.

Hawke shook. "Trooper Hawke."

"I was expecting an SUV or marked vehicle not a pickup and dog."

Dog woofed, hanging his head out of the driver's side window.

"It's my day off, and Dog wanted to go for a ride."

The officer raised one eyebrow. "The dog is named Dog?"

"He likes it. Do they know we're here?"

"My C.O. gave them a courtesy call to let them know you had more questions for them. A man peeked out about ten minutes ago." She grinned. "I was early but didn't make contact."

"Let's go," Hawke said, motioning for the officer to go first. It was her jurisdiction.

The door opened before they knocked.

"Trooper Hawke," Mrs. Holmes read the name badge on the officer, "Officer Rawlings, I really don't know what else we can tell you about the event at the Rendezvous."

"I just have some more questions. Is your husband home? I'd like to talk to both of you at the same time."

Mrs. Holmes studied him a moment before calling, "Mark, the police are here!"

"Where's your son?" Hawke asked. He didn't want the boy to hear the conversation. Whether Officer Rawlings liked it or not, he would have her take the boy out back to sit or play.

"He's with our sitter. We didn't want him to hear whatever you are accusing us of." Mr. Holmes entered the living room.

The couple grasped hands and sat together on the couch.

Officer Rawlings pulled out a logbook and poised her pen.

Hawke liked how efficient the woman was. "I'm still confused about the night of the fire. You, Mrs. Holmes—"

"Call me Dre." She winked. "Or Chessie."

"Dre, you were at the Rendezvous alone, but your sitter says she was watching your son." Hawke stared at Mr. Holmes. "Where were you?"

"I was called away to see to my mother." The man answered quickly.

Hawke shifted his gaze to the wife. "Why were you and James Pruss having daily phone conversations up until the Rendezvous?" He pulled the paper with the phone calls highlighted, out of the folder he held. A different color for each woman who had been calling or been called by the victim.

"I was helping with one of the competitions that weekend." She smiled. "Sure Shot was a stickler for the competitions running smoothly."

"Which competition was it?" Hawke asked.

"The William Tell. Shooting an apple off a dummy's head." She pouted. "Sadly, the competition didn't happen. It was to be held on Saturday."

"I thought William Tell used a bow and arrow? Wouldn't that have been more along the line of something Swift Arrow would have been in charge of?" Hawke could tell by the way Officer Rawlings brow furrowed she didn't understand his questioning.

"James wanted to put a spin on everything. I really don't understand why you are asking me these questions."

"Or why I need to be present," Mr. Holmes said.

"I'm trying to figure out why you, as Chessie, were seen entering Wylie Lambert's tent after he was dead."

"Dead, what are you talking about?" Chessie's eyes widened. She squeezed her husband's hand so hard her knuckles were white.

"I think, you and your husband worked out a plan with James to help it look like Wylie was still alive." He nodded toward Mark. "You spent Friday night in Wylie's tent, hiding, until everyone had gone to bed. Then you tore down the camp, loaded it in Wylie's pickup, and drove it back to his place in La Grande, where your wife picked you up."

The couple stared at their linked hands.

"I think the reason I found footprints from the road to Grizz Flat down the hill to the back of your camping area was because you didn't want anyone to see you coming from Wylie's camp. But you were seen. That's how I figured out you two were accomplices in hiding a murder."

"No! We didn't kill anyone!" Chessie said.

"But you helped James cover up the fact he knocked Wylie Lambert unconscious and put him in his Jeep, burning him up to make it look like James was dead."

Chessie shook her head.

"The irony, whoever James pulled into his scheme to help him disappear, made him disappear forever. I found his body four days ago."

"No!" Mr. Holmes raised up off the couch. "You're just saying this to make us say something we don't mean."

Hawke opened the folder and held out the photo of James's decaying body in the car. "That's how I found him. With his fake I.D. that he had Wylie manufacture for him. The reason Wylie had to die. I'm just not sure why James pulled you two in to help him. Did he have something on you?"

Chessie faced her husband. "If James is dead, we did all that for nothing."

"Shh. She doesn't know what she's saying. She and James were good friends, she's in shock."

Chessie stood this time, pulling her hand from her husband's. "I only slept with that man to get his financial help. He promised we'd get fifty-thousand dollars for making it look like Wylie had left the Rendezvous early. He said it was so the police would think Wylie killed him. But I swear, I didn't know he planned to kill Wylie. We needed the money to keep the house. All of Mickey's medical bills have wiped us out. I didn't know anyone was going to be killed."

"But you had to have known the body in the Jeep was Wylie. You took his stuff, and James had planned on someone taking his place." Hawke studied the husband and wife.

She looked genuinely broken up, the husband was stoic, giving him an icy glare.

Hawke nodded to Officer Rawlings.

"I'm placing you under arrest as an accomplice in the death of Wylie Lambert." She went on to read them their rights as she led them both to the door.

Chessie spun around at the door. "What about Mickey?"

"I'll talk to your sitter," Hawke said. He felt for the two, just trying to keep a roof over their son's head, but they went about it the wrong way.

He knew James killed Wylie, but he still didn't know who killed James. He could put a line through Chessie's name.

Chapter Thirty-five

On the drive back to Wallowa County, Hawke called Shoberg, who was back to work, and filled him in on what he'd just learned.

"We are down to Diamond Edwards, Cindy Albee, Mae Moody, and Wendy Levens?" Shoberg asked.

"No, just Diamond Edwards and Mae Moody."

"Why only those two?" Shoberg asked.

"Because Cindy Albee never called him."

"That's because she saw him every day. And she had access to the money going his way." Shoberg was stuck on the dealership secretary.

"She isn't conniving enough. You can see every emotion on her face. She'd never be able to kill someone and not have it show." Hawke knew he should consider all the women in the man's life as a suspect, but he just couldn't see the timid secretary killing her boss's son, even if he jilted her.

"Why not Wendy Levens?"

Hawke told him his suspicions she was hiding because she thought James was still alive and would come after her because she knew that Wylie had made the fake I.D.

"That's logical. But how do you explain Mae Moody killing him. Wouldn't she have had a restaurant to run on Friday night?" Shoberg asked.

"Yes, but she could have made the dessert that killed him and had someone else…" His thoughts went to how Mrs. Moody had bought out her husband and he had disappeared.

"We need to find Mr. Moody and Trudy Harris. I'll be in Alder in thirty minutes. I'll go by the Harris home and see if her mother and father know where she is. Can you put out a BOLO on Moody's vehicle?"

"Sure. I think I see where you're going with this. Let me know what you find out from the parents."

"Will do." Hawke grinned. Now it was all making sense. The baked goods, the cooking grease on the car seat. Why they'd all tried to make sure he knew James had been to the lodge multiple times in the blue car with a redhead. They had been setting up someone else.

He needed proof, or a really good tale, to catch them up.

Burke Harris answered Hawke's knock at the door of the one-story home. It appeared in good condition for its age. He'd place it a vintage 1960s home.

"Trooper Hawke, why are you visiting me here?" The man stepped out the door onto the porch as if he didn't want his wife to hear what they talked about.

"I wanted to know if you could tell me how to get ahold of Trudy? I've learned she quit her job at

Rimrock Inn, and I'd like to have a couple words with her."

"Did you try the house she rents? It's on the edge of town." The man didn't make eye contact.

"No, because I'm pretty sure she's not there. It seems Mr. Moody is also missing."

The man's eyes widened a bit before he caught himself. "Really? I didn't know that."

"You have no idea where your daughter might be?" Hawke asked, already making the decision to go see Cindy. She seemed to be the only one in the family who was honest.

"I quit knowing her whereabouts when she left home seven years ago."

"I'd like her phone number." Hawke had his phone out, waiting for the man to recite the number.

Burke glared, pulled out his phone, and read a number.

Hawke put it in his phone and dialed. It went to Trudy's voicemail. "Any chance your wife knows where Trudy is?"

The man's head rotated back and forth. "Michelle has gone to bed. She works hard at the café."

"I want her to call me in the morning." Hawke handed Burke one of his cards and pivoted. Once he was settled in his pickup, he dialed Shoberg.

"Hawke, did you find out something else?"

"We need to get the phone records for this number." He rattled off Trudy's number. "I think Trudy Harris's dad knows something, but he's not talking. He's probably calling Trudy and telling her to disappear. We have to find her. I'm headed to her cousin, Cindy Albee, to see if I can learn anything there."

"Copy."

Hawke started his vehicle, patted Dog on the head, and pulled away from the Harris residence. This time of night he expected to find Cindy at home, but he decided to swing by the car dealership since she'd made the comment about hanging around there late to avoid going home to her husband.

The lights were off. He pulled into the lot to circle back out and his lights caught Cindy's car by the man door near the garage. What was she doing here with all the lights out?

Hawke turned off his vehicle and exited, keeping Dog beside him. He didn't want anyone coming up on his six. Dog would let him know if that happened.

He tried the door.

It wasn't locked.

Easing it open, he heard voices.

"Trudy, you can't think you'll get away with this," Cindy said.

"Stop being so goody-goody. I'll give you enough to get far away from that drunk husband of yours." Trudy sounded confident. And just a bit crazy.

Hawke eased the door shut and texted Shoberg. *Found Trudy. Dealership. Bring backup.*

He pulled out his conceal carry weapon from his boot sheath and slipped through the open door, with Dog at his heels. He kept to the carpeted area along the perimeter so Dog's nails didn't give them away on the concrete showroom.

"I don't want to be looking over my shoulder like you are going to be," Cindy said.

"Give us the keys to any of the cars out there. I

know they're looking for us. Dad texted and told me."

Hawke found the two women and Mr. Moody in Cindy's office. He motioned for Dog to stay and stepped into the small room, making sure he was behind the man.

"Just the people I'm looking for," Hawke said, startling the two threatening Cindy. She'd caught sight of him, and to her credit, hadn't batted an eyelash. Not seeing a weapon, he held his firearm down at his side.

Moody swung around. He had a small caliber handgun pointed at Hawke. "How did you find us?"

Hawke itched to raise his weapon, but he could see the man was nervous. He didn't want the man to pull the trigger at the sight of his Glock. "Process of elimination. You two killed James." He stared at Trudy. "You going to kill your cousin, too, if she doesn't hand over the keys to a vehicle?"

Cindy gasped. "They killed James?"

"That's why they're in such a big hurry to get out of here. Right, Trudy?" He continued to stare at the younger woman, not moving his arm or hand that clenched his firearm.

She glared back and grabbed Cindy by the arm. "We aren't going to kill you. We didn't kill James, but we aren't about to stick around and go to jail for it." Trudy pulled Cindy out from behind the desk. "Let's go get a key while Charles ties up the snoopy trooper."

"You know she's going to take off and leave you taking all the blame," Hawke said, peering at Charles and nodding toward the two women.

Charles, definitely not a seasoned criminal, swung toward the two women.

A quick glance and Hawke saw the man didn't

have his hand on the trigger. He hit the man's arm, sending the weapon flying and grasped Charles's other arm, wrenching it behind his back.

Trudy started to run from the room.

"Dog!"

Dog appeared in the doorway, his teeth bared and growling.

Trudy screeched and backed up.

"Cindy, grab the gun and hand it to me," Hawke said, holding onto Charles and slipping his weapon back into his boot. He didn't have any cuffs. This was his day off and he'd planned to only talk to people, not arrest them.

The woman handed him the gun. He immediately released the magazine, dropping it and the bullets to the floor. "Could you hand me that?" He pointed to the cartridge on the floor.

Cindy handed it to him and asked. "Did Trudy really kill James?"

"I didn't kill him," the cousin insisted.

Hawke's phone buzzed. He shoved the cartridge in his shirt pocket, the gun in the back waistband of his pants, and looked at the message.

We're here. What do you want us to do?

Come in man door by garage. In Cindy's office. Bring handcuffs.

Three minutes later, Dog peered toward the showroom.

"All clear!" Hawke called out.

Shoberg, Deputy Novak, and Alder City Policeman Profitt appeared in the doorway.

Novak stepped in, cuffing Moody. Once they stepped out of the room, Shoberg cuffed a protesting

Trudy.

"What about her?" Profitt asked, pointing to Cindy.

"Can you come to the police station and tell me what happened tonight?" Hawke asked.

She nodded and then shook her head. "I honestly don't understand any of it."

Hawke gave her a half smile. "We'll figure it out together."

Cindy reached across her desk, picking up her purse. "What am I going to tell Uncle Burke and Aunt Michelle?"

Hawke followed her out of the office. "The truth, though I think your uncle already knows what your cousin did. I'm surprised she didn't ask him to give her a car."

The woman spun around. "He would never do anything to get on the bad side of Mrs. Pruss."

"Why is that? I thought he didn't like her." Confusion over the relationship between Burke Harris and Mrs. Pruss collided in Hawke's head. He'd reread all his notes and neither seemed to care much for the other. They were like thorns in one another's sides.

"They don't like one another, but Uncle Burke is about to get what he's always wanted and Mrs. Pruss will be able to keep her stature in the community." Cindy continued walking.

"What are you talking about?" Hawke asked, he and dog following close on the woman's heels.

"Mrs. Pruss signed the dealership over to Uncle Burke today. She's going to file for personal bankruptcy to get rid of the money she owes, but the dealership can't be touched because she doesn't own it."

Hawke escorted the woman to her car. "Drive over and park your car in front of the Sheriff's Office. Then no one will have to escort you back here to get your car."

She nodded, unlocked her car, and settled behind the steering wheel. "Thank you for showing up when you did."

"You're welcome." He closed her door and hurried over to his vehicle.

"Come on, boy. This could be a long night." Hawke held the door open for Dog to jump in, then he slid in and started up his pickup. "Let's hope no one has tried to get information out of those two yet. I know the triggers to push."

Chapter Thirty-six

Parking his vehicle behind the Sheriff's Office, Hawke left Dog in the pickup and entered the building through the jail.

"Hey Hawke, what are you doing back here out of uniform?" the young jailer, Ralph, asked.

"There are suspects up front I want to talk to, but Dog is in my truck and I didn't want to leave him out front."

Ralph nodded. "If you left the doors unlocked, I'll go let him out in an hour."

"Thanks, Ralph, he and I would both appreciate that." Hawke waited for the jailer to push the code to give him entrance to the front of the building.

"Not a problem. I like dogs, and I need to get out of here several times a night."

Hawke understood. It took a special person who could stay locked up looking after jailed criminals all night long.

Shoberg stood beside the door of the only interview room.

"Did you send the paperwork to get subpoenas to search Trudy's place and the Rimrock Inn?"

"Yes. Should have those in our hands by morning."

Hawke thought a moment. "We need to make sure Moody doesn't call his wife. She could toss out anything that might incriminate them."

"We took away his phone and told him he gets a phone call if he's arrested." Shoberg grinned. "He thinks he's here to give evidence against Trudy."

"My how fickle his love is. But we can use that." Hawke tipped his head toward the interview room. "Who's in there?"

"Trudy Harris. She seemed like a bigger flight risk. Moody's in the breakroom with Officer Profitt watching him." Shoberg held a file in one hand. "You want to take lead on this since you know more about what's happened than I do?"

"Sure. Has she been read her rights?" Hawke wanted everything she said to be admissible in court.

"Yes. The recorder is ready, just push the button." Shoberg opened the door.

Hawke walked through first, taking the seat right across from Trudy. Shoberg took the chair to his right.

"You can't keep me here," the woman said, her scared eyes showing she wasn't as brave as she sounded.

Hawke reached over and turned on the recording device. "Are you Trudy Harris?"

She nodded.

"Please say yes. A nod can't be heard," Shoberg said.

"Yes, I'm Trudy Harris. I didn't kill anyone."

"Have you been read your rights?" Hawke asked.

"Yes. I didn't kill anyone. I just waited for James in the car like he asked." Her gaze flit back and forth between himself and Shoberg.

Hawke shook his head slowly. "No, you didn't wait for him. I found proof that you met up with him at the gas can he used to set fire to Wylie Lambert. The boot prints from the blue Ford Escape to the gas can and the boot prints that left the car with James Pruss dying from strychnine were yours. We have a warrant and will go to your house and look for those boots and compare the tread to the photos I took."

"I didn't kill anyone," she said again.

"Who gave James the poison?" he asked.

She shook her head.

"We know it was mixed with the powdered sugar on a dessert. Perhaps a cookie?" Hawke wrote on the flap of the file and showed it to Shoberg. The trooper left the room and returned in a minute.

"Chocolate Crinkle cookies were James's favorite cookie," Shoberg said.

Trudy's gaze riveted on Shoberg.

Hawke had asked his colleague to ask Cindy what kind of cookie was James's favorite.

"Did you make James some chocolate crinkle cookies?" Hawke asked. "And added some strychnine to the powdered sugar they were rolled in?"

"No. I didn't make the cookies. I didn't know they had strychnine in them." Her eyes flicked at him then away.

"A half-truth. You may not have known the type of poison, but you knew they were poisoned." Hawke shook his head. "We'll have you when the DNA comes back from the chewed gum I found where you waited for Charles to come pick you up. Had you two already picked that spot, or did you have to call and explain to him where you were?"

She crossed her arms and stared at him.

"No matter, we're getting your phone records and that will tell us what we need. I just want to know, do you want to be arrested for murder, attempted murder, or accessory to murder?"

"I want a lawyer." She leaned back. Tears glittered in her eyes.

Shoberg said, "This ends our first interview with our murder suspect, Trudy Harris," and turned off the recording.

Hawke stood. "Let's go see how much Charles has to say about his involvement in James's death."

"He won't tell you anything," Trudy said, but she didn't sound as confident as before.

"All he has to say is you called and he picked you up. He didn't know who you were with or what you had done." Shoberg opened the door. "He's probably going to walk, and you'll be the one going on trial."

Hawke stood by the open door studying the woman. "If you didn't bake his fatal dessert, you should speak up."

She remained tight lipped. He walked out of the room and followed Shoberg down to the breakroom.

"How do you want to approach him?" Shoberg asked.

"Like we know everything. We do. We just don't have all the evidence tied up neatly. Yet." Hawke walked into the breakroom. Moody had helped himself to a cup of coffee.

Hawke sat down across from the man.

Shoberg sat next to him and pulled out his phone. “Since this isn’t a regular interview room, we’ll use my phone to tape this interview.” He placed the phone on the table between them. “Please state your name.”

“Charles Dale Moody. Why am I here?”

Hawke glared at the man. “You threatened an officer of the law with a firearm and you helped murder James Pruss.”

The man’s eyes grew larger. “I didn’t murder anyone. And the gun on you. I didn’t know if you were friend or foe.”

“My ass. You knew who I was. I’d interviewed you twice about the murder of James Pruss. There was enough light to see who I was. If you want the charges against you to be dropped to just threatening me with a firearm, then you better start talking.” Hawke slapped the folder on the table.

“I didn’t kill James. Taking his money was all Trudy’s idea. She said her father had figured out that James was planning on disappearing and leaving the dealership to the mercy of his gambling debts, the loss of money he’d stolen, and the cars he’d given away for favors. Trudy acted like she wanted to be one of his girlfriends. Then she told him inside stuff about the car dealership that Cindy had told her, and he began to think she was on his side.” Moody took a gulp of coffee and grimaced. Like most police stations, the coffee in the breakroom wasn’t the freshest. Neither were the day-old baked goodies.

“What did he tell her about Wylie Lambert?” Hawke asked. They had to get the truth about how

Pruss killed Lambert from someone. Otherwise Pruss's killer would go down for two murders.

"James told Trudy that he planned to fake his own death at the Rendezvous. That he needed her to pick him up on Eden Lane and then he'd pay her to take him to Portland where he'd get on a plane and not look back. She asked him how much and where was he getting the money even though she knew he'd stolen it from the dealership." Moody glanced at the cup in his hand, shrugged, and put it on the table. "He offered her twenty grand to pick him up and take him to the airport. She figured if they were going straight to the airport, he would have the money with him. She said we could blackmail more out of him and go off to live somewhere where no one knew us." He snorted. "It's no secret me and Mae haven't been getting along. But until Trudy told me James started acting funny after he ate the cookies Mae had sent along for him, I didn't realize she hated someone more than me."

"You're saying that Mae sent those cookies for James? That she made the cookies with strychnine in them?" Hawke asked, to make sure that information was on the recording.

"Yeah. When Trudy asked for the night off because she had a date with James, Mae handed her the box of cookies and said, 'Tell James these are from me.'"

Hawke sat up straight and peered at the man. "What did you tell Mae when Trudy called you to come pick her up?"

"I said that we were out of something and I was running to the store."

"She didn't know that Trudy was alive then?"

Moody's eyes and mouth widened like a fish

realizing it wasn't in water any more. "You think Mae planned to poison both James and Trudy?" He slapped a hand on his head. "Oh, my god. Do you think she planned to do the same to me?"

"That I won't know until I interview your wife. Did she know James was trying to disappear?" Hawke was trying to discover if the woman had felt her lover had fallen for a younger woman and had planned to run away with her or she just wanted to kill them both out of jealousy.

"I don't think so. Trudy and I only talked about it when we weren't at the Inn. But I know Trudy did call James a few times from Rimrock to get things cleared up."

That would account for the daytime phone calls to James's phone from the Inn. "What you've told us, is that Trudy didn't know about the poisoning and perhaps had also been a target?"

"Yeah. She thought she was making an easy twenty grand." The man's face reddened.

"Instead, she made off with all two-hundred-thousand dollars, didn't she?" Hawke had wondered where the money had gone.

"Yeah. She found it in James's bag after she'd parked the car in the trees. We were going to get away but didn't want to do it too soon, or someone would figure it out."

"Were you at the Inn when Trudy arrived the next day and told your wife she was quitting?" Hawke wondered what Mae had thought when the young woman she'd thought was poisoned had shown up at her Inn. Did she wonder about James? Was that why she was so jumpy?

"No. But Trudy said Mae just nodded her head, wrote out what was owed her, and walked back into the kitchen."

Hawke nodded. "Thank you for telling us the truth. You will be held over for arraignment for threatening me with a firearm. But the murder charge is no longer over your head."

He left the room as Shoberg took Moody to be booked in jail.

They needed the warrants to search the Rimrock Inn.

Chapter Thirty-seven

Thursday morning Hawke met Shoberg and Novak at the Rimrock Inn at ten. They all walked up to the door and entered. Two couples sat at the tables inside and a man sat at one of the tables on the porch.

Hawke led the way into the kitchen where they found Mae Moody preparing a plate of food.

"Mrs. Moody, I'd like you to step outside with Deputy Novak while we search your place of business and living quarters as well as all outbuildings," Shoberg said.

"I can't leave when I have customers. And you have no right searching where my customers are staying." She slapped a spoon down on the counter, splattering sauce across the pristine stainless steel.

"This court order says we can." Shoberg put the paper in the woman's hand and motioned for Novak to escort her out.

"I need to tell my customers—"

"I'll tell them you are indisposed." Hawke walked into the dining area behind Novak and Mrs. Moody. When the pair stepped out of the building, he told the customers he was there to do a search and would like to know who was staying at the Inn. The two couples in the dining room raised their hands.

"Officer Shoberg will go with you to your rooms, take a look around, and then you are free to do as you please." Hawke walked out to where the man sat on the porch. "Are you just passing through?"

The man sipped his coffee before answering. "I come through here once a month to visit my mother in the senior living center. I always stop on my way home to have some of Mae's fluffy light pancakes. What is this all about?"

"I can't tell you, but if you are finished, it would be best if you leave." Hawke waited as the man finished his coffee, placed a twenty next to his plate, and walked off the porch, heading around to the front of the building.

The logical place to find poison would be the kitchen, but then as clean as she kept the place, he doubted she would keep something lethal in the space where she cooked. He stared out the window and spotted the greenhouse. That would be where they would want to keep rodents away and not harm food in the process.

Hawke strode out through the door, across the grass, and into the greenhouse. The moist heat and smell of plants took him back in time to when he was a child and he'd wandered into a sweat lodge after it had been used to cleanse one of his uncles. He knew it wasn't a place to play, but he'd been curious what the males did in there that when they came out everyone seemed to have had an attitude adjustment.

"I didn't find anything upstairs, in the rooms they rent. Wondered if you wanted to join me while I search the living quarters." Shoberg stepped into the greenhouse, shoving Hawke's memories to the far reaches of his mind.

"I think we'll find what we need in here. She'd be stupid to put strychnine in the living quarters. What if her husband questioned her?" He waved his arm. "And here it would seem natural."

"True."

They moved every plant, pot, and barrel. Thirty minutes later, they still hadn't found anything.

"It has to be here," Hawke said.

"Unless she got rid of it after the poisoning." Shoberg took off his hat and wiped across his sweaty brow with his forearm.

"No. I think if her husband hadn't of left, he would have been next." Hawke snapped his fingers. "Call the sheriff's department and have them ask Mr. Moody what his favorite dessert is."

Shoberg nodded, made the call, and they walked back into the kitchen. "What's your theory?"

"That she did indeed get rid of the poison, but not before she made something to feed her husband."

Shoberg's phone rang. "Shoberg." He nodded. "Yeah. Thanks."

He pointed to the large freezer. "Chocolate ice cream."

Hawke walked to the freezer, opened the door, and read the labels on all the food. He found a plastic container with the label *Ice Cream Charles*.

Hawke put it in an evidence bag and handed it to Shoberg. "This needs to go to Pendleton ASAP. If they can discover strychnine in this, we have her."

"You want to keep looking?" Shoberg asked.

"Yeah, we should make sure there isn't anything else that might help put her away. I'll start upstairs while you have Novak take her to county jail and get that to the lab." Hawke walked into the dining area and found the stairs to the upper level.

The two couples were packing their things to leave. "Sorry your stay was cut short," he said to them and continued down the hall to the living quarters.

Shoberg returned to the living quarters. "You should have seen the color drain from Mrs. Moody's face when I handed the ice cream to Novak and told him to get it to the forensic lab ASAP."

Hawke nodded. "Then she did plan to poison her husband, too. We need to find more to connect her to James."

He was looking through the closet, which he noted had only women's clothing hanging in it. Either Mr. Moody had already cleared out all of his belongings or his wife had. There were shoe boxes setting underneath each pair of shoes. He picked up the shoes and opened the boxes. Some had more shoes, others were empty. The last box under a pair of tall boots, made noise when he picked it up. Inside were letters. Not in envelopes, just folded as if they were waiting to be slipped into an envelope.

He picked one up with his gloved hands and unfolded it.

Dearest James,

I know there is a difference in our ages, but as you

could see by our intimacy last night, I am woman enough for you. Why do you rip my heart out by bringing those young bimbos to my restaurant and spend money on them under my nose? They could never love you as much as I love you.

The letter went on and on.

"I found the connection. As long as we can prove these letters were written to or for James Pruss." Hawke put the lid on the box and tucked it under his arm. "I think we have the information we need to get the woman to confess."

At the Sheriff's Department, Hawke walked into the interview room with the box of letters tucked back under his arm. Shoberg followed him in, and they took the same seats as before.

Mrs. Moody's eyes widened then narrowed as she stared at the box.

Shoberg started the recording and asked the woman to state her name.

"Mae Crandall Moody, as if you didn't know."

"That was for the recording. We know who you are. I also need to tell you…" Shoberg told the woman her right to not say anything and the right to an attorney. When she said she understood, he leaned back, as if giving Hawke the stage.

"You recognize this box?" Hawke asked.

"It's from my closet."

"Yes. And do you know what's in it?"

"Personal letters. Ones that no one was to read."

"Not even James Pruss?" he asked, watching her mouth grimace and the spirit in her eyes dull.

"James meant a lot to you, didn't he?" Hawke

started.

She nodded.

"The recording can't see your head nod," Shoberg said.

She glared at him. "Yes, James meant a lot to me."

"But he didn't care about your feelings, did he?" Hawke continued. He knew the only way to get her to confess was to throw salt into her ripped and torn heart. He didn't like it, but she had killed a man and would have been happy if the woman with him had died as well. She had also planned on killing her husband. All that added up to someone who didn't deserve the courtesy he'd give most people.

She stared at him, her mouth in a tight line.

"He made love to you, made you feel cared for and young. Then he'd show up at your restaurant fawning over women ten and twenty years younger than you. This after he said you were too old for him.

"Even your husband was fooling around with someone nearly half your age. Trudy, your waitress. And then, you discovered James was also after Trudy. That he and she were planning to go away together. But it didn't make sense, did it? Your husband was still drooling over Trudy, and they acted like they were a couple, but James, he had his charm, his looks, and…what was it all the woman in the county swooned over him about?"

"When he was with you, you felt like you were the only woman he had eyes for. He made me feel…something I'd never felt—beautiful." Tears glistened in her eyes.

"But he tossed you to the side and showed up night after night with a different young pretty woman. Was he trying to make you suffer? Or did he think that was the only way to stop you from calling him late at night?"

Her gaze swung to him. "How did you know?" she whispered.

"Phone records. You were obsessed with James Pruss. The most sought-after man in the county, and he didn't want you." Hawke read one of the letters. It had been on the top of the stack. "If you won't be mine, no one can have you." He tapped the paper. "You decided to make sure if you couldn't have James's love, no one would." Putting the paper in the box and closing the lid he asked quietly, "When did you decide to poison James with his favorite cookie?"

She stared at the box. "The week before his death. He'd told me when I'd called that I should go bang my husband and leave him alone. I heard a woman giggle in the background. That's when I went down to the kitchen and made the cookies. I gave one to Charles's dog. Seeing how it died so painfully, I was delighted to know James would feel how his rejection had pained me. When Trudy asked for the night off to have a date with James, I smiled, handed her the box of cookies, and told her to give these to James from me." She flicked a glance at Hawke. "I'd fantasized she died in the same manner. When she arrived the next day and told me she was quitting, I thought maybe she'd figured out what I'd done. But then Charles disappeared, too, and I wondered if James would be coming for me." Her eyes rounded and her breathing became agitated. "You kept showing up. I thought sure he'd been found and I was going to jail. But he is dead, isn't he?"

"Yes, and you are under arrest for his death."

Hawke walked out of the room as Shoberg put handcuffs on Mrs. Moody.

Hawke sat on the front porch of Charlie's Lodge with Dani. Kitree was thirty feet away tossing sticks for Dog. Hawke told Sergeant Spruel he needed some time off, loaded up Jack and Polka Dot, and headed for the Eagle Cap Wilderness with one destination in mind. This place.

"You know what gets me the most about the whole thing?" he asked rhetorically and Dani stayed quiet.

"The second victim ruined the lives of so many people, and they'll never be able to see him pay for it."

"But, they could have all done the right thing and they wouldn't be where they are." Dani grasped his hand. "Come on, let's go for a walk. You came up here to forget."

"That's what I like about you. You're always practical." He put his arm around her shoulders, whistled for Dog, and waved Kitree to join them. "When would you have time to visit my mother with me?"

Thank you for reading book six in the Gabriel Hawke Novels. I enjoyed having Hawke get justice for another victim.

Leaving a review is the best way to show your appreciation to an author for entertaining you. All you have to do is leave a brief sentence or two about why you liked the book or what about the book interested you and a star rating. That's it!

While you're waiting for the next Hawke book, check out my Shandra Higheagle Mystery series.

Paty

Continue investigating and tracking with Hawke as his series continues. If you missed his other books they are:

Murder of Ravens
Book 1
Print ISBN 978-1-947983-82-3

Mouse Trail Ends
Book 2
Print ISBN 978-1-947983-96-0

Rattlesnake Brother
Book 3
Print ISBN 978-1-950387-06-9

Chattering Blue Jay
Book 4
Print ISBN 978-1-950387-64-9

Fox Goes Hunting
Book 5
Print ISBN 978-1-952447-07-5

About the Author

Paty Jager grew up in Wallowa County and has always been amazed by its beauty, history, and ruralness. After doing a ride-along with a Fish and Wildlife State Trooper in Wallowa County, she knew this was where she had to set the Gabriel Hawke series.

Paty is an award-winning author of 48 novels of murder mystery and western romance. All her work has Western or Native American elements in them along with hints of humor and engaging characters. She and her husband raise alfalfa hay in rural eastern Oregon. Riding horses and battling rattlesnakes, she not only writes the western lifestyle, she lives it.

By following her at one of these places you will always know when the next book is releasing and if she has any sales or giveaways:

Website: http://www.patyjager.net
Blog: https://writingintothesunset.net/
FB Page: https://www.facebook.com/PatyJagerAuthor/
Pinterest: https://www.pinterest.com/patyjag/
Twitter: https://twitter.com/patyjag
Goodreads:
http://www.goodreads.com/author/show/1005334.Paty_Jager
Newsletter- Mystery: https://bit.ly/2IhmWcm
Bookbub - https://www.bookbub.com/authors/paty-jager

Thank you for purchasing this Windtree Press publication. For other books of the heart, please visit our website at www.windtreepress.com.

For questions or more information contact us at info@windtreepress.com.

Windtree Press
www.windtreepress.com

Hillsboro, OR

For questions or more information contact us

CPSIA information can be obtained
at www.ICGtesting.com
Printed in the USA
FSHW022235101021
85372FS